THE PHENOMENON TRILOGY

ON THE RUN

To Devin

Best wishes!

Chris Raabe

THE PHENOMENON TRILOGY

CHRIS RAABE

LUNKER
PRODUCTIONS

Omaha, NE

Paperback: 978-0-9884740-2-4
Kindle: 978-0-9884740-1-7
LCCN: 2012953628

Lunker Productions LLC
PO Box 391251
Omaha, NE 68139

The Phenomenon Trilogy
www.phenomenontrilogy.com

Printed in the USA
10 9 8 7 6 5 4 3 2 1

This novel is dedicated to
Emma, Reagan, and Olivia.

"Back in over there," Christian said, pointing to an area of grass to the right.

Ray backed in so the car pointed toward the exit.

"Now what?" Ray said.

"Now we wait," Christian said. "We wait for my dad to show up."

"How long?" Sam asked.

"Until they come," Christian answered.

The sun set behind the trees, and slowly, the day faded to twilight. No one spoke. No words would calm their fears now. They escaped, not knowing whom to trust or what had happened.

"You know," Alexis said, "if you're right, this changes everything we know about Phenomenon Children. Everything Mr. Banner told us may turn out to be a lie. We will have nobody to trust and nobody to turn to."

"We have each other," Sam said, enthusiastically. "I trust all of you."

"Same here," Ray chimed in.

"Can we trust him?" Alexis said, pointing an accusatory finger at Christian. "He led us out here. For all we know, he is leading government agents to us right now."

"Alexis, that's unfair," Sam cried.

"She may be right," Ray said. "What if he cut a deal with them for his own freedom?"

The headlights of a vehicle appeared through the trees on the road. Christian sat quietly.

"If that is my father," Christian said, "will you trust me then?"

Christian turned in his seat toward Alexis. Even though he could only make out the silhouette of her head, Christian could tell Alexis anticipated the worst.

"If that turns out to be your father, then I am with you," Alexis said, "but if it isn't, we are all screwed."

No one breathed.

The headlights turned off the road and onto the tractor path their SUV traveled down earlier. Ray started the engine.

"If it isn't someone we know, we're out of here," Ray said coolly, "and you can hitch a ride home, Christian."

Christian gasped when he saw the headlights did not belong to his father's car.

CHAPTER 1

The four Phenomenon Children rode silently in what might be considered a stolen SUV. Technically, the vehicle belonged to Mr. Banner, the quasi-father of Ray, Alexis, and Sam Banner, but they took it without permission from the farm outside of Red Oak, Iowa. Compound that problem with the fact that government agents were combing the Red Oak area and surrounding communities in search of this SUV. Christian mulled over the daunting task facing the four teenagers. Evade law enforcement and trust no one until they reach Grandpa and Grandma Pearson's farm outside of Wisner, Nebraska, which would take most of the night on these county roads.

Ray let off the accelerator slightly at the next gravelly intersection before accelerating up the hill. Christian's stomach twisted as the SUV flew over the crest and barreled down into the valley, building up speed for the next incline. Only fifteen minutes had passed since the four of them left Christian's father and grandfather at the Old Highway 34 turnoff, but the silence in the car felt like it lasted an eternity to Christian.

He glanced over at Samantha, who sat next to him in the backseat. Her face leaned up against the window, and her sandy-blonde curls glowed green in the dim light of the dashboard. She sighed and turned toward Christian. Without saying a word, she gently laid her hand on his knee and leaned close to him to give him a peck on his cheek.

Ray sat statuesque in the driver's seat; his pale hands gripped the steering wheel in a death lock to keep the vehicle from sliding on the occasional washboard in the gravel. Alexis sat next to him with her arm stretched across the armrest and her hand on Ray's thigh. An outsider would have guessed the two couples were headed back from a double date at the movies. They all sat calmly, except Ray.

"Alexis," Ray broke the silence, "check to see if there's a map in the glove-compartment."

While she fumbled around in the glove box, Christian decided to check the seat pocket in front of him. Sam perked up and searched the area in front of her before climbing over the back of the seat to look in the rear storage area of the SUV.

"Nothing!" Alexis said, emphatically. "Just a tire pressure gauge, the registration, and an insurance card."

"There is nothing in these seat pockets," Christian said, disappointedly.

"Maybe check the back," Ray replied.

"Already looking," Sam stated in a muffled tone with her butt up in the air and half her body stretching into the area behind the back seat. "Just a tool box and some paper towels. Oh, I think this is a first aid kit."

Sam eased herself back over the seat and straightened her shirt as she reclaimed her position next to Christian.

"Does anyone have any idea where we are?" Alexis asked.

"Iowa," Ray said, dryly.

Ray's comment was not funny, but for some reason all four of them laughed like "Iowa" was a whimsical punch-line to a good joke. They all seemed to be looking for an escape hatch out of this nightmare, and Ray's attempt at humor gave them a brief reprieve. Even Alexis, who usually punched someone for saying something stupid like that, couldn't hold back a snicker. The laughing subsided to uncomfortable chuckles, and Christian sensed their short stint of chipper moods turn to uneasiness again. He thought about the irony of the situation. They were on the run from government agents, and one of the most dangerous agents might be the adopted father of the other teens in the car. Ray could withstand extreme temperatures with no effect, Alexis could hear a whisper from a hundred yards away, Christian could breathe underwater, and Sam could sense people's emotions, but not one of them could choose the proper escape route through the country roads of Iowa because there was no map in the car. Their phenomenal abilities served no use in this situation. Now, that was irony.

Ray slowed and pulled to the side of the road, as the pinging gravel on the undercarriage gave way to the soft dirt and grass of the shoulder. Christian noticed the red reflection of a stop sign ahead.

"We've probably gone about fifteen miles or so," Christian said from the backseat. "Unless we get onto a paved highway, it will be difficult to tell how far we travel."

"Well, we need to get a map," Ray stated. "Otherwise, we're going to have trouble finding our way in the dark on these county roads. We already crossed one paved road, so this will be the second. How long do we stay off the highways?"

Ray turned off the headlights but left the parking lights on. He turned around in his seat to face Christian.

"What's the plan, guys?" Ray asked.

"We need to get a map," Alexis huffed, as she leaned into the opening between the seats. "Otherwise, we won't have a clue where we are going."

Sam asked Christian, "Do you know the area at all? None of us have ventured this far north of Red Oak."

Christian shook his head but noticed a hint of illumination in the distance out of Ray's window.

"Hey, are those lights?" Christian asked, as he pointed over Sam's shoulder to the west.

Ray turned to look out his window, and Alexis leaned up over the dash to see around Ray.

"They sure are," Sam said, turning back from her window.

"I would guess that's Griswold," Christian said. In the excitement of the evening, he had not thought about his countless fishing trips over the summer. "My dad took me to a lake near Griswold before my trip to South Dakota. If we go right on this paved road, we should end up meeting the highway to Atlantic."

Christian knew Atlantic High School was in the same conference as Red Oak. Even though he never had the opportunity to travel there for a game in the short time he had spent in Red Oak, he remembered looking at a map on one of the fishing excursions with his father. He recalled that Atlantic was northeast of Griswold and just south of the interstate.

"We can go north to the Interstate from there," Christian said, hesitantly. "I know the Interstate sits just north of Atlantic. I remember seeing it on a map."

"I say we stay on the gravel until we get further north," Alexis said. "No offense Christian, but you're not the most experienced of the group at avoiding detection."

"We can go faster on the paved roads," Christian answered, ignoring Alexis's jab.

Christian could feel the glare from Alexis' dark eyes even though he couldn't see them. Even though she decided not to say anything in response, Christian knew Alexis didn't appreciate people disagreeing with her.

Ray said, "They'll probably think we headed west."

"So if we turn right, we will be headed the opposite direction," Sam chimed in, obviously siding with her boyfriend's idea.

"That still doesn't solve the map problem," Alexis huffed.

"No, it doesn't," Ray replied.

"But neither does staying on the gravel," Christian said, flatly. He sensed victory in the debate.

"Okay, fine," Alexis said, caving in. "We go right, but then what?"

"We take the Interstate west when we get to Atlantic, and we find a rest area," Christian stated.

"Why a rest area?" Sam asked. Christian glimpsed a wrinkling of Sam's brow in the thin light emitted from the dashboard.

"A map," Ray said energetically as he put the vehicle into gear and turned on the headlights. "A rest area might have a map. Nice thinking, Christian."

"I guess it's worth a shot," Alexis said. "I've seen maps at rest areas before."

"Make sure you don't speed," Sam chimed.

"Yes, mother," Ray said with a laugh, as he turned onto the highway.

Christian was surprised by this second attempt at humor from Ray, since Ray didn't seem like the joking type. Christian smiled as he leaned back in the seat, wondering how long he would be on the run with The Three. How long had it been since he first met them at school? He couldn't remember. So much had happened in the last week. Had it been only one week?

One week ago, Christian was looking forward to his second week of school. He remembered betting his dad a million dollars about the weather and not being so worried about Calvin Robinson at school. Christian wondered how long it would be before he saw his parents again, or if he ever would see them again, for that matter. He had quit paying attention to the discussion in the car and was focusing on the faces of his family. Alexis interrupted his brief trip down memory lane.

"You said go north?" Alexis questioned from the front seat.

Sam sat up as Christian leaned to the middle. They were stopped at a T-intersection, and Christian saw "71" on a white sign above a yellow sign with black arrows going right and left.

"It's just a guess," Christian said, hesitantly, hoping he was right. "Go left."

"Great, a guess!" Alexis said, sarcastically, and Christian sensed a roll of her eyes by the way she shifted her head.

Sam interjected, "Hey, we're all guessing here. Take it easy."

"Only one way to find out," Ray said with a grin, patting Alexis on the leg.

Something about Ray was different; he still seemed in control, but there was something odd in his behavior. It was like he was enjoying their situation, reveling in the unknown, but taking care to contain Alexis's fears. Ray appeared calm on the exterior, but Christian could sense Ray was more on edge than he looked. Not on edge about being captured, more like he was trying to contain his enthusiasm about the situation and control his excitement. His mannerisms reminded Christian of how some of his teammates acted before a football game. Their faces would be stoic, while their muscles showed another side to the story, wound tight and ready to explode. Ray had that look.

Ray turned left, and the headlights flashed on a green sign that said, "Atlantic 10."

"Niiice," Ray said, letting the first vowel roll for a second before completing the word. "Maybe you should come up front and be my navigator. Alexis can get lost in the restroom."

Alexis punched Ray in the shoulder, as he yelped out a laugh.

"Then why are you in the bathroom so long?" Ray chuckled and switched hands on the wheel, as he fended off another blow with his right arm. He reached over and pulled Alexis close to him, and she jabbed him in the ribs, pulling away as soon as Ray let go. Alexis's mood was definitely not as jovial as Ray's. She feigned a laugh, but Alexis was more irritated than humored by Ray's cavalier attitude.

The car swerved a bit, and Sam chided them both.

"Hey, keep it on the road," she said. "What in the world are we going to do if you wreck this thing?"

"Sorry, Mom," Ray whispered, faking sheepishness. "Christian, why did you have to bring your mom with you on this trip?"

"I heard that," Sam muttered.

Christian wrapped his arms around Sam and pulled her close to him.

"It's okay," Christian whispered, sensing she didn't appreciate the playful teasing. "He'll play nice from now on. I promise."

They drove in silence until they came to a stop at another T-intersection. One arrow pointed left to the lights of Atlantic and the other directed them right for access to Interstate 80.

The road jogged to the east a half mile before curving north to the Interstate. It only took five minutes of driving before they found a rest area. Christian welcomed the opportunity to use the bathroom. Sam's elbow had been pushing on his kidney the last couple of miles, and he needed to take a leak.

They all stretched when they got out of the SUV. Sam skipped out in front, and Alexis frantically searched for a map in the rack mounted on the outside of the building marked "Visitor's Center." Ray's focus matched Christian's as he pushed open the door marked "Men." Alexis swore as the door closed behind the two boys.

Neither Christian nor Ray spoke the whole time they were using the restroom, sort of an unwritten rule with high school boys. When someone stood next to you at the urinal, it was eyes straight forward, no sudden movements, and absolutely no talking. Girls were a different story, and Ray and Christian could hear their muffled voices from the other bathroom through the vents in the ceiling. It wasn't until Ray and Christian had washed their hands that either of them decided to speak.

"Where do we go from here?" Ray asked, as he punched the button on the automated hand dryer.

"Hopefully Alexis found a map," Christian answered. "If she didn't, I have no idea."

"Judging by her foul mood as we were walking in here, I doubt she found any map for us to use," Ray chuckled.

"She really gets worked up sometimes, huh?" Christian said.

Ray nodded and motioned to the vent while pointing to his ear, reminding Christian that the concrete wall between them and the girls was not going to keep Alexis from eavesdropping on their conversation.

A high-pitched squeal followed by laughter blasted through the vent as the hand dryer shut off.

"Are you having a party in there?" Ray asked.

"No!" Alexis hollered from the other side. "Sam found a toad in the stall!"

"Kiss it, Sam!" Ray fired back. "It may be a prince."

"Gross!" Sam yelled, and then there was another scream.

Christian wiped the water from his hands onto his shirt and pushed through the door to the fresh air. He could hear another shriek from behind the women's door, so he knew it might be awhile before the girls were done. Ray exited seconds behind him. Christian decided to walk over to the welcome center, even though Alexis had checked it when they arrived.

"Let's see if we can find a map," Christian said. "Maybe there is a stand on the other side."

Christian turned the corner, but he stopped cold next to the pop machine, and Ray bumped into him from behind.

Ray stammered, "Hey, why did you…" but quieted when he spied what had drawn Christian's attention. Another vehicle had pulled into the parking stall next to Mr. Banner's stolen SUV. Christian's feet suddenly became as heavy as cinder blocks, and an uneasy feeling nauseated his stomach.

The two boys stood wide-eyed as a man slowly moved toward them with his right hand reaching for something on his hip.

CHAPTER 2

A light brown patrol car was parked in the diagonal stall next to the only other car at the rest area, Mr. Banner's SUV. Christian could see the words "Iowa State Patrol" in large block letters on the rear panel of the passenger's side of the vehicle.

Ray whispered, dejectedly, "Over before we even had a chance."

The girls exited the restroom in laughter, and Ray turned around to quiet them. Christian could faintly hear Ray whisper, and he knew Ray had filled Alexis in on what was approaching us.

"How you kids doin'?" the trooper asked, as he pulled a flashlight from his hip.

At first Christian thought the man had reached for his gun. His heart pounded in his chest as he almost put his hands up, instinctively. Christian realized his misjudgment when he was blinded by a flashlight beam. Then he raised his hand to his face to shield his eyes from the light as if blocking the setting sun with his glove on a baseball field.

"Hello, officer," Christian managed to say, masking the fear in his voice by answering with a short phrase.

"Easy, Christian," Alexis whispered from directly behind him. "Don't assume anything."

Christian sensed movement behind him as Sam and Alexis moved into the officer's view. The beam swung in Ray's direction.

"There's four of you?" the trooper said, somewhat surprised.

"Yes sir," Ray answered.

"What were you girls screaming about?" he asked.

"Toad in the stall," Alexis giggled, like a seventh grade girl would snicker in the hallway of the junior high, if a cute boy walked by.

"That your vehicle?" the man questioned.

"Yes sir," Ray replied. "Actually, it's my dad's."

"You kids from around here?"

"No sir," Ray said. "We have a long drive home, and we needed to stop to use the restroom."

Sam moved around behind Christian to get out of the beam of light, but she leaned close to him when she got to his right shoulder.

"Relax," she said, so quiet that only he and Alexis could have heard, "his colors are fine. No threat."

Sam's ability to read human emotions by simply looking at a person still amazed Christian. He wanted to thank her for sharing the information, but he hung onto his words.

"Where you guys headed?" the officer asked.

No one answered at first.

Christian wished the man would turn that flashlight off. He felt like he was being interrogated.

"Omaha," Ray said, calmly.

Christian glanced at Ray, who stood confidently with a slight grin on his pale face. He was enjoying this. Christian's nerves were coiled into a ball in his stomach, and Ray looked calm.

The trooper turned off the flashlight, and walked toward them. With the light off, relief washed through Christian, and he took a better look at the Iowa State Trooper. He was about the same height as Christian, and he was slender. His trooper hat was tilted down slightly, but Christian could tell the man had a buzz cut. The facial features matched his physique, thin. The man's eyes were narrow slits above a small nose, like he had a permanent squint. When he spoke, his mouth didn't open very wide, and there was no expression in the muscles around his jaw and cheeks. He looked extremely serious and all business.

"You kids been drinking?" the officer asked, as he moved closer to Ray, probably attempting to get a whiff of his breath.

Christian found it amusing that the officer would ask that question. Even if they had been drinking, why in the world would they tell a state trooper?

"We're on our way back from Des Moines," Christian stammered.

"Well, you still got a ways to go," the officer said, as his face widened to show off two straight rows of white teeth. "We've been having problems with the local kids painting up the bathrooms with their graffiti. When I saw one vehicle, I thought maybe I'd get lucky. You mind if I check'em while you wait here?"

"No sir," Christian responded, more calmly this time.

"If you check the girls' side, watch out for a killer toad," Ray said with a chuckle.

The officer feigned a smile and strode past them, entering the men's side first.

"Did you find a map?" Ray whispered.

"No," Alexis huffed.

The officer peeked around the corner before entering the ladies side, and the conversation stopped. It wasn't long before the officer returned from his investigation of the lavatories.

"You kids can go. I don't want you to have to wait any longer. It'll be pretty late when you get home, as it is. Where in Omaha do you live?"

"Huh?" Ray faltered.

"The west side," Christian quickly jumped in, trying to take the questions about his former hometown. He didn't know if Ray had a clue about places and locations in Omaha.

"Really, out near Bellevue," the officer said with a grin.

"No, that's south," Christian corrected him. "Millard area, about 156th and Dodge."

The trooper's eyes narrowed a bit, and then his face relaxed into another grin. Christian recognized the officer's attempt to check out their story without being direct. Christian seized the opportunity to leave no doubt in the trooper's mind about the truth of their story.

"Boys Town is almost in my backyard. Can't believe how much the city has grown since I was younger," Christian said, confidently. "Used to be cow pasture and corn fields when I was a kid. Now, the houses stretch out to almost Elkhorn."

"Did you just move there?" the man asked.

"Nope, it was long ago," Christian replied, puzzled.

"You better get those plates taken care of, then," the trooper said, calmly. "You need to get your Nebraska plates. The ones you got are Iowa."

"Oh, it's not my car," Christian said, quickly.

"It's my dad's," Ray said, sensing the officer's next question.

"We're going to his house to hang out tonight, and then we'll head back home tomorrow."

"I see," the officer said, looking intently at Ray. "Montgomery County, huh? What town?"

Christian wondered how he knew the county, but he didn't ask.

"Red Oak," Ray said, calmly.

There was a long silence, and Christian thought they were caught for sure. He wondered if the officer had already known that four teens were fleeing from Red Oak.

"Well, you kids better be on your way," the man said, surprising Christian.

Christian sighed with relief, as the trooper walked around the back of the visitors' center, and Ray didn't wait for the officer to change his mind. He hastily made a bee-line for the SUV and popped the automatic locks to open the doors.

It didn't take long before the four Phenomenon Children were back on the Interstate, headed west.

"Geez, I thought we were in trouble when I saw that patrol car," Christian said with a sigh of relief as he peered out the back window just to make sure the patrolman wasn't following them.

"No kidding," Ray said. "You were stammering like a guilty man. I was hoping you would say as little as possible. Then all of the sudden, you turned on the charm and put that guy in his place about Omaha. I didn't have a clue when he asked what part of town."

"How did he know we were from Montgomery County?" Christian asked.

"I don't know," Ray replied. "Maybe he checked our license plate with his computer."

"Guys," Alexis said. "Iowa tags have the county listed on the plate. He probably just read the license plate."

"How could you guys stay so calm?" Christian asked. "Until he turned that flashlight off, I couldn't think straight."

"Experience," Ray answered. "I guess we're used to keeping secrets. It comes with being a Phenomenon Child. You'll get used to it."

"We shouldn't stay on the Interstate," Alexis interrupted, seriously. "We're lucky there was no A.P.B. out on us already."

"I agree," Sam said. "If word gets out about four kids in a black SUV, that trooper will know it was us, and we won't make it much further."

"What do you think, Ray?" Christian asked.

"He had a good enough look at us," Ray responded. "If the government releases descriptions, that officer will know it was us."

"It's hard to hide the whitest kid in the state," Alexis said. It sounded playful to Christian, but there was an edge to her statement.

"Especially when I am standing next to your dark skin," Ray said, jokingly. "Let's take the next exit."

"Shoot!" Sam cried. "Shoot, shoot, shoot, shoot, shoot!"

"What?" Alexis asked, impatiently.

"We should have asked him for a map," Sam answered.

Ray chuckled in the front seat, and Christian could tell that Alexis was rolling her eyes, again.

"What?" Sam asked. "What is so funny, Ray?"

"Well," Alexis started, "don't you think it would have been kind of odd for us to ask the state trooper for a map?"

"No," Sam huffed, "not at all. Aren't they supposed to serve and protect?"

"Yes, that is their motto, I think," Ray replied.

"Well, a map really would serve us well," Sam stated, "considering we're off the Interstate and back on the road to who-knows-where."

Ray was exiting the Interstate as Sam spoke. They stopped at the end of the off ramp and stared at another county highway, and Ray pointed to the sign.

"Either we go back to Atlantic, or we go north to Exira, wherever that is," Ray said.

"I don't think Atlantic is a good idea," Sam said.

"I agree," Alexis added.

"I say we go north and then west," Ray said. "If the government does send out word about us, they'll assume that we were on Interstate 80 headed west. They'll also think Omaha is our destination, so if we were to leave the Interstate now, they would think it would be to go south. We'll have to find our way on the back roads and cross into Nebraska on a less traveled highway."

Everyone agreed on it, and Christian was glad they were all thinking straight and along the same line. He struggled to keep his mind focused; he thought his life was over when that trooper came into view at the rest area.

Ray turned right and headed toward Exira.

"Well, without a map, it's going to take us a lot longer to get to your grandparents' farm," Ray said.

"Maybe there will be a gas station open in Exira," Sam said.

"Well, we'll find out in about eight miles," Alexis commented.

Alexis leaned forward and tried to locate a radio station. Christian leaned back and rested his head against the window while Sam quickly reclaimed her position close to him. Christian marveled at the calming effect Sam had on him when she was at his side. He was on the run with three other fugitives in a "borrowed" SUV with government agents hunting for them and a sly state patrolman in their rearview mirror. Christian knew nothing about the situation his parents were in, and even though they had a cell phone, he couldn't risk a call. His parents could be arrested and jailed for all he knew, and yet, he finally quieted the thumping in his chest while stroking Sam's left arm. Christian closed his eyes, and his thoughts drifted to his grandfather. He remembered Grandpa Pearson's blue eyes searching Christian for answers on the dam in South Dakota. He wondered how Grandpa dealt with all those images from World War II.

"I wonder how he did it," Christian mumbled to himself, forgetting that Alexis could hear everything.

"How who did what?" she asked from the front seat.

"Oh, nothing," Christian said at first. "I was wondering how my grandpa could go through life with all those images in his head, all those horrible scenes from the war."

Alexis didn't have time to respond. As Christian finished his sentence, the car swerved to the shoulder, and a thump rattled the undercarriage of the vehicle. Ray let off the gas, and the car coasted. The continuous thumping from the front of the SUV slowed its repetition until they came to a complete stop.

"Great!" Ray shouted. "Just, freakin' GREAT! Everyone alright?"

"Yeah, we're fine," Christian answered. "What did you hit?"

Christian had experienced this before, mostly on fishing trips with his dad and his grandpa. He easily recognized the sound of a flat tire.

"Looked like a two-by-four," Ray answered, as he smacked the steering wheel with the palm of his hand. Ray turned on the flashers as he opened the door.

"What do we do, now?" Sam asked.

"We hope the spare isn't flat," Christian answered.

"And we hope we only have one shredded tire!" Ray shouted, as he slammed the door shut.

"That boy has got a serious temper," Alexis huffed. "Knowing Mr. Banner, that spare has air in it. I bet he even has two spares in this thing."

"No kidding," Sam laughed. "He probably has it hidden in some secret compartment."

"Mr. Banner plans for everything," Alexis said, nervously; the edge returning to her voice.

Christian thought about her wording and the emphasis on the word "plans." If Mr. Banner was the bad guy, which Christian was positive he was, then the word "plan" carried a lot more danger for the four of them. What plan had Mr. Banner concocted for his Phenomenon Children? Christian was convinced there was no way Mr. Banner was the good guy in all of this.

"Well, I better go help him," Christian said, unenthusiastically.

Christian opened his door and stepped out into the night air. It was much cooler than it had been when they visited the rest area. Christian figured it was because the car had stopped in a valley. He remembered his father explaining one time that the cooler air always pooled in the valleys in the late summer and early fall.

Ray opened the back hatch and moved the tool box to get at the spare. Christian held up the plastic floor cover, and Ray easily yanked the tire from its hiding spot. He bounced it on the ground.

"Looks to be full," Ray said. "Can you grab the jack?"

Ray rolled the tire to the front of the SUV as Christian unscrewed the wing nut holding the jack in place.

"We're lucky we only lost one tire," Ray said.

"No kidding," Christian responded. "We really don't need to add auto theft to our resumés."

"Oh, I don't know," Ray said. "Stealing a car might be fun."

What is with this guy? Christian thought.

Ray dropped to his belly and slid the jack under the car. Christian loosened the lug-nuts, explaining to Ray that it was a trick he picked up from his father.

"It makes it easier to loosen them when the wheel is stationary on the ground," Christian stated.

"You were talking earlier about your grandfather," Ray said. "About how hard it must be with those images in his head."

"Yeah," Christian responded. "I don't know how you go through life with that in your brain."

"You just do," Ray said, flatly, and Christian sensed pain in Ray's words.

Ray turned the swivel on the jack with the tire iron, and the car nudged up slightly.

"I don't know how your grandpa has done it for almost half a century, though," Ray said. "A person must get better at it over time. I keep trying to get the picture of my parents out of my mind."

Christian felt uneasy as Ray relived the night of his accident.

"We were just driving home from town, when we hit a patch of black ice. The snow was blowing, so it was hard for Dad to see the road as it was, but then to hit ice right before the bridge. Neither of my parents were wearing their seatbelts.

"I used to give my dad a hard time about it, joking about going through life without him. He wore it sometimes, but usually he'd forget about it until we were on the road. I would remind him, and he'd put it on. I guess we were in such a hurry to beat the incoming storm that I didn't notice his seatbelt was unhitched.

"The car caught the edge of the bridge and rolled down into a creek. I always put my seatbelt on, so I just got shaken up a bit, but…"

Ray looked up from the jack. His face was stoic, and he continued in a calm tone.

"But they were hurt bad. Both of them hit the windshield. There was a lot of blood, and after a while, I could see their breath because the inside of the car was getting colder. I pleaded with them to wake up, but neither of them ever did. Water started seeping into the car, but I was pinned behind my mother's seat, so I couldn't reach them to help them. And I couldn't get out.

"My mother's breath was the first to disappear from the cold air. I remember gently running my hand along her hair over and over again. It was matted with blood, and when the sun came up the next morning, I could see the dark stains on the seats and spatters on the spider-webbed glass of the windshield. As much as I try to remember them before the accident, my mind always reverts back to those last few hours with them."

"I'm so sorry," Christian said, sadly shaking his head. "I didn't intend for my question to bring back those memories."

"Don't," Ray said, abruptly. "I am lucky to be here today. People don't understand us, Christian. The government just sees us as a military asset. Even the kids in school wouldn't understand if they knew the truth about us, about our special abilities. They would just see us as a circus act or some kind of freak show. In a small town like Red Oak, we're always viewed as weird anyway, since we have to keep to ourselves. It really works to our advantage being outcasts from day one. But I get angry when I think about what I've missed out on since that fateful day. The football games, the wrestling meets, a normal life…"

Ray's voice trailed off as he grabbed the tire iron and tightened the nuts.

"So how do you cope with it all?" Christian asked.

"You just do," Ray responded. "You stick with your kind to avoid unwanted scrutiny. I don't try to make friends with people, and I don't let people who aren't like me get too close."

The two boys stood quietly, and Christian felt like Ray was sizing him up.

"I don't envy you, Christian," he said.

"What?" Christian said in surprise. "I was just thinking the same about you."

Ray saw the puzzlement in Christian's expression, and he smiled as he lowered the vehicle, bringing the tire back to the ground. He stood and handed the tire iron to Christian before reaching down to retrieve the jack.

"I have dealt with what you are going through," Ray said, his face more serious. "I have made the journey through dealing with the loss of my family. I have accepted my life as a Phenomenon Child on the run, and I am ready to spend the rest of my life with Alexis, in complete secrecy. I am in survival mode. I have accepted my fate as a Phenomenon Child…"

"And?" Christian asked, wondering where this conversation was going.

"And you haven't. I know you haven't had much time to deal with all of this, but you are clinging to something dangerous."

"What's that?" Christian asked, puzzled.

"Hope," Ray said, calmly. "You still think there is hope. Hope that you will be reunited with your family, hope that things will go back to being the same, hope that you will wake up and the nightmare will be over. I have been down that road, Christian. If you want to survive as a Phenomenon Child, you need to get that particular kind of hope out of your system."

Ray grabbed the tire iron from Christian's hand and walked to the back of the SUV, leaving Christian to stew on Ray's revelation. Christian did not turn around. He felt waylaid by Ray's words, blind-sided. Ray was right; Christian held out hope that things would go back to normal. He wanted his life back.

"Why did you tell me all of this right now?" Christian asked, the anger coming out in his voice. "Why did you hit me with those words of wisdom?"

"Hey, cool it," Ray turned on Christian. "You need to know what lies in front of you. Sam won't tell you because she has the same problem. She clings to the same hope of reuniting with her family. That is why you two are perfect for each other."

Ray chuckled, and Christian's anger rose as he clenched his fists. He wanted to sock Ray right in the mouth. He could take him right here, because he had the element of surprise. Ray was not expecting a fight, but Christian intended to give him one. Christian was scared, and Ray's words held no comfort. In fact, the possible truth in Ray's statements fanned a terrified anger that had no reason to surface until now.

"It was easy for me to lose hope," Ray said, coolly. "I lost my family before I knew about how different I was."

Christian moved closer to Ray, prepared to attack him as he turned around.

With his back turned, Ray added, "Besides, you're my little phenomenon brother, now. I need to teach you the ropes."

Ray started walking away to the driver's side of the car, and Christian followed him, red hot with anger. He was NOT some kid brother.

"Don't you remember what your dad said before we left?" Ray asked, as he reached for the door.

"Huh?" Christian answered.

"He told us to look out for each other so he could see you again," Ray said.

Christian recalled those words and his temper cooled a little bit.

"I had to tell you about how dangerous hope is," Ray said, as he turned to face Christian.

"Why?" Christian asked, his anger relenting.

"Because you have no idea what kind of dire situation we are in," Ray said.

"Huh?" Christian responded.

Ray smiled.

"You don't have a clue as to what we're going to do next," Ray attacked, his voice rising. "You were dumbfounded by the state trooper. Well, those government agents that are after us are no state police! They know who we are now, and they will stop at nothing to catch us! There are no rules that bind them! Remember what happened to Charlie?"

Christian nodded, as he recalled the story of their friend in Phoenix. He had been kidnapped in front of a group of people at a convenience store.

Ray continued, his voice almost booming, "There was no front page article, no judicial process, no chance for the truth! They just took him!"

The two boys stood silently. They just took him. The words echoed in Christian's thoughts.

Ray grinned, and that restored some of the dying anger in Christian.

"Then why are you enjoying all of this so much?" Christian retorted. "How can you get any pleasure from this situation? I've noticed how excited you are!"

"This is our opportunity to break away from Mr. Banner and live our lives with no one looking over our shoulders," Ray said, his emotion rising, again. "I have spent too much time hoping for Mr. Banner to give us our exit, waiting for our own escape from all of this. Don't you get it? Your life will never be what it was! As long as you keep hoping for that, you are in a dangerous spot… And so is anyone who is with you."

Ray opened his door, calmly climbed in, and started the car. Christian stood motionless by the back door.

"You didn't have to be so point blank," Christian heard Alexis say before Ray slammed the door shut.

Christian yearned for his family. He wanted things to go back to normal, all square, but he knew that was a long ways away. He also knew that Ray was wrong. Hope was necessary in times of crisis. It was the thread that would keep the four of them together, and it was the key to avoiding capture. Without hope, the only option would be to give up. Christian would do whatever it took to be reunited with his family, and he knew hope was crucial to succeeding.

Sam opened her door and stepped out, gently closing it behind her.

"Christian, you okay?"

He didn't answer.

"I am sorry about what Ray said to you. Alexis did play by play until you were both loud enough that her hearing wasn't needed," she said, smiling.

Christian turned to Samantha and pulled her close.

"I will not give up hope," he whispered. "No matter what he says, no matter what happens, I will see my family again."

"Don't be too hard on Ray," Sam whispered back. "You are probably his favorite person right now."

Christian pulled away from Sam and looked at her in puzzlement.

"If it wasn't for you, Christian, we wouldn't be on the run like this," Sam explained. "Ray has been chomping at the bit to get away from Mr. Banner ever since I joined them. Not sure why, but I think Ray has never appreciated all that Mr. Banner has done for us."

"Like he doesn't trust him?" Christian asked.

"No, I don't think it's a lack of trust," Sam answered. "I think Ray felt like Mr. Banner was trying to replace his dad, and Ray has always been uncomfortable with that."

Ray opened the door.

"Hey, Freud, you can psychoanalyze all you want, but let's do it in the car," Ray said. "We have spent enough time out here. We're lucky a car hasn't come this way."

"Alexis's ears are annoying," Christian said, as he opened Sam's door.

"I heard that," Alexis sang from the front seat.

Sam climbed in before Christian, and Ray spun the tires on the soft shoulder after Christian's door closed, fishtailing before the rubber met the asphalt.

"Oh, man!" Ray exclaimed. "I've got to use the bathroom again!"

Alexis laughed as the SUV raced over the hill.

"Too bad your bladder isn't as big as your mouth," she laughed, grabbing Ray's cheek and giving it a pinch.

Soon, the faint lights of a town were visible ahead but a ways off to the right.

"I hope Exira has a gas station that is open," Sam said.

"And that gas station better have a restroom, or I'm using the trees," Ray said.

"You are not peeing in public," Alexis scolded.

"It's only public if someone is watching," Ray laughed, and Christian laughed, too.

CHAPTER 3

They drove past Exira without stopping, since they would have had to drive two miles from the main road to get to it. They decided to continue north. In a matter of minutes, lights of an extremely small town glowed in the distance. The SUV slowed as it skirted the east end of the town of Hamlin. A blinking red light marked the intersection of Highway 71 and County Highway 44. Ray decided to turn to the west without asking, and no one in the car objected.

"I think we have gone far enough to the north," Ray stated. "Maybe we need to drive parallel to the Interstate, or we might never get to Nebraska."

In less than a minute, they had traveled a few blocks to the opposite end of town. Sam marveled that the town of Hamlin only had two roads.

"Actually, the town has four roads," Ray said. "There are two more roads running perpendicular to the ones we saw. I noticed them as we came to that intersection back there."

"I counted six," Alexis said, smugly.

"Six?" Ray questioned.

"You forgot the two highways we have driven on," she answered, smugly.

Ray rolled his eyes as the dim light of the small town retreated behind them. Kimballton was only ten miles from Hamlin, according to the sign at the side of the road outside the edge of the tiny village of Hamlin.

"Maybe Kimballton will have a gas station," Sam said, hope in her voice.

Christian wondered if it was getting too late for a small town to have an open gas station. The highway curved south for a mile before turning back to the west again. This pattern repeated two more times before the road appeared to straighten to the west for the final stretch to Kimballton.

"Well, this looks more promising," Sam said energetically as they rolled into town.

Kimballton rivaled Hamlin in size, but the main drag appeared to be just as desolate. A Casey's General Store marked the entrance to Kimballton, but all the lights were off. They drove past sleepy, little houses, a few with white picket fences and front porch swings.

"At least they have a gas station," Sam huffed. "Too bad it's closed."

The only breath of life in the entire village emanated from a glass door propped open with a cinderblock. The rest of the businesses along the brick walls on either side of Main Street were closed. Three cars and a rusted-out pickup sat in the diagonal stalls in front of a bar called Hotel Whiskey. Every other door was dark. Ray rolled down his window, and the sound of twanging country music and a few ye-haws reached Christian's ears.

"You are not stopping here," Alexis informed Ray, as he slowed the SUV.

"I don't plan on it, but I don't think anything else is open," Ray answered. "At least it would have a restroom."

"Hold it!" Alexis demanded, pointing at him.

In addition to finding a map, Ray still needed to use the bathroom. Thinking the same thought, Christian scanned each side-street for a possible bathroom, as the SUV rolled slowly through town. Maybe they could use a hedge row on a darkened street.

"I don't see anywhere for us to use the bathroom or get a map," Christian said in frustration. "Maybe the next town."

Ray sped up as the car reached the west edge of town.

"That sign says sixteen miles to Harlan, you'll have to hold it until then," Alexis said. "Isn't Harlan in the same conference as Red Oak?"

"I'm pretty sure it is," Christian answered. "It sounds familiar."

"Maybe we can get a map there," Sam added in anticipation. "If it is the same size as Red Oak, it has to have an open gas station."

"I can't wait sixteen miles," Ray said. "I have got to go, now! My bladder is killin' me."

"Hold it!" Alexis hissed through gritted teeth.

"I am pulling over," Ray fought back, and Christian noticed him shift uncomfortably in his seat.

"Not here!" Alexis cried. "Don't be stupid! At least go up a gravel road, away from the highway."

Ray slowed the SUV and turned right at the first gravel road he came to.

"How far do I need to go?" Ray questioned, sarcastically. "I don't think anyone will see me hangin' out from this far away from the highway."

"At least over the hill," Alexis said. "Can you hold it that long?"

Alexis was provoking Ray, and he hammered the accelerator in response to her demands. Christian felt the weight of his body shift backwards into the seat, as Ray refused to let off the gas.

"Is this far enough?" Ray questioned, as he turned to smile at Alexis. "Maybe I should go another mile to be safe."

"Safe?" Sam shouted. "Watch the road!"

The vehicle shot up the incline and sped over the top of the hill, hurtling down the other side. Christian lifted in his seat as they cleared the peak and descended. The sensation reminded Christian of a roller coaster dropping down its tracks, and he didn't like the feeling.

Then Ray locked up the brakes, and Christian heard Ray shout and Alexis scream as a sickening thud met the front end of the SUV. The seatbelt gripped Christian and held him in place. It took half a minute for him to regain his focus. When he did, Christian saw the passenger side of the windshield was a spider web of cracked glass.

CHAPTER 4

After the initial locking of the brakes, Christian's body had jerked forward. The seatbelt held him in place, but his head continued forward and down. Initially, he didn't catch sight of what the car had hit. Christian had heard a high-pitched voice scream, and then the sickly "thud," before catching sight of the blood-spattered windshield. The scene continued to replay for Christian.

"Everyone okay?" Ray's voice called through the fog in Christian's mind.

"Christian," Sam said, as she shook him. "You alright?"

Christian nodded, as the haze cleared.

"Alexis," Christian whispered, his voice cracking, "She okay?"

"Why wouldn't I be?" Alexis said, peeking around from the front seat.

"I thought," Christian stammered, "I thought you hit the windshield. It's smashed. I, I didn't see what happened."

"Deer," Ray said, unhappily, as he turned off the engine.

Ray opened his door, and Alexis did the same.

"You sure you're okay?" Sam questioned.

"All I saw was the broken windshield," Christian explained. "I thought Alexis had slammed into it, and that was what made that loud thud."

"Fortunately, we all had our seatbelts on," Sam said. "Otherwise, someone would have gone flying. Ray was going pretty fast when we came over the hill."

"Well, Alexis didn't want me to pee near the highway," Ray pleaded his case.

"But I didn't tell you to gun it over the hill, did I?" Alexis shot back, as her hair whipped around with the jerk of her head.

Christian unhitched his seatbelt and pushed on the door. Sam followed him out of the SUV, which sat cockeyed in the middle of the gravel road. The cool night air chilled Christian but helped clear the cloud that seemed to be suffocating his brain activity. Sam hugged his arm as they walked around the front of the car. Ray and Alexis stood motionless and quiet in front of the SUV on the passenger side.

The driver's side headlight had crumpled on impact with the deer, but the other headlight illuminated the back half of the brown body crumpled in a heap near the ditch. Alexis shifted her weight, allowing the full force of the headlamp to shine, and the light glistened off two red stumps where the front legs should have been. Sharp points of white bone poked from the tip of each fleshy knob.

"It came out of nowhere," Ray said in a hushed tone.

Alexis put an arm around Ray's waist. No one spoke. The deer's black eyes stared intently at them, as the body shivered with uneven breaths. It attempted to lift its body, as if it was going to make a run for it, but then its head flopped back to the ground, hopeless in its endeavor. Christian saw terror in the black eyes, as if the deer realized escape was impossible and death, inevitable.

Christian marveled at how somber everyone was at the side of the defeated animal, including himself. Christian hunted a lot with his father and grandfather, so the death of an animal was just part of life, but this time it felt different. In a way, Christian could relate to the whitetail deer lying on the road in front of him. It was just going about a normal life, when BAM, its world was turned upside-down. One accident and its life was dramatically changed. It couldn't have avoided this, just like Christian couldn't have avoided what happened to him on that lake in South Dakota.

Christian decided he was not going to end up helpless like the animal in front of him. If the four of them could not figure out a solution to this new problem, Christian knew they would all end up like the deer in the road. They needed to act quickly.

"We need to get out of here," Christian stated, calmly. "If someone finds us, they are going to want to report the accident, that can't happen."

"Well, we have a problem," Ray said, pointing to the broken headlight.

"It's just a headlight," Sam said.

Christian saw what Sam missed; the tire on the passenger side was shredded.

"The front end must have crushed the tire," Christian said.

"Now what?" Sam asked.

"Of all the stupid things," Alexis sobbed, "You have to get all cocky and go flying down a gravel road."

Ray furrowed his brow and opened his mouth but changed his mind. Instead of arguing, he put an arm around Alexis.

"Now what are we supposed to do?" Sam added.

"Well, first, we need to stay calm and focused on the task at hand," Christian stated. "We need to get this car off the road, and we need to do it now!"

"What about the deer?" Sam asked.

"It's as good as dead, already," Ray said. "Christian's right. We need to move this car before someone comes by here."

"Well, we can't drive it," Alexis said through tears. "We're screwed."

Ray knelt down to inspect the tire, and Christian walked to the edge of the ditch and around the back of the disabled vehicle. His steps crunched the gravel, as he slowly made his way in the dark until his eyes adjusted. Maybe the SUV wouldn't take them to Nebraska, but they needed to get it off the road so they could come up with a plan. He just needed to find a driveway across the ditch into the field. Christian could see trees about twenty yards from the road. All they had to do was get the car into those trees, but how? Then Christian found a way to get the vehicle across the ditch.

"There's a path back here that goes into those trees," Christian called to the three teens huddled around the front of the SUV.

Ray quickly jogged over to take a look.

"This path goes back off the road," Christian explained, as he pointed to the faint outline of a trail between the trees and rows of corn. "It must be a tractor path. Maybe we can get the SUV far enough into the trees that no one will see it. At least, not until the sun is up."

"I'll go see if I can back it up to here," Ray said. "Christian, you stay put, so I have an idea of where I am going. I will be able to see you in the taillights.

Ray started the engine and backed up. The vehicle shuddered, but it was moving. With only three functioning wheels, Ray struggled to keep it on a straight line. Soon, Ray pulled the front tires even with Christian's location. With the shine of the headlight, Christian jogged down the path to the tree line. About twenty yards past the start of the trees, Christian could see an opening for the SUV. He raced back to Ray.

"There is an opening in the trees about twenty yards in," Christian explained.

"Well, I can't get this thing to go more than a few feet forward," Ray said, frustration in his voice.

"Can you turn it around and back it in?" Christian asked. "It seemed to go in reverse pretty easily."

"I can try," Ray said. "Just keep an eye on those ditches. They look pretty deep."

When Christian had walked down the road moments before, he saw the danger the ditches posed. Tall weeds hid the threat the ditch posed; they were quite a bit steeper than they appeared at first glance. Christian watched the road edge as Ray struggled to turn the car around. Four or five feet forward, crank the wheel, a foot or two back, crank the wheel, forward again. Ray repeated the steps until he finally positioned the vehicle to go in reverse onto the tractor path. Christian called out to Ray when he needed to turn his wheels, and soon Ray had backed up even with the edge of the trees.

They were lucky it had not rained for a couple days in this area, or they never would have gotten the SUV that far off of the road. Ray almost had the SUV far enough back to turn in behind the tree line, when Christian heard Sam screaming.

He looked up to see her blonde hair in the gleam of the single headlight, and then the words registered, "CAR! CAR! CAR!"

"Lights!" Christian said to Ray.

Ray killed the one headlight, and they were plunged into darkness. Ray turned off the engine, as Sam crouched behind the SUV. Christian moved beside her.

Sam explained in a hushed voice while gasping for breath, "While you two were moving the car, Alexis and I decided someone should be on the lookout for any cars coming over the hill. I was standing up on the road, and I could see the highway. I saw a car turn onto this road."

"Where is Alexis?" Christian asked.

"She stayed up by the deer," Sam said. "She didn't want to leave it to die all alone, but I am sure she took cover when she heard me holler."

"She probably heard the car, herself," Ray whispered.

Christian wondered why Alexis, who seemed so tough, with such a cold persona, felt such pity for the animal that had caused them so much trouble. He thought Alexis would have responded with anger. Christian was surprised to see a caring side of the huntress.

Lights glowed on the road in front of them, and a sedan cruised past their hiding spot. Just before it passed behind the trees, Christian saw the brake lights glow red. He moved to the driver side of the SUV and crept toward the front for a better look.

The car stopped and both doors creaked open on ancient hinges. Two people got out, and Christian saw them talking in the glow of the headlights. After a minute, they both walked back to their open doors, and the dark-colored sedan raced up the road and over the hill.

"Where's Alexis?" Ray said aloud from the driver's side window of the SUV, startling Christian, who almost fell forward to the ground.

"I forgot you were in there," Christian whispered back. "You scared the crap out of me."

"I am over here," a voice called from the road. "I waited too long, and I didn't think I could make it to the trees, so I hid in some bushes on the other side of the road. Almost broke my leg in the ditch. Those things are a lot deeper than they look."

Christian looked knowingly at Ray, who rolled his eyes as Alexis walked down the path toward them.

"That was Melvin and Ethel on their way back from some birthday party," Alexis explained. "Melvin wanted to call the DNR about the deer, whatever that means."

"Department of Natural Resources," Christian said. "It's the game and parks people."

"Great," Sam huffed. "Now, the game warden's going to be out here."

"Not until tomorrow," Alexis said, calming Sam's fears. "Ethel was adamant that her husband wasn't going to wake up Rick at this late hour. I'm thinking Rick is the game warden, then. I would guess ole' Melvin will make the wise decision and call in the morning. I think Ethel wears the pants in that relationship."

"Let's get this rig hidden, before someone else comes along and decides to stay awhile," Ray sighed, "and before I wet my pants."

Christian guided Ray the rest of the way into the trees, and Alexis and Sam stood near the road to make sure Mr. Banner's SUV was well-hidden.

"Looks good from here," Alexis hollered.

Ray shut off the engine and the lone headlight, before he hobbled back a few feet into the trees to relieve himself.

"Here comes another car!" Sam shouted, as the two girls jogged down the path toward the trees.

They stood in silence behind the SUV as the headlights flashed on the road. They would be able to see only bits and pieces of the scene from their position behind the rows of trees. Alexis crept around to the other side of the vehicle, and Christian knew her movements were simply to get a better listen of what might be said on the road. Christian decided to follow her, because he wanted a better look. She leaned against the thick trunk of an old tree. Christian knelt beside her and found an opening in the underbrush. He had a good view of the pickup on the road and the deer lying in the glow of the headlights.

A tall, wiry kid walked around the front of the truck. He looked like he was in high school. Christian saw the boy retreat back to the passenger side, open the door, and lean into the cab. It appeared that he was looking for something. Finding what he was after, the boy quickly walked back to the deer. He looked down the road toward the highway and up the other way. Christian did not possess the same hearing ability as Alexis, but he recognized the unmistakable sound of a clip being slammed into the butt of a pistol.

"Oh no," Alexis whispered as the boy extended his right arm in front of him and lowered the pistol at a downward angle toward the animal.

Christian and Alexis both jumped a bit, as the shot pierced the still night air. Even though they both knew it was coming, they still recoiled at the sound. Unaware of what was transpiring on the road, Sam yelped once at the sound of the gunshot.

The unexpected sound from the trees surprised the boy on the road. He whipped his head around and walked to the passenger side of the pickup once more. With the pistol still firmly held by his right hand, he reached into the truck. He pulled out a large yellow contraption that was shaped like a hand-held hair dryer.

"What is that?" Alexis asked in a whisper.

Before Christian could give a hushed response, a beam of light reflected off the side panels of the pickup. With the high-powered spotlight in his left hand, the boy crouched and crept quietly on the edge of the gravel, masking his footsteps on the soft ground near the ditch. He raised the spotlight, and a beam of light illuminated the trees above Alexis and Christian.

"Don't move," Christian whispered in such a low voice, he wasn't sure if even Alexis would hear him.

He saw Alexis slowly nod.

"He's checking the trees for a raccoon," he whispered, almost inaudibly. "Don't give him any reason to shine that light at ground level. Just stay still."

Alexis nodded, again. He could see her rigid body press harder against the tree.

A phone rang from the road, Christian raised his head to look through another opening in the branches. Christian recognized the should-I-answer-or-not body language of the boy on the road. The boy looked at the phone, then the trees, then back to the phone, then the trees again. Finally, the boy raised the phone to his ear.

"Hello."

The boy clicked off the spotlight.

"I am on my way, Dad!" he said with irritation. "No, I am about five miles from the farm. I just passed through Kimballton."

The high school kid slumped his shoulders and turned toward the pickup.

"No, I found a deer on the road near the highway."

"No, it's dead."

"Someone must have clipped it pretty good. Knocked its front legs clean off."

"No, the vehicle isn't still here."

"Oh, I stopped to look at the deer, and I heard a coon in the trees."

"I know, I know, I'm getting back into the truck right now."

He put the phone back into his pocket, but he shined the beam of light on the trees one more time before closing the passenger door. Then he walked around the front of the pickup and entered the driver's side, still pointing the spotlight into the tree tops. Christian finally heard the slam of the door, and the truck peeled gravel before rocketing up the hill.

CHAPTER 5

"What do we do now?" Alexis asked.

The four teenagers huddled together outside Mr. Banner's crippled SUV. Twenty minutes had passed since the pickup raced off to the north, and they had not seen another vehicle. Christian wondered if Alexis's confidence had been shaken by the boy with the pistol, or if she struggled with what she thought was brutality when the high school kid shot the deer. Christian understood the logic behind his actions on the road. The deer's injuries were too severe. To let it go on living was cruelty, but Christian was positive Alexis viewed the boy's act as heartless.

"We need another car," Ray said.

"But I don't see any dealerships around here," Sam said, attempting to be funny.

"We aren't going to buy one," Ray said in exasperation. "We need to steal one."

"I don't like the idea of stealing a car," Sam said, her voice faltering.

"I don't think we can walk all the way to Nebraska," Ray commented.

"I know, I know," Sam retorted, "I just don't like the idea of leaving someone without a car. I am well aware of our situation, and I know we need a car. I just feel bad about it."

"If it makes you feel any better," Christian interrupted, "I am sure my cousin will return it when we are done borrowing it."

"Yeah," Ray said, with a wide grin, "just like we borrowed Mr. Banner's SUV, only we won't total the front end of our next car."

Christian marveled at how well he could see now that his eyes had fully adjusted to the darkness. Alexis sat quietly on the ground. Her legs were crisscrossed with her body hunched forward. Her chin rested on closed fists, almost like she was trying to curl up into a little ball.

Ray and Sam stood across from Christian, who leaned against the hood of the SUV. Ray's arms were folded across his chest, but he was not angry. Christian could tell that Ray was thinking about the situation, mulling over things in his mind. Sam's curly locks of hair had been ruffled by the night, and she kept brushing the curls from her eyes. While Ray stood still, Sam slowly rocked her weight from one leg to the other, almost like an awkward middle school slow-dance movement. Christian guessed Sam was cold, so he reached for her hand and pulled her into his arms, so her back was against his chest. Alexis continued to sit motionless.

"Better?" Christian asked.

"Definitely," Sam responded.

Sam rested her head just below Christian's chin.

"So what happens to this?" Sam questioned, as she pointed her thumb toward Mr. Banner's SUV.

"We just leave it," Ray said.

"So, how do we find another vehicle?" Sam asked.

"Good question," Ray commented, as he pondered the predicament.

"Can either of you hotwire a car?" Sam asked.

Christian shook his head.

"I forgot about that," Ray said, dejectedly. "We are going to need keys for the car we want to steal."

"Yeah, and who is going to give us the keys to their car?" Sam posed.

"Wait!" Christian shouted, excitedly, as he pushed Sam off of him. "Wait… a… second!"

"What is it?" Sam asked.

"I bet we can find a car around here," Christian answered, as his excitement grew.

"Sure," Ray huffed. "Every farm has a vehicle on it, but no one is going to just hand over the keys."

"I mean, I bet the people around here are just like my grandpa," Christian explained. "Oh, why didn't I think of it in the first place?"

"Think of what?" Ray and Sam responded in unison.

Christian's grandparents never locked anything on the farm, not even the farm house, unless they planned to be gone for days at a time. The keys to Grandpa's car were usually in the ignition in an unlocked garage.

"I bet we can find a car with the keys in it," Christian stated, jumping around excitedly. "It may take some checking, but I am positive someone around here has a car with the keys in it. They might even be dangling in the ignition."

"What are you smoking?" Ray said with a laugh.

"Seriously," Christian pleaded. "I have been around farms all my life. Yeah, I lived in Omaha, but most of my extended family has lived in the country at one point or another. I spent a lot of summers on Grandpa's farm, and he never locked anything up, except the fuel tanks. His brothers never locked anything up, either.

"Remember when we drove out to my grandfather's farm, and the door to the A-Barn was open and the camper was unlocked? Every vehicle they own has the keys in it. You never lose them that way, I guess. I bet you a million dollars we can find a car with keys tonight. It may take some time, but we'll find a car we can use."

"Alexis, what do you think?" Ray asked.

Alexis looked up from her position on the ground and half-smiled. She rubbed her eyes as she stood.

"A million dollars, huh?" Alexis questioned, rhetorically. "Are you sure you're good for it? I could use a million dollars."

"Whoa, I am not losing this bet," Christian grinned. "Besides, my father owes me about ten million from all the bets he has lost to me, so I'm good for it. You better be searching for your checkbook."

Alexis smiled, and Christian guessed that she was looking for some way to get the deer off her mind. What better way to do that than by taking a field trip. Christian thought Alexis figured on going along. She would be able to hear trouble long before Christian would see it.

"So who goes?" Sam asked.

Sam had a knack for asking good questions. Sometimes, her questions bordered on "duh," but at least she asked them.

Christian liked that about her. She had no fear of looking silly around others because she simply wanted to know what was going on. She wasn't goofy, like most girls Christian had encountered; in fact, Samantha was genuine. Sam did have the ability to read people's emotions, so maybe it was easier to ask when you could tell how people were feeling.

Alexis spoke first, "I think Sam and Ray should stay with the car. Christian and I can look for a new ride."

"Shouldn't we all stick together?" Sam asked, nervously.

"Alexis is right," Ray said. "It will be too hard to sneak around with four people. Christian and Alexis should go find a car."

"What are we going to do?" Sam quizzed.

"Maybe we should get the bags from the back," Ray said. "Take anything of use from the SUV."

"And then we'll wait here for them to come back?" Sam said, uneasily.

"What do you think, Ray?" Alexis asked. "Do you guys need to move away from the SUV while we're gone? In case someone else stops and decides to investigate a little more."

"Or the game warden shows up," Sam said, concerned.

"But where?" Ray asked. "I have no idea what's around here."

"You could hide in the cornfield," Christian said.

He pointed toward the south in the direction of the highway.

"This cornfield stretches up over the hill," Christian explained, as he walked out toward the gravel road to peer down the fence line. "Once you get a couple rows deep, no one will see you."

"But how do we find them?" Alexis asked.

"Easy. They walk until they reach a fence," Christian answered. "The first fence you come to over that hill will be our meeting spot. It will be easy to spot from the road, since there should be a break in the corn where the fence is. Alexis and I just have to make sure we keep track of where we are at, and we can find the fence when we come back."

"I don't know about this," Sam said, concerned.

"Trust me," Christian said. "I have spent many nights keeping track of where my dad's pickup was parked when we go fishing. He does a good job getting the location of new fishing holes, and

I navigate. If it wasn't for me, my dad might still be looking for his pickup somewhere in the country."

Christian was trying to add a little humor to reassure everyone, but they weren't buying it. He didn't see what the big deal was.

"Seems risky," Alexis said. "I am with Sam on this one."

"If we get turned around," Christian pleaded his case, "we go back to Kimballton and drive from there. This gravel road was the first right turn once we passed the sign for Harlan. It's a piece of cake. I am telling you guys, I have a knack for these sorts of things."

Ray said, "I am with Christian. It makes sense. We can't all go traipsing around in the dark, and Christian has already proven that he knows more about farms than all of us put together. Alexis can hear what trouble lies ahead. Do we have any other options?"

Ray's question hung in the air as he looked at each of the girls. Neither of them spoke, and Christian knew his plan was the only option.

"Do you think we need to scrape off serial numbers on the car?" Sam asked.

"Only if we can find something to use for the scraping," Ray said, "but we should take the license plates off and hide them in the brush somewhere."

"Good idea," Christian said.

"Well, let's get going," Alexis whispered.

"Why are you whispering?" Christian asked.

As he finished the question, a car raced over the hill from the north.

"Anything but a minivan like that one," Ray said, as Alexis moved around the SUV.

"Really? You're going to be picky?" Alexis retorted.

"Not really a minivan kind of guy," Ray said with a smile.

Alexis crept to the edge of the trees, and Christian followed her. The car didn't slow down as it approached.

"Must not see the deer," Alexis stated.

"Or doesn't care," Christian responded.

Alexis's body tensed at Christian's words, and she winced.

"Sorry," Christian whispered. "I didn't mean for that to sound as harsh as it did."

"That's okay," Alexis replied. "Let's go."

The van rattled as it roared past, and Alexis and Christian jogged up the road to the north behind it.

The stones and gravel crunched beneath their feet. It was an eerie sound in the still night as they ran. At the same time, it was calming. The two stopped at the top of the hill, and Christian attempted to keep his breathing quiet, so Alexis could hear more easily. She turned to look back to the south, where they had come from.

Christian hesitated then asked, "Another car?"

"No," Alexis turned toward him grinning. "Just Ray being a typical big brother."

"Huh?"

"Ray is questioning Sam about you," Alexis whinnied. "Making sure she's keeping the relationship appropriate."

"What relationship?" Christian asked, but he knew the answer.

"Ray is a good guy," Alexis said. "He cares about the people close to him, but he just has a hard time expressing anything, good or bad, unless he really knows you."

"You don't struggle with that," Christian said, expecting Alexis to lash back at him.

"When you grow up like I did," Alexis explained, "you have to be tough on the inside and the outside. I know I can be intimidating, but that's who I am. I'm okay with that. Sam can see people's emotions, so it is easy for her to avoid bad seeds. Ray doesn't let people get close very often, and that is his shell of defense. Me, well, I guess I am always on the offensive; the alpha female is what one of my teachers called it. I attack before I get attacked, so people stay clear."

"I guess that's why I always thought of you as a panther ready to pounce when I first met you," Christian said, realizing he was moving into uncharted waters with Alexis.

Alexis almost buckled with laughter. Christian wondered why his comparison to a panther was so funny.

"I don't believe it," Alexis said, regaining her composure. "I didn't think Ray had it in him."

"What are you talking about?" Christian asked.

"The birds and the bees from Ray," she said with a smile. "I wish we had time to listen to that conversation, but we better get moving. There is another car coming from that way."

Alexis pointed down the road, past the spot where they hit the deer. After a couple of seconds, Christian saw the haze of lights over the rise of the hill. They jogged up the road another fifty feet before moving off the gravel behind a couple of bushes at the edge of a pasture.

"It slowed down, but it didn't stop," Alexis said.

Soon the car crested the hill and sped past them. Alexis and Christian waited for the car to disappear into the night and then crossed the ditch once more and continued their jog down the hill. Christian spotted a mailbox on the right side of the road. A driveway wound through the trees back to a small farmhouse with a single light illuminating a wooden horse barn and two small sheds. The lights were off in the house, and Alexis pulled Christian off the driveway to the trees.

"Wait a second," she whispered. "Let me listen."

Christian waited at least ten seconds before he spoke, "Anyone home?"

"I don't think so, but I can hear a dog in the house," she answered.

They clung to the shadows as they walked toward the house. A bark behind a large window broke the silent air. Christian and Alexis backed up a couple steps, back into the shadows. A few seconds later, a light popped on upstairs. Christian didn't wait for Alexis to tell him what to do, and the two teens raced out the driveway and darted right, back onto the gravel road.

Alexis laughed, "I hate dogs."

"Me, too," Christian responded.

They stopped to rest at the top of the hill, and Alexis tuned her acute hearing back toward the farmhouse with the dog. Christian scanned the road to the north, as he stood back to back with Alexis.

"Hey, I see a light back in the trees over there," Christian said, surprised.

"Where?" Alexis answered, turning to look in the direction Christian was pointing.

"Off to the left, just over the top of the next hill," he replied.

"Not seeing it," she scoffed. "You must be dreaming."

"Wow," Christian said, "unbelievable hearing, but you can't see that light. There is a house back up in those trees, guaranteed."

"Wanna put another million on it?" Alexis asked with a grin.

"Like taking candy from a baby," Christian returned the smile. For the first time, Christian felt like Alexis appreciated him, and he was actually enjoying the fact that he was with her for this assignment.

"You mean panther," Alexis said, harshly, before her suddenly stern look melted into a laugh.

"Did I say panther? I meant kitten," Christian said, as he took off on a full sprint down the road.

The air rushed past him, and he sensed his heart pounding in his chest, but he refused to let Alexis catch him until he wanted to be caught. He reached the bottom of the hill and began to climb the incline of the next. When he noticed two wagon wheels sticking halfway out of the ground ahead on the left, Christian skidded to a halt at a dirt path that twisted up from the road into a stand of trees. Alexis put on the brakes a few seconds later.

"I was wondering when you would stop," she panted. "I am pretty quick, but I didn't realize you were that fast."

Alexis seemed genuinely impressed with Christian's speed, and he felt good about that.

"Looks like you owe me a cool mill," Christian said, as he gasped for breath.

"Let's see where it leads," Alexis said, catching her wind. "I don't see a house, so I don't owe you squat, yet. It probably leads to another field."

The wagon wheels marked a narrow drive that led up through a grove of trees. The dirt road climbed the hill near a barbed wire fence before winding through some ancient cottonwoods. The thick canopy blocked out quite a bit of the full moon's light, so the two teens had to make their way more slowly than before. Twice Alexis tripped on a gnarled root, and Christian poked fun at her lack of night vision.

They followed the route through the trees, stopping once for Alexis to check for sounds of life, especially dogs. The path widened as it snaked between two grain bins and emptied into an open area in front of a house. Lights on three poles lit up the entire space.

"I owe you," Alexis admitted. "You were right on this one."

"Small bills will do just fine," Christian responded with a proud chuckle. "Twenties and hundreds."

Christian noticed that the road they had taken was not the primary entrance to the farm. Another driveway rolled down the hill for at least a hundred yards before disappearing into the darkness.

The two-story farmhouse matched the barns on the farm with its white siding and red shutters and red trim. The barns were the same color scheme, only reversed, with red walls and white trim and white doors. The colors reminded him of a farm near his grandpa's place, where a guy had painted his barns with the colors of the University of Nebraska, scarlet and cream. Christian almost expected to see a big red "N" adorning the side of one of the barns or a Herbie Husker mascot painted on a building.

"I don't hear anything," Alexis said, "but let's go around the back of the house. I feel pretty out-in-the-open right here."

They crept around a large steel grain bin and into a row of trees that ran along the back of the house. After listening for sounds from inside the house, Alexis said she was confident that no one was around, and that there were no signs of a dog. A long building extended from the other side of the house, but it was not connected. Christian assumed it was the garage, even though it looked long enough to park ten cars side-by-side. A sidewalk extended from the back of the house to a windowed door in the side of the long building.

Christian walked confidently to the door and tried to turn the knob.

"It's locked," he said, in frustration.

"I guess this guy isn't your grandpa," Alexis laughed. "Can you see anything in there?"

Christian put his face against the window and shielded his eyes from the light on the pole above. He could tell that a vehicle was missing from this garage.

"There's an open space and then an old, beat up pickup, but I can't make out any other vehicles in the dim light," he said. "It looks like this building is open all the way down to the other side, but I can't tell for sure."

Alexis huffed, "Yeah, open all the way down, except for the door. I say we break the glass."

She searched the immediate area and picked up a brick from a stack near the back of the building. Alexis raised her arm.

"Whoa!" Christian exclaimed, blocking her throw just in time. "There are other doors. Let's check them first. We couldn't all ride in the cab of that pickup anyway. It's only got a bench seat across the front. Four would be a tight fit, and it would draw a lot of suspicion."

Christian led Alexis around to the front of the building. The first door looked like a normal garage door. Christian pulled up on it, but it wouldn't budge.

The remaining entry points were large sliding doors, big enough for a tractor to fit through. Christian tried the first, but it was locked. The second one squeaked on its rollers when he gave it a shove, and with a little muscle, Christian was able to push it open. The lights from the farm pushed away the darkness of the entry way. Christian recognized what looked like a John Deere planter in front of him. His grandfather owned a similar one.

"Wait," Alexis said, in a whisper. "Push it closed."

Christian didn't wait for her to explain. He knew all too well that Alexis had heard something. The huge door groaned as he pulled on it to get it back into place.

"Follow me," Alexis said, leading Christian back the way they came.

As they turned the corner, Christian peeked back down the driveway. He saw headlights turn down the drive, and his nerves began to fray.

"Looks like the owners of the farm are coming home," Christian whispered.

"There is a good hiding spot behind the house," Alexis said, calmly.

It was a good thing Alexis stayed calm, because Christian's heart was pounding as his adrenaline kicked in. She led him into a stand of trees. Christian couldn't see that much from his vantage point, but he knew Alexis would be able to hear everything.

The headlights glowed on the side of the house, and a silver SUV stopped in front of the garage. A light flipped on behind the window on the side door of the building, as the mechanized opener moaned from inside. The vehicle's engine purred, waiting for the door to finish lifting. In a matter of seconds, car doors slammed shut and muffled voices drifted to Christian's ears. After a few minutes of hushed discussion from the garage, a woman walked from the front of the building toward the house.

"Don't be too long," the woman called over her shoulder.

"Don't worry," a male voice called back.

The grind of the garage door sounded again.

Alexis looked at Christian and grinned, "I guess I owe you two million dollars."

Christian wondered what Alexis had heard.

CHAPTER 6

A young woman in a floral-print dress crossed the small grassy area between the garage and the two-story house. She was slender everywhere but her midsection. It was obvious that she was pregnant. The woman's hands cradled the basketball protruding from her belly under the dress.

"She is headed to the laundry room," Alexis whispered. "She plans to sort laundry and start a load before going to the bedroom to read for a while."

"What about the husband?" Christian asked, in a hushed voice.

"He saw the deer on the road," Alexis said. "He plans to take a tractor down and move it."

"Where?" Christian questioned.

"He told her he was going to move it off the road and call someone to come and pick it up in the morning," Alexis explained.

A diesel engine roared to life from the far end of the garage-type building, and soon Christian saw a tractor roll into view. A young man opened the door and jumped to the ground. He quickly crossed the open gravel to a barn on the far side of the farmstead. Alexis put her hand on Christian's shoulder.

"Wait here. I'll be back in a minute," she whispered as the man disappeared into the red barn.

Alexis bounded from their hiding spot and disappeared around the far side of the house. Christian waited, impatiently, wondering what Alexis was doing. A few minutes later, the man returned to his tractor. There was a grind of the gears, and the green monster lurched forward. It slowly climbed the gradual incline toward the grain bins before lumbering from the light of the farm into the trees and down the path Alexis and Christian had taken to find the farm.

The growl of the engine faded into the night air as the tractor cleared the hill and the noise all but disappeared as it traveled down to the gravel road. Christian was alone.

A light popped on inside the house, and then another illuminated the room near the back door. The farmer's wife hauled a large laundry basket down the stairs. She didn't bother to look out the back window as she disappeared into the basement.

Alexis reappeared from the far side of the house and crept toward the back door. She stood motionless for a few seconds before continuing past the door into the open area between the house and the garage.

"Christian," Alexis whispered. "Are you still there?"

"Yes," he whispered in response.

"You can come out now," she answered in a hush. "The wife is downstairs doing the laundry."

Christian jumped up and raced to Alexis. She guided him to the front of the garage, and they quickly moved down to the open door on the far end.

"You will have to go through the door he opened for the tractor," Alexis explained. "I will stand by the window of that side door that you stopped me from breaking earlier. If the woman comes upstairs, you won't see me at the window. Don't start the car or open the garage door unless you see me in that window."

"What if the keys aren't in the SUV?" Christian asked.

"They will be," Alexis said with a giddy smile. "Her husband told her that he left the keys in the Santa Fe, so they wouldn't lose them again. You were right."

"What am I going to do?" Christian asked, wryly.

"What do you mean? You start the car and open the garage door," Alexis said with a roll of her eyes.

"Not that," Christian responded. "What am I going to do with the two million dollars you owe me?"

Alexis socked him in the arm playfully.

"Don't do anything unless I am standing by that window," Alexis smiled. "We're wasting time; you better get going."

Christian took off for the open sliding door where the tractor had been parked. He stopped just inside the interior of the building, trying to allow a little time for his eyes to adjust to the darkness. At the far end of the garage, Christian saw the outline of Alexis standing near the window. Christian took small steps at first as he shuffled sideways past the planter. When he saw the pickup only two stalls away, he widened his stride. On his second step across what appeared to be open space, his right knee and left shin smacked into solid steel. With his left foot off the ground in mid-step, he had no way to keep his balance. Christian's momentum propelled him forward onto the back end of a flatbed trailer. He put his hands forward, keeping his face from slamming into the wooden boards. The pain was brutal, and he grabbed his shin as he rolled off the trailer and onto the ground.

He groaned a little as he tried to get back to his feet. Then he looked up to see if Alexis had witnessed his fall, hoping her back was turned.

She was gone from the window. Christian dropped back to the ground, disregarding the pain as he flopped onto the powdery dirt floor.

Christian laid still, his heart pounding in his chest. He peeked up to see if Alexis was back at the window, thinking she may have moved closer to the house to listen in on the woman.

A figure appeared in the window again, and Christian sighed in relief.

Then the door swung open. In an instant, Christian realized that it was not Alexis. He flopped back into the soft powdery dirt as the lights above him buzzed to life.

Christian prayed the noise was not noticed by the person on the other end of the building. He peered across the expanse of the earthen floor and spied the woman's dress shoes standing next to the SUV. She was humming a song as she opened the vehicle's front door.

"I think I will leave my purse in here, too," she said to herself. "I always seem to forget it, so that will keep me from making a second trip to the house in the morning. Right, Christian?"

Christian froze.

Had the woman seen him? How did she know his name? Had Alexis been caught and spilled everything?

"Well, we better get back to our laundry," the woman said. "You are getting heavy. And by the way, I could use less kicking tonight. It won't be long, and we will get to meet you, Christian."

She started humming again as the lights went off and the door to the garage slammed shut.

Christian rolled onto his back, closed his eyes, and exhaled in relief.

After lying on the soft ground for a minute, he rose to his feet and made his way to the pickup. He spotted a better hiding spot, and still crouching, he moved to the hood and looked to the window. No one was there. He lowered his body so he was concealed by the front tires, in case the wife made a return trip.

After a minute, he looked again. Finally, Alexis had returned to the window.

Christian wasted no time. He moved around the front of the truck and made a beeline for the driver's door of the SUV. He quickly checked to make sure Alexis was still at the window. She was, so he turned the key in the ignition. The vehicle hummed to life, and Christian checked the visor for the garage door opener. With a push of the button, the opener groaned to life. Christian waited for the door to finish rising before backing out.

Alexis was waiting. She opened the passenger door and jumped in.

"Let's get out of here," she said, nervously.

"Wait," Christian said.

He grabbed the woman's purse and ran into the garage, setting it gently in the middle of the SUV's parking spot. Christian ran back to the idling vehicle. He pushed the garage remote, and the door lowered as they sped down the driveway, away from the house.

"I don't understand you," Alexis said.

"Well, we don't need her purse," Christian explained as he shifted into drive.

"I can just hear it. They stole our SUV, officer, but they left my purse," Alexis said with a smile.

"Maybe they will go light on our sentence if they catch us," Christian responded with a grin.

When they passed the edge of the outbuildings, Christian flipped on the headlights. Then he slammed on the brakes, and they skidded to a stop. Three deer stood twenty yards in front of them in the middle of the gravel driveway.

"That would have been bad," Christian said quietly as he exhaled a relieved breath.

"They really are magnificent animals," Alexis whispered, as if she didn't want to spook them. "They're so peaceful."

All three deer turned their heads toward the vehicle like they had heard Alexis's words. Christian edged forward.

"What are you doing?" Alexis whispered, harshly.

"Relax, Alexis," Christian comforted. "I am just moving slowly. I won't hit them. I just want to scare them off the road without honking and drawing attention to ourselves. We did just steal a car, and we really can't wait around to admire the animals."

"But we left the purse," Alexis laughed. "You really are a good guy, aren't you?"

"Yeah, I guess I am," Christian smiled again. "If you can look past fleeing the scene of Johnny Stratton's accident in Red Oak, two counts of auto theft, and being on the government's most wanted list, I guess I have always thought of myself as one of the good guys."

The deer loped off the road, and Christian let off the brake. He continued slowly to the end of the driveway. They turned and drove a couple hundred feet to a stop at the road that would take them back to Sam and Ray. Christian started to turn the wheel toward the right when Alexis grabbed the wheel and protested.

"We shouldn't go that way," Alexis said. "That farmer will recognize his own SUV."

"Good call," Christian said, as he cranked the wheel back to the left. "Let's take this road and circle around."

"And let's watch for deer," Alexis responded. "There must be some kind of deer convention around here."

"I'll be careful," Christian answered.

They followed the road north for half a mile before turning left. Another mile, another left. By Christian's calculations, they were headed back toward the highway. As the paved road came into view, Alexis turned in her seat and faced Christian.

"Did you hear the woman talking to herself in the garage?" Alexis asked.

"Yeah," Christian answered. "I about crapped my pants at first, until I realized she was referring to the baby."

"They seem like a happy couple," Alexis said. "I mean, they seem like they will probably be good parents. I know you couldn't hear them, but they made little comments about the baby. I bet they'll be good parents."

"Sure," Christian smiled, surprised by Alexis's rambling. "If you pick the name Christian, you have to be good parents."

"You love your parents, don't you." Alexis said, not as a question but more as a statement.

"As much as anybody else, I guess," Christian answered.

Alexis sat quietly, as if she was mulling over the answer to a difficult question. Christian slowed at the stop sign and signaled his left turn. He waited a little longer than he should have, but he wanted to see if Alexis would decide to expand on her thoughts.

As he accelerated onto the highway, Alexis sighed.

"I never had that," she whispered, sadly.

"Had what?" Christian asked.

"Loving parents," she answered flatly, and Christian sensed hurt in her words.

Christian wondered what had happened to Alexis, but he didn't plan on prying. If she wanted to talk about it, she would. Alexis didn't struggle with stating her mind, but she had not opened up to Christian like this. He knew the best thing to do was let her share when she was ready.

"Is this the turn?" Alexis asked.

"I'm positive this is the road," Christian said. "But we will know for sure in a minute. Let's drive over the hill and turn around. Then we can come back to the first fence."

They slowly drove over the crest of the hill, checking to see if the tractor was waiting there. The road was dark. They continued down the hill a ways, and Christian recognized the trees. He turned onto the trail and spotted Mr. Banner's damaged SUV in the reflection of the Santa Fe's headlights.

"I guess we are on the right road," Alexis said.

"Let's go back up the road and find Sam and Ray," Christian said.

They drove back over the hill, and Christian slowed when he spied a fence out his driver's window. He rolled down the window so he could be heard.

"Ray! You out there?" he yelled.

"It's about time," Ray hollered back.

Sam and Ray emerged from the corn field. Christian pulled to their side of the road.

"Can you help us out?" Sam asked.

Christian jumped out and reached down into the ditch, grabbing two bags. Alexis opened the back of the SUV and Christian handed them to her. Sam held out her hand, and Christian assisted her out of the tall grass. Ray scrambled up the incline and shook Christian's hand when Christian reached back to help him.

"Good to see you guys again," Ray said as he pulled himself up the last two feet with Christian's help. He grabbed Alexis and hugged her.

"Nice ride," Ray said. "Silver is good."

Sam hollered, "Shotgun!"

"I could use a nap," Ray said with a yawn.

"I better drive," Alexis said, still in Ray's arms. "You don't have a license, Christian."

"You better not hug me, too," Christian said to Ray.

"Don't worry; you're not my type," Ray chuckled.

Sam was already in the front seat. Ray climbed behind the driver's seat. Christian was closing the back hatch when Alexis called to him.

"Hey, Ray's a good guy, too," she said. "I know you might be thinking otherwise after what happened earlier."

"He just rubbed me the wrong way with his approach after the flat tire," Christian said. "I wasn't expecting him to jump on me like he did."

"You're one of us, now," she explained. "He is going to be protective of you, too. He just doesn't have much tact, and he doesn't want you to be hurt by hoping for too much. Ray has talked to Sam about it many times. He is not a dreamer like you two are. It's all about the facts with Ray."

"Then you need me," Christian responded. "I have enough hope to go around if Sam's runs out."

"Oh, don't worry," Alexis said as she rolled her eyes and smiled. "Sam won't run out of it, either."

"I guess that's why I like her," Christian smiled.

"You and Sam were made for each other; that's for sure," she said with a laugh.

"We better get going," Christian said as a car raced by on the highway in front of them. "If that farmer sees his car is gone, we need to be as far away from here as possible."

Alexis was buckling her seatbelt as Christian closed his door.

"Sweet!" Alexis cried. "Full tank of gas!"

They turned right and headed west again.

CHAPTER 7

Christian awoke in the backseat to Sam and Alexis bickering about which way to turn. He sat up groggily and looked out his window, rubbing his eyes to remove the sleep. The countryside was bathed in a thick coat of black, and he could not see any stars in the sky.

"Clouds have moved in," he said, quietly, and the two girls in the front stopped arguing.

"Hey, sleepyhead," Sam cooed from in front of Christian.

"Where are we?" he asked.

"Not sure," Alexis answered with a sigh. "We passed through Harlan but had no luck finding a map. All the convenience stores were closed."

"Why are we stopped?" Christian questioned.

"Well, Alexis and I aren't sure which way we should turn," Sam said in irritation.

"I think we should go right," Alexis interrupted, "but Sam thinks left."

"Either we go north or south," Sam explained.

"I'm thinking we want to stay north," Christian replied. "South would take us back toward I-80, and we decided earlier to stay away from that Interstate."

"My thoughts exactly," Alexis stated, enthusiastically jabbing at Sam's choice.

"But the road appears to go northeast, so isn't that backtracking?" Sam said, hinting at the support she probably wanted from Christian.

Christian noticed the letters NW glowing in green on the rearview mirror. Sam was right; a right turn meant they would be headed northeast, away from the Nebraska border. But a left turn would take them back toward Interstate 80, and that didn't really appeal to Christian's sense of avoiding the law.

"Sign says that Woodbine is that way," Christian said as he pointed Alexis's direction. "And Logan is that way." He pointed southwest. "Neither of those towns rings a bell, so I say we avoid a possible intersection with I-80 and go right."

"Fine," Sam sighed, realizing it was a two to one vote and not in her favor.

Alexis put the vehicle in gear and pulled off the shoulder back onto the highway. She turned right and set the cruise control at fifty-five. Sam did not put up any fight when the decision was made to go right, and Christian appreciated that. He thought Alexis would have acted very differently had the decision been the opposite. Alexis usually struggled with being out-voted.

"You two fell asleep about five minutes after we got onto the highway," Alexis said. "Any chance this SUV has been reported stolen?"

"I don't think so," Christian said. "Hopefully, they don't know it's gone from their garage. We should be out of Iowa by the time they wake up. How long was I out?"

"Maybe a half hour," Sam answered. "We drove around Harlan looking for an open gas station, but we didn't wander too far off the main highway. We haven't passed through any other town since Harlan."

After a while, they reached the small village of Woodbine, but nothing was open. The next town was Dunlap, according to the sign, and Denison was beyond that.

"Shoot!" Alexis cried. "The highway north out of Harlan goes to Denison. I remember seeing a sign for it. We are backtracking!"

"No problem," Christian calmed her. "If there is a turn at Dunlap, we can take it. I am sure a highway will go west from there."

It would be another five miles before that question was answered.

"So what did you two talk about while we were snoozing?" Christian asked.

The two girls giggled a little bit before Alexis answered.

"You," Alexis said.

They refused to divulge any other details, and they giggled again when Christian prodded for more specifics.

"We don't kiss and tell," Alexis said, wryly, and Sam snickered.

"They were talking about how good of a kisser you are," Ray interrupted. "Well, Sam was anyway. Alexis better not have any idea about how good you are at kissing."

"Ray!" Sam shrieked in disgust. "We thought you were sleeping."

Christian could feel the warmth of embarrassment flowing into his cheeks.

"That was the last thing I heard before I fell asleep," Ray explained. "I woke up just now, when you two were laughing like little school girls. Where are we?"

"Dunlap," Christian said as they passed the top of a hill to see lights in the distance.

"Where is Dunlap?" Ray asked.

"Not sure," Alexis answered.

"We're hoping there is a highway west from there," Sam added.

"So, we are going north?" Ray said. "Good, that means further from the Interstate. We need to avoid I-80."

Christian guessed Alexis felt even more pride with Ray making that statement.

"Dunlap looks small, too," Sam said, as they closed in on the town. "I don't see a highway turnoff, yet."

They drove slowly through town, obeying the low speed limit to the number. Christian was glad that Alexis was not the daredevil Ray seemed to be. As they passed by tattered houses, Christian spotted a sign up ahead on the right-hand side of the road.

"There's our turn," he said, triumphantly.

"Looks like a county highway, but at least it's paved," Alexis said, as she turned on the blinker.

The county highway was narrower than the state highway they had been traveling on. The paint dividing the lanes was chipped and faded. In some places, it was nonexistent. Cracks riddled the blacktop, and grass peeked through the openings. County Highway 37 was not the ideal route to take in the middle of the night, but they wanted to get back to a westerly heading. Alexis took it slow, driving most of the way in the thirty to forty mile-an-hour range. The road routinely meandered back and forth through fields of corn and soybeans. An occasional light appeared from inside a grove of trees, like a house was playing hide-and-seek somewhere in the shadows as they cruised past.

"So how do I rank?" Christian asked with a grin.

"Huh?" Alexis yawned.

"In the kissing department," he continued.

"Oh, that," Alexis grinned.

"Don't you dare!" Sam growled.

"Pretty good," Alexis said, paying no attention to Sam's warning. "I believe she used the words soft lips."

Sam groaned and buried her head in her hands, Ray let out a bellow of laughter, and Christian reached his arms around the front seat to hug Sam.

"I can't look at you again," Sam said to Christian without emotion.

"But you can still kiss him," Alexis laughed, "because you do that with your eyes closed."

Ray roared a second time.

"I am so embarrassed," Sam sighed.

Christian chuckled as he released Sam and leaned back.

The car remained quiet until they reached the little town of Soldier, Iowa.

Ray had closed his eyes, and Christian was positive it was real sleep this time, since Ray was snoring. Sam had also drifted off in the front seat, so just Christian and Alexis were awake.

"Tell me about your parents," Alexis requested.

"Well, they are just like anyone else's folks, I guess," Christian said, not sure what to say.

"No, what do they do? What are they like?" she pressed.

"My mom stays at home. 'Domestic Goddess' is what she calls it," Christian started. "She likes to sew and goes to every event under the sun. I mean, she goes to all of her kids' events. She makes every football, basketball, and baseball game for me and every concert and dance recital for my sisters. My father, well, you know he is a principal, but before that, he taught sixth grade science and social studies. He likes to fish and cook out. They both like to play cards. I guess everyone in my family likes to play cards. My grandparents, aunts, uncles, cousins – they all like a good card game."

"How would you know what all those people like to do?" Alexis asked, not believing his claim.

"Reunions, birthdays… you know, get-togethers," Christian answered.

"Huh?" she responded, and Christian sensed Alexis was confused.

"Didn't your family ever get together for a reunion? I mean with the extended family, like great aunts and uncles and second cousins," Christian said.

"No," Alexis said, flatly.

"Oh, well, my family gets together to celebrate everything," Christian explained. "Major wedding anniversaries, birthdays, graduations, and every year we have a family reunion in July. I see my extended family all the time… at least, I used to."

"And they all play cards?" Alexis asked, and her tone was genuine, like she wanted to know more.

"Most of them do," Christian said with a smile. "They play this game called Pitch, typically ten-point, ace-deuce partner. It seems complicated at first, but once you get the hang of it, it's really a blast. They do prizes for the most times getting a bid of seven or more, most times going set, high point total for men and for women, and low point total for men and women. Everyone sits at tables of five, and you play five hands. The low scores move down a table and the high scores move up a table. Every round is a different set of people to play with. My family loves their cards."

"I've never played cards," Alexis said quietly, and Christian thought she was almost ashamed to admit it.

"Never?" Christian asked.

"Nope," she answered.

"What did you do when your family used to get together?" he wondered aloud.

"We didn't," she replied.

"You never got together with family?" Christian said in amazement.

"I don't have any family," Alexis said calmly.

"Just your parents, huh?" Christian said.

"No, I don't have any family," she said again. "My father was never around, and he ended up in prison. My mother had me when she was fourteen and… well, she was so strung out most of the time, that when she was there, she wasn't really there. From what I can remember, my dad was sent to prison before I started first grade. He's probably still there. Once the state got involved, after my mom was arrested for dealing dope, she lost custody of me. I was seven when I was sent to my first foster home since there was no other family to care for me.

"I jumped around from home to home for a while before I ended up at Hidden Acres Boys and Girls Ranch. It was a home for abused children, kids who had been kicked out of their homes, or kids like me, who struggled in the foster care world and needed a more consistent, structured environment. I was thirteen when I went to live there."

Christian didn't know what to say, so he just sat quietly while Alexis stared out the windshield at the road. She had the same tone that Ray had when he shared with Christian about the accident he had experienced with his parents.

Alexis sighed and continued, "I liked the ranch. For the first time in my life, I felt like I belonged. Foster care was a revolving door of relationships. Each new house meant new siblings in a family that I didn't belong to. Some families were okay, but usually I bided my time until the eventual move to the next foster home. I didn't want to get my hopes up that the next stop would be permanent. The pattern continued until I entered eighth grade. That was when I moved to the ranch."

"What happened in eighth grade?" Christian asked, hesitantly.

"A fight," Alexis said, as if she savored the word. "I got into a fight."

Alexis paused.

"At school?" Christian asked, curiously.

"No, at my foster home," Alexis answered with a tinge of anger in her words.

Christian didn't prod any further. He knew Alexis would share if she wanted to.

"It was a new home," she started. "I really liked the foster parents, and they had talked about adoption, but the guy got laid off from his job, so they couldn't afford another mouth to feed. It was another case of bad breaks for a troubled teen.

"My new home was not in the middle class neighborhoods I had been accustomed to. No, it was very upscale. They were a nice couple at first, but I think they were into foster care for the wrong reasons."

"Why is that?" Christian asked, wondering what would be a wrong reason.

"They sort of paraded me around as 'the foster kid' whenever friends came over. It was like I was some trophy for them to show off to their rich buddies. 'Oh, look at us, we are so wonderful to take in this poor little urchin child.' And their two children never fully accepted me. The girl probably would have eventually, but the big brother, he had issues. In fact, he tried to put me in my place.

"His name was Matt, and he had a blonde crew-cut. I can still picture the little rat's face. He thought he was hot stuff, but he was a whiny brat with a pimply face. He was a year younger than me, and it burned him that I had been invited to join the family. Matt was a bully, pure and simple, even to his younger sister. He used to mumble 'trailer trash' under his breath whenever I was around.

"We were walking home from school and his buddies were coming over to the house to hang out. I was a ways ahead of them when a rock skipped past me on the sidewalk. I whipped around and saw Matt smiling. He tossed another rock up into the air and caught it as he eyed me. Then he hurled it in my direction, and it fell harmlessly in the grass beside me. I didn't even flinch.

"He yelled, 'You better run, trailer trash,' and his buddies joined in with the taunt. I held my ground, and Matt picked up another rock. His little sister started yelling at him to knock it off, but he pushed her to the ground, yelling, 'Don't take trailer trash's side!' I turned around and continued my walk, picking up my pace a bit, since it as an opportunity to put some distance between me and them.

"When I looked back, they were gone, everyone but his little sister, Erika. I decided to wait until she caught up with me, so she didn't have to walk alone. We didn't talk the entire time. I didn't ask where her brother was, because I didn't really care. Once we reached the house, I went upstairs, straight to my room. They were waiting for me."

Alexis hesitated for a moment, and Christian leaned forward in his seat.

"What happened?" he asked,.

Alexis sniffed, as if she was holding back a tear.

"Matt grabbed me from behind and pinned my arms behind my back, pushing me facedown onto my bed. Two of his friends held my legs when I started to struggle and kick. Matt leaned real close and reminded me that I was trailer trash. He told me that I was worthless and that I could disappear and no one would miss me. Bad things were running through my head. It wasn't the first time I had seen a boy do that to a girl. I grew up seeing that sort of stuff with my parents, but I had never been on the receiving end of it. I thought the worst. Then he grabbed me by the hair and pulled me back to my feet.

"One of his friends grabbed a small trash can from under my desk and handed it to Matt. He dumped it out on my head, before putting the plastic can over my head. Then he pushed me to the ground and laughed."

"What did you do?" Christian asked, not wanting to believe a teenage boy could be so cruel.

"I snapped," she answered, calmly. "It all happened so fast. With the plastic grocery bag still in the trash can covering my mouth, my survival instincts kicked in, and I attacked. With my hands free, I pulled the can off my head, and I grabbed my book bag from the floor, swinging it as hard as I could. The power of three textbooks landed against the side of Matt's pimply face. He fell backwards, twisting sideways into my desk, hitting his head on the corner. One of his friends ran out the door, but the other was caught between Matt and the exit. I fell on him with a flurry of punches. My rough childhood taught me a little about fighting. He started crying and balled himself up on the ground, but I kept clawing at him. In fact, I think I even bit him when he put his hand in my face. I was kicking him when Matt's dad came into the room and grabbed me from behind to pull me off. That was when I saw the pool of blood on the carpeting, and Matt lying there unconscious. Matt's father let go of me when he saw his son's condition.

"Was he okay?" Christian asked, even though he rooted against it inside.

"He had a gash across the side of his face," Alexis explained. "I think he ended up getting thirty stitches. I bet he still has the scar to remind him of what he encountered that day. He must have hit the corner of that desk just right. He regained consciousness pretty quickly. Matt's friend ended up with a broken nose and a loose tooth, and I ended up in juvie."

"But they attacked you," Christian cried.

"Trailer trash's words meant nothing to those rich people," Alexis sneered. "The boys lied about what happened, and I was the one who ended up in court as the defendant. Matt's friend, the one with the broken schnoz, had a father who was an attorney. I didn't stand a chance. The court sent me to a juvenile detention center before my date in court.

"The attorney father wanted to try me as an adult for assault, but the judge wanted nothing to do with that. The honorable Judge Stone felt I had been through enough and served enough time at the detention center, so he ruled that I would be sent to Hidden Acres Ranch. He also questioned the attorney about the accuracy of the boys' stories, and Judge Stone saw it as a chance to give me an opportunity to get a fresh start. I heard the entire closed-door discussion from my seat in the courtroom.

"During my time in juvie before the hearing, I realized my auditory skills had gotten a lot better. At first, I thought I was hearing voices, but then I figured it out. My ability to hear had changed, and by the time I was in court for my appearance, I was already honing my craft of eavesdropping."

"Mr. Banner found her at the ranch," Sam said from the front,.

Christian thought Sam was a sound sleeper. He was surprised that his conversation with Alexis had roused her from her snooze.

"Mr. Banner had planted Ray at the ranch," Alexis explained. "Mr. Banner had to hide Ray for a while, and there was no time to go to the safe house in Arizona."

Alexis laughed as she recalled the memory.

"I met Ray by chance at Hidden Acres," she said. "He arrived the same time I did, so naturally, I gravitated to him. Sounds odd, doesn't it? But it was easier to get to know someone who was also new to the place."

"Doesn't sound odd," Christian said. "That was the draw I had to you three when you arrived in Red Oak. I didn't have very many friends, so new people meant we had something in common. We were all outcasts."

"Ray didn't really hang out with anyone, and I could hear all the comments about him from the other kids," Alexis said. "I could also hear the comments about me, so I decided he was safe, and he was kind of cute, too. One night we were talking about how we ended up at the ranch, and I told him about my hearing."

Sam interrupted, "So, when Mr. Banner returned, Alexis disappeared with them."

"There wasn't a lot of security, so it was pretty easy," Alexis added. "Who wants to spend a lot of energy hunting down a girl who beat up two boys?"

"Onawa," Sam said, out of nowhere.

"What?" Christian asked, confused.

"That's what the sign says," Sam said, as she pointed out the windshield.

As they drove closer to Onawa, Iowa, Christian saw another sign with "I-29" on it and an arrow pointing straight ahead. Interstate 29 was the freeway that ran from Omaha to Sioux City, along the Missouri River. Christian knew the Interstate meant they were close to the Nebraska border, really close.

CHAPTER 8

"I bet there will be a truck stop near the Interstate," Christian said, as they passed the darkened windows of a convenience store on the edge of town.

"Where does I-29 go?" Sam asked.

"North to Sioux City," Christian answered, "but we won't be taking I-29. This highway should take us across the Missouri River into Nebraska."

The teens weren't disappointed this time; a truck stop called Dave's World sat on the right side of the road before the I-29 interchange, and it was definitely open. Dave's World was the oasis they had been hoping for. Even though it was the early hours of the morning, the truck stop was a buzz of activity. The diesel pumps for the tractor trailers were just off the highway, so they drove around to the west side of the complex to gas up the SUV.

"I'll fill it up," Christian volunteered. "You guys can go inside and pay and use the bathroom. Maybe we should grab some chips. I'm kind of hungry."

"Should we wake him up?" Sam asked, as she motioned to the backseat where Ray was sawing logs.

"Nah, let him sleep," Alexis said. "The evening's events have taken quite a bit out of him."

"He isn't faking it this time," Sam muttered, obviously still bugged about Ray spilling the beans on the kissing conversation.

Christian filled the tank before he went inside to use the restroom. Alexis passed him on her way back to the car with an arm full of chips.

"Did you grab a map?" Christian asked.

"Aw, crap!" Alexis cried. "I can't believe I spaced it off. I'll unload this stuff and go back in to get one.

Christian used the restroom and washed his hands before throwing some water on his face. There were streaks of dirt on his cheeks and forehead, probably from rolling on the ground in the garage on the farm where they acquired the SUV.

When Christian exited the bathroom, Alexis and Sam were waiting for him.

"We have a problem," Alexis said nervously.

"No map?" Christian said with a chuckle, but his humor was met with serious looks. "What problem?"

"Two state troopers just pulled in," Sam whispered. "I can tell they are calm by their colors, but we need to be careful to not all be together, in case they have descriptions of us."

"What should we do?" Alexis asked in a hushed voice.

At that moment, the two troopers entered the building, and one of them made a beeline toward the three teens.

"Here they come," Christian said, quietly. "Go use the bathroom."

Christian turned and entered the restroom a second time, opening the door to the nearest stall. He locked the door and sat on the toilet. The door to the restroom creaked. Peering through the narrow slit of the stall door, Christian saw two sets of polished shoes cross the floor to the urinals.

"Odd story," one officer said. "Too bad we don't have pictures."

"Needle in a haystack, if you ask me," a husky voice added.

"High school kids driving a dark colored SUV; you see that in every small town."

"No kidding," responded husky voice. "Did you say that one of them could pass for an albino?"

"Yeah, very blonde, almost white hair and pale skin color, but there are four of them total. The bulletin said that they are only wanted for questioning in the death of a high school student in Red Oak. Something about an accident a couple nights ago, and they have information about what happened."

"Like they are going to end up in Onawa. Say, how's your kid?" husky voice asked.

"Oh, doc said it was just a run-of-the-mill ear infection, nothing to worry about," the other replied. "My sister keeps tellin' me to take him to a chiropractor. I'm not sure I want to do that; he's only two."

"I try to see my chiropractor at least once a week," the husky voice explained, and Christian thought that the gruff voice came from the older of the two officers. "Anymore, I only go to the medical doctor for my annual physical, and I haven't had to take a real sick day in almost a year and a half. You may want to listen to your sister on this one."

"Aw, my wife thinks chiropractic is witch doctor stuff," the officer said.

"Well, it ain't gonna hurt your little guy, so you may want to try it," the older lawman replied.

A toilet flushed and soon the water ran in the sinks. The door creaked and Christian waited at least two minutes before leaving the stall. After another couple minutes, he finally had enough courage to open the door and walk into the corridor.

With no troopers in sight, he walked down the hallway and scanned the store. When Christian peered around a corner to check out the restaurant on the west side, he saw the troopers being led to a booth near the window. From that window, the state patrolmen had a good view of their stolen, silver Santa Fe.

"Psst, Christian," called a voice from behind him.

He turned to see Alexis standing near the fountain machines.

"Hey, where's Sam?" he questioned with a jest of his hands.

"She's out at the car," Alexis whispered.

Christian started to speak, but she held her hand to his mouth.

"I heard," she said, quietly. "I listened from outside the door when I saw them both go into the bathroom. Have they been seated yet?"

Christian nodded, "But they are in the first booth with a window looking out at our SUV."

"Crap," she said in a hushed voice. "Crap, crap, crap."

Christian could sense Alexis losing it, and Ray wasn't around to assure her.

"We can't all go out there at the same time," Christian said, calmly. "It sounded like they don't have the greatest descriptions of us, except Ray, and he's sleeping in the car. We just need to relax and look normal."

"You wait here," Alexis said. "I will go out with Sam and bring the car around to this side." She pointed to the glass door exiting to the diesel pumps.

"Did you grab a map?" Christian asked.

Alexis didn't have to answer. It was written all over her face.

"Okay, I'll go find a map," Christian said. "Where are they?"

Alexis pointed toward the restaurant. Christian peeked around the corner and spied the rack of maps, directly behind the first booth where the officers were sipping coffee.

"Do you want to drive or get a map?" Christian asked.

"I'll drive," she responded quickly.

"Don't pull around until you see me leave the rack to go pay," Christian said.

"I'll go out the door over there," she said pointing to the same door Christian planned to use. "I'll walk around to the car and wait for you to move to the register."

She turned to go, but Christian put a hand on her shoulder to stop her.

"Alexis," he said, smiling to calm her nerves. "It'll all work out fine, just calm down."

"Okay," she said with a deep breath. "Sometimes I get really worked up."

With that, Alexis turned toward the far door. Christian strolled toward the rack of maps. He found an Iowa map first but almost forgot to grab one for Nebraska. He was ready to go pay when he heard a catcall whistle from behind the high wood back of the booth.

"Would you look at her?" called the husky voice from the other side. "Girls didn't look like that when I was in high school."

Christian leaned to the window and saw Sam leaning against the front end of the SUV. Alexis was just entering the scene from his left, and she snapped her head toward the restaurant windows as she crossed the pavement to Sam. Christian realized that Alexis had heard the officer in the booth in front of him.

"Was that the 1860's when you were in high school?" the other man said, coolly.

"Oh, to be young again," the older officer crooned. "Check out her friend. The good-lookin' ones always travel in packs."

Alexis turned toward the windows again, and again, it wasn't Christian in the crosshairs of her eyes. She was definitely dialed into the troopers' discussion. Alexis turned back to Sam, and Christian saw Sam's blonde locks peek over Alexis's shoulder in the direction of the first booth of the restaurant. Christian figured Alexis was filling her in on the peeping perverts behind the glass.

"You know, they think those four are headed for Omaha," the younger trooper said. "You're headed back that direction, so you may want to see if pictures have been sent, yet. You never know; it may be your lucky day."

"I should pull those two over before they leave," the husky voice said with a laugh. "Maybe pat them down just to be sure they aren't carryin' drugs."

"You are a sick old man," replied the other trooper.

A heavyset woman waded through the tables toward the booth with a large circular tray in her hands. She set it on a little stand next to the state troopers' table. At the same moment, Christian heard a car door slam outside, and he figured Alexis and Sam had finished their conversation.

Husky spoke, "Hey, is there someone in the back seat of that SUV?"

Christian leaned over and looked out the glass window. To his horror, Ray was sitting up in the back seat and looking directly out the window.

"Yes there is," replied the younger officer, "and he matches that description of the albino-lookin' kid. The dark skinned girl does too, come to think of it."

Christian could hear them shift their weight on the vinyl seats.

"Let's check it out," said the husky voice.

"Who ordered the bacon cheeseburger?" the large woman asked, clanking ceramic plates as she spoke.

Christian grabbed the rack of maps in front of him and pulled as hard as he could. He pushed open the glass door, and a crash erupted behind him.

Alexis had just started to pull forward when Christian exploded from the convenience store, running to his left, away from the SUV and pointing ahead of him.

"Go!" he yelled repeatedly as he raced down the sidewalk parallel to the car's path, motioning to an open area beyond the fuel pumps.

Ray opened the door and Christian jumped into the SUV. Alexis gunned the accelerator, and the door slammed closed behind him.

"What do we do?" Alexis cried.

"Go left!" Ray shouted.

"What?" Sam questioned the decision.

"Left! Left!" Ray hollered again, as he looked out the back window. "We have a better chance of losing them in town than we do on the open road. Those cop engines are built for speed."

Christian turned to see the patrolmen stop chasing them on foot and dart for their vehicles, which were parked on the far side of the restaurant's windows. They hadn't reached their patrol cars by the time Alexis turned around the south side of the building, out of the officers' view.

Sam covered her face and screamed as Alexis rocketed from Dave's World and headed back toward Onawa, almost hitting a minivan during the maneuver. Christian turned around again to look out the back window. As they neared the town's main intersection, flashing lights sprang onto the road at least a half mile behind their SUV, fishtailing as they tried to make the turn onto the highway.

"They're coming!" Christian shouted, turning to look out the windshield to see what was ahead of them.

The light changed to red at the intersection in front of them, and Alexis let off the gas.

"Don't stop!" Ray ordered. "Go, left!"

The silver SUV screeched through the intersection, as the tires whined, trying to maintain a grip on the asphalt. An eighteen-wheeler slammed on its brakes as the teens passed in front of the behemoth's bumper. A horn sounded from the monster, as the SUV's back end avoided disaster by mere inches. Alexis gained control, and hammered the accelerator one more time.

"Take the next left," Ray commanded. "Christian, do you see them?"

Alexis didn't question his demand. She turned down the dark side street.

"Christian, did they reach the corner when we turned?" Ray asked.

"No, I didn't see them," Christian answered.

"Alexis, turn off the lights and pull in front of that pickup on the right," Ray said.

Alexis turned off the lights and quickly drove to the spot in front of a rusty three-quarter ton truck.

"Put it in park," Ray said, in a calm but direct voice.

Sirens wailed from the highway intersection, and Christian turned to see two sets of flashing lights reflect off the side of a house. Soon, the patrol cars sped past their hiding spot on the dark street.

"They just passed us," Christian sighed.

Ray let out a yell and hollered, "That was freakin' awesome! Nice drivin' Alexis!"

"Now what?" Sam asked.

"Simple, get back on that highway and we can go west," Ray said. "But we need to be quick about it before they realize we gave them the slip."

"Wait, I have maps," Christian said, realizing he still gripped the two maps in his hand. "I can't believe I hung onto them the whole time. Alexis, turn on the dome light."

Ray interrupted, "It won't take long for them to realize we doubled back somewhere. Christian can look at the map while you drive."

Sam opened the glove box and searched its contents, and Alexis quickly took a left to go back toward the highway.

"You can turn off the dome light, Alexis," Sam said, as she flipped on a flashlight and handed it to Ray.

Christian unfolded the Iowa map and quickly located the Omaha/Council Bluffs area. His finger trembled as he moved up Interstate 29 to Onawa. He traced the highway from Onawa across the Missouri River into Nebraska.

"Okay, we are on 175," Christian said excitedly as Alexis turned right onto the highway. "Stay on this. It will take us to Nebraska. Let me check the other map to see where we go from there."

Christian set the Iowa map on the seat between himself and Ray. He glanced out the window at Dave's World as they passed by.

"Now, let's see," Christian said, returning to the map. "Where is Onawa? Found it! Alexis, when we cross the river, you're going to turn left on 75, but you'll only be on it for about a mile before taking a right on 51."

"How long on 51?" Ray asked.

"Hold on," Christian said, with a little agitation. "Don't rush me."

Christian traced Highway 51 with his finger.

"Wow, we really are close to the farm," Christian said in amazement. "I bet it's less than an hour."

"Really?" Sam said, excitedly.

"I never realized how close grandpa's farm was to the Iowa border," Christian marveled.

Christian had traveled there many times, but all of those trips had been from Omaha. He had never driven from Iowa to his grandparent's place.

"It's really close, once we get to 51," Christian commented.

"How long on 51?" Ray asked again.

"Oh, maybe thirty miles, and then we will turn south and come in from the backside of Wisner," Christian answered. "From there, I don't need a map to find my way."

Christian finally relaxed his body and leaned back in his seat. Ray folded up the Iowa map, while Christian did the same with Nebraska. Alexis turned on the radio, and after a couple times pushing the seek button, she found a station playing her kind of music.

When they reached Wisner, Christian searched his cell phone contacts and found his cousin David's number. Even though faint light reached into the night sky with the first fingers of morning, Christian called him. He listened intently, as David relayed directions and information.

"My cousin wants us to meet him on the Old River Road," Christian said, concerned. "It's less traveled."

"Just point the way," Sam said with a smile.

"I am ready to get out of this car," Ray said as he stretched, "maybe take a shower."

"You need a shower," Sam giggled. "I can smell you from up here."

Alexis didn't say anything, and Christian knew she had heard his entire conversation with David. It wasn't all good news.

CHAPTER 9

The SUV turned onto a paved road leading south out of the little town of Wisner. A couple of dilapidated sheds in dire need of repair and fresh paint stood in the glow of the last streetlight marking the city limit. The morning light was faint, but Christian could see the treetops of age old oaks and maples silhouetted against the lightening sky. It wouldn't be long, and the sun would spark the horizon with brilliant gold.

"Take the first left after this bridge," Christian stated solemnly.

They crossed the Elkhorn River, and Christian recollected a trip to one of its many sandbars with his grandfather.

"Grandpa used to take me out on this river to seine for minnows," he said, and sadness leaked into his words. "We would find a shallow channel, and I would cross it with one end of the net. We would walk against the current, and then I would cross back over. We would lay the net on the sand and collect the minnows in a five-gallon bucket."

"Did you ever catch anything besides minnows?" Ray asked with interest, as the Elkhorn faded behind them.

"Yeah, sometimes little suckers and bullhead," Christian answered. "Every once in a while, we netted something with size, like a carp or catfish. Once we caught a five pound channel cat."

As he reminisced, Christian almost missed the turn they needed to take.

"Turn here," he said quickly, but Alexis was already signaling her turn and slowing down.

"How far do we go?" Sam asked.

"Three or four miles," Christian answered. "David will meet us at the entrance to his pasture ground."

"What is he driving?" Sam asked.

"He's on foot," Alexis said. "I was listening to the conversation."

Alexis looked into the rearview mirror, and Christian could see compassion in her eyes. She didn't mention the rest of the conversation, and Christian was thankful for that.

"Why isn't he driving?" Ray asked.

"He plans to drive the SUV back into town to hide it," Christian said. "He dropped his truck off in Wisner late last night. He will come back out to meet us after he gets the SUV safely hidden."

Alexis drove slowly on the loose gravel of the winding road. Rows of corn filled the fields, with an occasional patch of milo or soybeans growing in the expanse of corn.

"Why aren't there any driveways or mailboxes on this road?" Ray asked. "Don't people live in this area?"

"Nah, the river floods too much to risk living in this area," Christian explained. "Most people around here call this the 'bottom.' The Elkhorn River is less than a mile from here, and this ground floods just about every spring when the ice thaws. Most springs, you can't even drive down here unless you're in a tractor."

As they rounded the curve, the road inclined, and Christian saw a man standing near a gate.

"There's David," Christian pointed over Alexis's shoulder toward the left side of the road where his cousin stood in faded blue coveralls.

David waved to them as they drove closer, and Sam powered down her window as they turned onto the grass path.

"Christian in there?" David asked.

"Here, in back," Christian answered.

"You kids pull forward and I'll shut the gate behind you," David said.

Alexis stopped ten feet past the fence line and waited for David. Ray opened the back door and slid over so there was room.

"I'm not riding with you," David said. "I decided it was too far to walk, and I drove the four-wheeler down here."

He pointed to the rows of corn, and Christian saw the outline of a camouflaged ATV.

"Just follow me to the house," David explained.

David slammed the door shut and walked past the SUV to his ride. A simple push start and the engine came to life. The Yamaha bounced along the trail in front of them as they drove through tall grass along a barbed wire fence. They followed David through another gate that stood open before the path wound around a thicket of tangled bushes and uphill to a patch of cottonwood trees. Here the trail continued past a house and the skeleton of another building. David stopped next to the framed garage, and Alexis followed suit, parking next to the ATV.

Christian opened his door and stretched as he got out.

"How are you doing?" David asked as he came around the back of the SUV.

"Not good," Christian answered.

Alexis opened her door to get out, and Ray and Sam followed on David's heels.

"Let me introduce you to Alexis, Sam, and Ray," Christian said as he pointed to each of them.

David shook hands with each as they were introduced. His smile was a dimpled, ear-to-ear grin beneath a short, round nose and circular glasses. When David spoke, his lips barely moved and the words tumbled out quickly but succinctly.

"Your grandma filled me in on most of what she knew over the phone," David explained. "I thought you guys would be here sooner. I've been up all night waiting for a call."

"Sorry," Christian said, apologetically, as David dismissed the inconvenience with a wave of his hand. "We've had a rough night. This isn't our original ride."

Christian pointed to the SUV.

"We had to steal it from a farm when we wrecked our first SUV," Ray said with a smile.

"I see," David said, grinning like he knew a secret.

"We hit a deer," Sam added.

The dimples deepened in both cheeks as David laughed.

"Well, you guys aren't making it easy on me," David said. "Now, we'll have to return it. I can't have some farmer wondering where his vehicle is on my conscience."

"Sorry," Sam said.

"Not to worry," David replied. "My cousins wanted to take a road trip, anyway. I'll tell them to use the address on the registration to find the owner."

"We ran into a bit of trouble in Onawa, too," Alexis said.

"There's more?" David said, surprised.

"A couple state troopers can ID this baby," Ray said as he patted the vehicle. "Not sure you want to have someone driving it."

"Not a problem," David answered, still smiling. "We can haul it on a trailer and cover it with a tarp. Why don't you guys grab your bags and come inside."

David turned and walked to the two-story house.

"It isn't much," David said, "but it will keep the mosquitoes and rain out."

The teens quickly grabbed their bags and followed David to the front door.

"It's not quite ready for occupancy," David laughed.

"But it'll do," Christian said, thankfully.

"I brought some sleeping bags down here last night when I got the call from your grandma," David said. "You'll have to make do without pillows, and there is no running water."

"I am ready to crash," Ray huffed, as he grabbed a sleeping bag from the pile.

"Sorry about the wood floors," David grinned. "We weren't expecting guests, so I didn't have time to lay the carpeting. I'm gonna take your rig into town before people are up and around. My cousin owns a garage, and I can hide it there, until we figure out when to return it and how to get it there."

Alexis tossed him the keys, and David walked to the door and motioned for Christian to come with him.

"You guys can get some sleep," David said. "I'll bring a meal out to you at lunch time."

Christian followed David outside.

"Thanks a lot David," Christian said.

"Hey, you're family," David smiled.

"So Grandpa was arrested?" Christian asked, not wanting to discuss it in front of The Three, even though he knew Alexis would be listening.

"Your grandma said they were all taken into custody for questioning, but your grandfather hasn't been released, yet," David answered, the hint of a grin still etched in his cheeks. "Your grandma says she'll be back here before noon, in case you need her help. She said your grandpa can handle himself. Your father will drive him back here when they let him go."

"So everyone is okay?" Christian asked.

"Sounds like it," David answered. "Your folks are fine, and your sisters are too. Strange how the police hung onto your grandpa, though."

David let the sentence hang in silence, and Christian bit his lip.

"Now, I don't know the whole story, but I know your grandma said you were in dire straits. She said that the police were after you for something you didn't do, something about a kid getting killed in a car accident. Your grandma said your grandfather was giving them a hard time, and they decided to keep him a little longer. That grandfather of yours can be a pistol."

Christian realized that David had no idea what was going on, and he didn't think that was fair for David to be unaware of the danger.

"Well, there's more to it than that," Christian started off slowly, picking his words carefully.

At twenty-four, David was college educated. He had a degree in engineering, but he was helping his father with the farm. Christian knew David probably had an idea that there was more to this than met the eye.

"I figured as much," David said with a smile.

Christian sighed, "We are on the run from government agents, all four of us."

Christian expected a barrage of questions; but instead, David's smile faded and a pained expression took its place.

"David, what is it?" Christian asked.

"Big black SUVs?" David asked.

"Huh?" Christian responded.

"I thought Terrell was kidding," David said in disbelief.

Terrell was one of Christian's distant cousins who lived in Wisner. He was a year younger than Christian.

"Last night, Terrell made a comment about seeing some boys in town during the afternoon driving a big black SUV with government plates," David said, seriously. "Terrell said they looked serious, wearing black suits and sunglasses. I kidded him about watching too many movies. I thought he was just joking around."

Ray bounded out of the house and jogged toward them.

"Hey guys," he said. "What's up?"

"We have guests," Christian said, knowing that Alexis had been eavesdropping and letting Ray know what they were talking about outside. "Government is here."

Ray showed no surprise at Christian's statement.

"How many people know about this house?" he asked David.

"Not many, and you can't see it from the road," David answered.

"No need to take the SUV into town, then," Ray said.

David nodded in agreement.

Ray asked, "Can you get your truck?"

"Not a problem," David said with a smile. "My wife can take me into town to get it. And I can drive the SUV deeper into the trees, just in case someone comes looking out here. I am supposed to meet your grandma at the donut shop in town anyway, Christian. She is going to be back before noon."

David walked to the SUV and opened the door.

"I'll do some snooping and let you know what I find out when I come back at lunch time," David said. "Use the upstairs rooms. You can sort of see the trail up to this place from those windows. I drive a blue pickup."

David slammed the door shut and backed onto the trail. He disappeared behind a grove of trees just past the garage.

The teens had relocated to the upstairs rooms when the ATV engine started outside. Christian watched David bound through the tall grass and disappear behind some trees.

"We are screwed," Christian whispered to himself as he watched the branches of giant cottonwoods sway with the morning breeze.

"Get some sleep," Alexis said quietly.

Now, Alexis was being the calm one.

"Sleep?" he answered. "How can I sleep?"

Christian had endangered his entire family, and his grandfather had been arrested. To make matters worse, agents hunting for them were already in the area.

"Maybe this wasn't the best place to go," Ray said, "but we're here, so let's use it to our advantage."

"We are hidden," Sam added, trying to reassure Christian. "You need to get some sleep. We will be safe here for a while."

Alexis said, "Christian, your grandfather will be okay."

"It's my fault he's caught up in all of this," Christian said, sadly. "If I hadn't let him help me…"

"Help you?" Alexis asked. "How did he help you?"

"Grandpa Pearson erased the memory from Calvin Robinson's mind," Christian blurted, emotionally. "Back in Red Oak, before I came out to your house to warn you that government agents were in town, Grandpa Pearson touched Calvin Robinson and erased his memory of me coming out of that tunnel after Johnny Stratton died. Not only can he read the images in your mind, but he can erase them, too."

The Three sat speechless on their sleeping bags.

"What?" Alexis finally uttered in disbelief.

Ray said, excitedly, "No way! That is too cool!"

"Cool?" Christian shot back. "I pray they don't figure out that he is a Phenomenon. If they do, it's all my fault."

Christian glanced back to the window. The morning light was gaining strength with every passing minute, and Christian felt the tug of sleepiness pulling at his body.

"I don't want to talk about it," Christian sighed as he knelt to spread out his sleeping bag.

Alexis stood and walked over to the window. She slid the glass sideways to open it and walked out of the room. Christian heard the same sound of windows opening in the other upstairs bedrooms.

"If we are going to sleep up here, we need some air flow," Alexis said as she returned to her sleeping bag. "It's already stuffy in here, and the sun is only going to make it warmer."

Christian bunched up the end of the sleeping bag to make a little pillow. It didn't take long for the others to fall asleep, but Christian was consumed by the thought that Grandpa was paying the price for Christian's freedom. He wondered why Grandma had decided to come back home. Christian figured that if Grandma was coming home without Grandpa, that meant she thought Grandpa Pearson was going to be okay. That thought brought some comfort to Christian as he relaxed a bit and drew closer to sleep.

Then Christian wondered why Grandma was more worried about his safety than Grandpa's. The small comfort Christian had felt was shattered when he realized that Grandma's return probably meant that Grandma thought Christian was in greater danger here than Grandpa was in custody. Even though the revelation was even more disheartening, Christian's exhaustion took over, and he fell asleep.

CHAPTER 10

When Christian awoke, the house was dark. The muggy air stuck to him, and he could feel wet spots where pools of sweat had soaked into the crumpled sleeping bag where his head had been. Voices drifted to his location from the vent near the room's door, which appeared to be closed, but he couldn't tell due to the lack of light. His body ached as he sat up before rolling onto his hands and knees to get up. He felt along the wall in the blackness and found the door was open.

Bits and pieces of hushed sentences wandered up the stairs through the pitch black. He found the rail and descended to the first floor.

"Christian," Alexis called. "Glad to see you're finally awake."

The voice came from another room. Christian wished he could remember the layout of the house, but he had not ventured long in the downstairs area before the group had moved upstairs earlier in the day.

"Where are you?" Christian asked in a scratchy voice as he tried to fully wake up.

"Keep coming down the hallway," Sam said. "We are just around the corner."

"Watch out for the ladder," Ray said, just as Christian found it with his right shin.

If he hadn't quite woken up, yet, the ladder did the trick. Pain shot through his leg and he almost fell over trying to keep his balance. His hand found the wall, and Christian steadied himself before continuing his trek through the house more cautiously than before.

"You okay?" Sam asked, concerned.

"Yeah, I'm alright," Christian grimaced, as he gingerly rounded the corner to the room where The Three were gathered.

"We all slept pretty well, considering the heat," Sam said in amazement. "We decided not to wake you when we got up."

"Did David come back?" Christian asked.

"Yeah, he came around ten o'clock, and we were sure the tractor would wake you up, too," Ray said. "We saved you some food. It's in the cooler."

Ray thumped it, and Christian slowly walked toward the sound. His eyes were adjusting, but he wasn't confident in his movements, yet. Christian could see Ray sitting on the floor, and he assumed Alexis was perched on Ray's left.

"Ten o'clock? What time is it now?" Christian asked.

"About ten-thirty," Ray answered.

"Sam?" Christian called.

"Right in front of you," Sam answered.

Christian had guessed wrong; Sam was next to Ray. He glimpsed movement near the door, and Alexis's outline moved past a window, taking a seat on the other side of Ray.

The cooler lid squeaked as Christian opened it. His hand felt the cool air emitting from the container, as he felt inside.

"Sandwiches are in plastic bags, and there are some cans of soda left," Sam explained.

"Thanks," Christian answered.

"It's summer sausage," Ray said.

Christian loved summer sausage. It reminded him of the long fishing trips he took with Grandpa Pearson and Dad in the summers. Grandma always made sure there were plenty of sandwiches to go around.

"David's wife made them," Alexis added.

Christian fished out a cold can of pop before closing the lid and sitting on top of the cooler. Food had never tasted as good as it did at that moment. Christian polished off the first sandwich and the shrill creak of the lid announced that he was going in for more.

They all sat and made idle chit-chat as Christian finished off a second and third before chugging the can of cola.

"This really is one of those blind taste tests," Christian laughed. "I can't tell what brand this is."

"I would guess Coke," Ray said.

"Really, I thought it was Pepsi," Sam retorted.

"Alexis?" Ray asked. "What do you think?"

Alexis didn't answer.

Christian's eyes were more aware of his surroundings, since he had enough time for them to make the adjustment to the darkness. He noticed Alexis's head was turned toward the open window near the front door.

"What is it?" Christian asked, trying to listen for the sound Alexis was dialed into.

"Engine on the road," Alexis answered. "But it isn't coming this way."

It was eerie sitting in the murkiness of the house, and Christian stood up.

"Well, let's go outside and see what we're drinking."

"Probably not a good idea," Alexis said, matter-of-factly.

"Why not?" he asked.

"David said the government agents were out all afternoon, driving around the gravel roads," Alexis answered. "He took an extra cooler into the fields today, and he dropped it off on his way back to 'the place.' I still find that term, 'the place,' funny."

Alexis laughed.

"What else did he say?" Christian asked.

Ray took over, "David overheard the agents say that a new group was coming in after midnight to take over surveillance of the area. He thought that would be our best opportunity to make our little trip."

"Trip?" Christian said, puzzled. "What trip?"

"We were pretty nervous when we woke up to that tractor and it was dark out," Ray explained. "David told us he wanted to come to the house when it was dark. He met with your grandma this afternoon in town, but he didn't want to risk coming out here right away with those agents driving around the back roads. Your grandma has a plan, and it's a pretty good one."

Alexis huffed at Ray's statement, and Christian realized that not everyone in the group was in agreement.

Ray continued, ignoring Alexis's disapproval, "David thinks it won't be long before those agents start poking around the fields. He's convinced this house will be found eventually. Sounds like they have spent time driving the roads and questioning people around here about us. David said his phone has been ringing off the hook with neighbors asking what the heck is going on.

"Your grandma told David that we should sneak up to her farm tonight on foot and take her Buick. She mentioned something about a relative you have in Grand Rapids."

"Grand Island," Alexis corrected Ray.

"Yeah, that's right, Grand Island," Ray said. "Do you know who she is talking about?"

"Grand Island?" Christian said. "I don't have any family in Grand Island. I wonder who she is talking about."

"Well, that's what she told David," Alexis said, showing her opposition with her tone of voice. "See, I don't like this. I think we need to go to the safe house in Arizona. Whenever phenomenon children get into trouble, that is where they are supposed to go, the safe house in Arizona."

"Well, we can't just jump on a plane, can we?" Ray said in irritation.

Christian figured they must have had a similar conversation already, and Ray and Alexis had dug in their heels on opposite sides of the equation.

Sam calmly broke the tension, "Let's get the car and go to Grand whatever."

"Island," Christian reminded her.

"From there, we can drive to Arizona to the safe house," Sam explained. "We can't make that trip to Arizona in one night, anyway, so maybe this crazy relative, that Christian can't remember right now, can at least give us a place to shower and clean up, because you guys all stink to high heaven. Or maybe we can stay in a hotel or something."

Christian heard Sam take a deep breath, and he assumed she was about to continue her speech. In the second of silence, Christian made the connection.

"Oh… I know who Grandma is talking about," Christian blurted, not believing that he hadn't thought of him right away. "Uncle Mick!"

"You can't remember your own uncle?" Alexis said, her hostility toward Ray shifting toward Christian.

"He isn't a relative," Christian explained. "He went to school with my dad."

Christian laughed before continuing.

"Crazy Uncle Mick, he played baseball with my dad when they were younger. Mike McCarney is his real name, but everyone in my family calls him Uncle Mick. He was from somewhere in New York, and he came out to Nebraska to play football and baseball at Concordia in Seward, where my dad went to college.

"Being from New York, Uncle Mick didn't have any family around here for the holidays. Dad always brought him back to the farm for Thanksgiving and Christmas and whatever other breaks they had. He sort of became part of the family. When he graduated from school, he took a teaching job in Grand Island, and he has been there ever since.

"We'll have to use a phone book to find an address when we get there since my cell phone doesn't have internet on it, but Uncle Mick won't bat an eye at putting us up for a long time. The government would never look for us there, since he isn't family, not technically anyway. They wouldn't have any knowledge of Uncle Mick being a possible person we would go to."

"Geez, how much family do you have?" Ray snickered. "It's bad enough that you are related to everyone around here, but you have to take in New York transplants."

"Well, that New Yorker is an option I never would have thought of," Christian stated. "I am glad that Grandma thought of Uncle Mick. Anyone I would have taken us to would have been related to me, and I am sure the government is keeping tabs on any family that any of us have."

"I don't know how they would have enough agents to watch all of your family, Christian," Ray joked.

Christian felt sorry for Ray, who didn't understand the bond formed with extended family when you were around them so often. He also knew that Alexis had not had any experience with those family relationships. Their ties to family were nonexistent in Alexis's case and stained by too much pain for Ray. Christian wondered if Sam could relate to the feeling of having a large loving family.

"If all else fails," Sam stated, "we can go to Phoenix and look up my family. It isn't large, but my parents would take us in."

"We need to get out of here first," Ray said. "So let's not get ahead of ourselves. And from what David said, we probably need to get going. It's almost eleven-thirty. They are switching out agents in half an hour."

The Three had put the bags near the door, so each of them grabbed their own on the way out. The night air refreshed Christian as he closed the door behind him. He was amazed at how much cooler the temperatures were outside compared to inside the house.

"I love the night air," Alexis stated as she took a deep breath.

"Hey, it's just cola," Sam said. "There is no brand. I guess we were all wrong."

They all laughed as Christian led them past the grove of cottonwoods behind the garage. The temperate night air reenergized them, and Christian was glad to have been given the opportunity to rest during the heat of the day.

Storm clouds flashed to the west behind them as they walked further into the trees, but the clouds were a long ways off, and the moon would give them some guidance until the thunderheads pushed closer. The trail wound around a pile of rotting logs and branches that had been torn out in the spring to make room for David's house.

"We will follow this trail until we come to a barbed-wire fence," Christian whispered. "That fence is the property line between Grandpa's farm and his brother's property. There is a dirt road that runs along that fence to the A-barn, where we tried to sleep in Grandpa's camper the last time we were up here."

"How far?" Alexis asked.

"Maybe three-quarters of a mile," Christian answered.

"Then wait a second," Alexis said. "I need to put on some jeans. These mosquitoes are eating me alive."

Alexis dropped her bag to the ground and fumbled through its contents until she found what she was looking for. She held it up to get a better look.

"This will do," Alexis said, calmly, as she unbuttoned her shorts. "Turn around, Christian, not for your eyes."

"That's a good idea," Sam added, as she unzipped her bag and found a pair of jeans. "Ray, you can also look the other way."

"Come on," Ray moaned in discontent. "You're like a sister to me."

"Shhh," chastised Alexis. "You want to alert the whole countryside that we're out here? Now, turn around."

Ray did as he was told, but he whistled a catcall even though he wasn't looking. Christian laughed and pushed Ray, jokingly.

"You better not be peeking at my girl," Christian said.

"Maybe I should change, too," Ray said as he pulled his shorts down, exposing his rear end to the girls.

"Looks like a full moon," Christian snickered.

Sam and Alexis both shrieked, and Alexis had a couple of choice words for Ray.

"Hey, your butt's so pale, we could use it as a lantern out here," Sam giggled. "Maybe your special ability is actually a fanny lantern. Turn it off; it's blinding me."

"Gassy fanny lantern," Alexis added, pinching her nose with her fingers. "Dangerous weapon if pointed at you."

Alexis waved a hand in front of her face, acting as if she had smelled something bad.

"Would that be called a buttocks bomb?" Sam said, and the two girls laughed again.

"Enough jokes," Ray said in irritation, as he buttoned his shorts back up and started walking.

Alexis picked up her bag and ran to catch Ray.

"I'm sooooo sorry," she cooed pretentiously. "Did we hurt your feelings?"

Alexis pecked him on the cheek, and Ray stopped walking. He turned around and grabbed her in his arms.

"You were showing yours, so I thought I should show you mine," Ray chuckled.

"You are such a freak," Alexis said, pushing away, pretending to be disgusted with him.

"But I'm a lovable freak," Ray said, smiling and pulling her closer.

"Unfortunately, yes," Alexis said, and Christian recognized the typical roll of the eyes from her. "You are a lovable freak."

"Can we continue our little trip?" Christian said mockingly. "Now, that the nudie show is over."

Sam looped her arm in Christian's. In all the excitement of the last day, Christian had forgotten how good it felt to touch Samantha Banner. While walking he tried to gently kiss her. Instead of it being romantic, they bumped heads and noses.

"Ow!"

"Sorry," Christian said, apologetically. "That didn't quite work the way I intended."

"We will have to keep practicing," Sam answered, pecking Christian's cheek.

"Sounds good," Christian said, sweetly.

"You two are so cute," Alexis said, rolling her eyes again, and Christian got the idea that Alexis was getting tired of him and Sam showing affection to each other.

"This is where we turn," Christian said. "This dirt road will take us to Grandpa's farm."

A gate marked the pasture ground for Grandpa Pearson's cattle. The dirt road was actually more of a path, two earthen lines formed by the constant pounding of truck and tractor tires on the ground with a wide patch of prairie grass filling the area between the tire tracks. A cornfield ran the length of the road to the right and a barbed-wire fence to the left with open pasture behind it and some dying cottonwood trees spaced intermittently along the way.

Christian was reminding The Three about the layout of Grandpa Pearson's farm when Alexis interrupted.

"Shh," Alexis said, as she stopped.

The four of them stood like statues, waiting.

"There's a vehicle behind us," she stated coldly, and they all instinctively ducked down.

"Is it coming this way?" Sam asked, and the reality of the danger dripped from her question.

"I don't think so," Alexis said. "No, it's headed back toward the road."

"Probably David coming to check on us," Ray said nervously. "He probably wanted to make sure we were on our way."

"You're probably right," Alexis said.

She leaned toward the house, as if it would allow her to hear more easily.

They waited for another minute in silence.

"It's on the road now," Alexis exhaled in relief.

"I say we take it a little more cautiously," Christian said.

"Good call," Sam said. "Ray, no more full moons."

"Storms are closer," Christian commented. "We are going to possibly lose the light we have."

They all looked over the still corn to the west. The shafts of lightning bouncing around the clouds were much closer than before, but the thunder was still out of earshot, at least for Christian, Sam, and Ray. Christian wondered if Alexis could hear the thunder from this distance, but he decided not to ask.

They reached the tree line and were greeted by deeper darkness. The moon was close to being swallowed by the thunderheads, and the thick foliage of the canopy blotted out any dim light from penetrating to the earth below.

"Spooky," Sam whispered nervously.

A little light emanated from the tree tops near an opening at the far end of the trail, where a farm light illuminated the front of the A-barn on Grandpa Pearson's farm.

"Not far, now," Christian said in a hushed voice. "When we get up there, Alexis should probably check it out to make sure there isn't someone waiting for us."

"Good idea," Ray whispered.

They reached the edge of the darkness and Alexis crept to a row of bushes just beyond the reach of the light. After a couple minutes of silence, she retreated to where Ray, Christian, and Sam were waiting.

"All clear," Alexis said.

"Let's go behind that long shed," Christian explained, pointing across the dirt road driveway to more trees. "We can walk around to the garage and go in through a door on the side."

They raced across the gravel, and when they had safely reached the shadows of the trees, Sam asked, "Was that the road we came in on when we came up here with you the first time?"

Christian nodded.

"That's that nasty curve, then?" Ray asked.

Christian nodded again. He led them around the shed and garage. Firewood was stacked next to a chicken coop in a well-lit, five-foot-wide space between the two buildings. The door to the garage creaked open, and the four of them were plunged into more darkness. Christian opened the driver's door to the car and checked to make sure the keys were in the ignition.

"I better drive," Ray said. "I have a little more experience behind the wheel than you do."

Christian agreed, as he popped the trunk.

"Put the bags in back," he said.

Alexis and Sam climbed into the back seat, while Christian got in the front seat on the passenger side.

"Don't we need to open the garage door?" Ray asked.

"There is a remote up there," Christian answered, pointing to the visor against the roof.

Ray pulled down the visor and a scrap of paper fell gently into his lap.

"What's this?" Ray asked, handing it to Christian.

"Looks like an address," Christian said. "Uncle Mick's address."

"We can double-check it in Grand Island," Alexis said. "Just to be sure."

"Well, it says 'Mick' on it, so I'm pretty sure it's his address," Christian said, and this time he was the one who rolled his eyes at her. "When we leave, let's go back down the road we came up on. They might be watching the other ways off this farm."

No one disagreed. Christian knew that it was a gamble regardless of the road they chose, but they needed to get out of this area.

"Maybe David left a note for us," Sam said, hopefully.

"I doubt he would leave a note for us," Ray said. "He was pretty concerned about leading them to us."

"Go with the lights off, just in case," Alexis whispered.

Ray started the engine, and Christian pushed the button on the opener. Ray backed out and Christian hit the button a second time. The door slowly closed, as Ray turned the wheels toward the A-barn.

Gravel crunched under the slow-moving tires until they passed onto the earthen road through the trees. Then it was an eerily quiet ride with the headlights off. Ray turned on the parking lights for a second and located the control panel when it lit up. He pressed the button for the air conditioning before turning off the parking lights, sending the car into darkness again. Soon, cool air flowed from the vents.

Christian's hand bumped something in his front pocket, and he remembered his grandmother's cell phone. He pulled it out but dropped it when the car hit a bump in the darkness of the canopy of branches above them.

"Sorry," Ray said. "I don't want the brake lights to come on."

Since they traveled on a downward slope, Ray had to let gravity move the car, but he decided to hit the brakes sporadically to avoid another jolt. They coasted all the way to the bottom of the hill, and Ray cranked the wheel to take the route past David's unfinished house. With the slight incline, Ray had to use the accelerator.

Christian finally located the phone and retrieved it from under the seat. If he had remembered it earlier, he could have called David, even though the government was probably listening in to David's line. Christian flipped the phone open, and a message appeared.

"1 new text"

His finger touched the key pad, and words flashed onto the screen.

"House NOT safe"

The car accelerated up a slight hill to the cottonwoods, reaching the skeleton of the garage.

"Is that David's truck?" Sam asked from the back seat.

It was too late to stop now, and Christian knew that was not his cousin's vehicle parked outside of the two-story home.

"Gun it!" Christian hollered. "The house isn't safe!"

Ray cussed as he floored the accelerator, and the Buick bounded along the rough terrain. The cell phone screen changed, and Christian saw "David's phone" appear on the screen. He clicked "answer" as he turned back to look toward the house. Christian caught a glimpse of two men running out the door of the house as the car bounced past a black Tahoe. The undercarriage pinged and then Christian's side mirror exploded.

"They're shooting at us!" Alexis screamed. "Go! Go! Go!"

CHAPTER

11

Even with the intermittent screams from the back seat, Christian could still hear David's voice on the line.

"David!" Christian hollered.

"They are at the house!" David yelled.

"They're shooting at us!" Christian fired back, his voice cracking. "We came back down that path, and they were there!"

"Where are you, now?" David asked.

"We are trying to get to the main road!" Christian shouted.

"They are new agents, and they may not know the roads," David said. "If you can get some distance you may be able to lose them."

Ray shouted, "What's he saying?"

Christian answered, "They're new agents! They may not know the area! We need to get some distance and lose them."

"Hold on!" Ray bellowed, and Christian glanced up to see the gravel road ahead.

The jarring left turn onto the main road knocked Christian off balance. The force caused his weight to shift into the door, and he dropped the cell phone in the darkness.

"Seatbelts!" Ray commanded.

Christian looked back toward the trail to see the headlights of the Tahoe leaping up from behind the corn rows before dropping down again. Unfortunately, he also saw the plume of gravel dust shooting up from behind Grandma's Buick.

"There is no way we can lose them with that dust from the road following us!" Christian exclaimed, as he pulled the strap of the seatbelt across his body. "No wind. It just hangs there on the road."

Ray had the gas pedal floored, and they were moving without lights at a dangerous speed for this type of road. One washboard could send them into the ditch.

Ray flicked the headlights on, illuminating what was ahead of them.

"What are you doing?" Alexis screamed. "They will know where we are going.

"What's ahead?" Ray demanded with biting authority in his voice, as they rocketed past a farmhouse. "Turn, stop sign, what?"

"Half-mile there's a stop sign," Christian answered. "T-intersection. Left is toward Grandpa's farm; right takes us to the highway. We might be able to lose them on pavement."

Ray let off the gas and braked before turning toward Grandpa Pearson's farm, the back end fishtailing a little.

"The highway was the other way!" Alexis groaned.

After completing the turn, Ray doused the headlights.

"Are you crazy?" Sam screamed.

"You're going to kill us before they can catch us," Alexis cried.

"They'll just follow the cloud of dust," Christian said, thinking Ray had lost his mind to think that turning the lights off would help.

"That's what I'm hoping for," Ray uttered calmly under his breath as he moved the car to the left edge of the road.

"They're making the turn," Sam said, nervously from the back seat.

"You're hoping for?" Alexis screeched, wondering the same thing as Christian. Why was Ray hoping for them to follow?

The car had almost reached the top of the hill, when Ray let off the gas, coasting down the back side. Christian saw the yellow sign on the right side of the road and opened his mouth to warn Ray of the curve, but Ray tapped the brakes and leaned to his right as he zeroed in on the inside part of the turn. The passenger-side wheels tried to grip the grassy edge of the curve and the back end fishtailed again, slightly. Ray swung the steering wheel into the swerve and the car straightened out. Then he hammered the accelerator, and the Buick's motor shuddered before shifting to gain speed. Christian realized what Ray's plan was, and he looked back to see if it worked.

The lights of the Tahoe glowed in the gravel dust, as the big rig leapt over the top of the hill. It appeared to Christian that the wheels may have left the ground momentarily.

"They're flying," Christian said in amazement. "There's no way they make that…"

The lights of the government vehicle dimmed for a split second in the trail behind the Buick but brightened as it tore out of the cloud of gravel dust. The Tahoe did not make the corner; instead, it turned and skidded sideways. The headlights rolled multiple times.

"Turn," Christian sighed in relief.

The road behind them was empty as they climbed the crest of a hill.

"They're gone," Christian said calmly. "It worked."

Sam and Alexis turned in their seats and peered out the back window.

"What do you mean they're gone?" Sam asked. "Just like that, they're gone. How?"

"They didn't make the turn," Ray said solemnly.

Christian repositioned himself facing forward, and Ray turned on the headlights. He continued to race south on the gravel.

"Hey, Christian, you there?" a grainy voice shouted from the floor. "Christian!"

Christian leaned down and retrieved the phone he had dropped. Amazingly, the cell didn't shut, and David was still on the line.

"Yeah, we're here," Christian said, as he relaxed.

"Did you lose them?" David asked. "I could only hear screams and yelling for awhile."

"Yeah, we lost 'em," Christian said.

"Don't stop for anything!" David stated. "Put as much distance between you and them as you can."

"That won't be a problem," Christian answered. "Ray's got it floored."

"You know where you're headed, right?" David questioned.

"Yeah, how did they find us?" Christian asked.

"They stopped by my dad's place, and my wife and I were out on the porch," David explained. "One of them thought they heard a shout out in my field, and two of them went to investigate. It wasn't long, and they came back up to ask about the house out there. I tried to lie, but then all four of them went down there to investigate more thoroughly. That's when I sent you the text."

"I didn't get it right away," Christian said, apologetically. "The phone was on silent."

"Well, you kids take care and good luck," David said.

"Thanks for everything," Christian replied. "Oh, and David."

"Yeah."

"You need to call for an ambulance," Christian said. "Those guys didn't make that curve near the back drive into Grandpa's farm. They rolled a couple of times at least, and they were flying when they left the gravel."

"Okay," David answered, gravely. "I'll call, and then I'll go over and check it out."

David hung up, and Christian switched the ringer to buzz.

Christian told Ray, "Just follow this south until we meet up with some pavement."

"Then what?" Alexis asked.

"Then we drive until we find a town and can figure out where we are and how to get to Grand Island," Christian answered. "There should be a map in the back pocket of my seat."

Sam leaned forward and pulled out an atlas. She handed it over Christian's shoulder.

"Thanks."

They rode in somber silence, even though they should have been thrilled by the escape. Christian imagined the horror those agents felt as the vehicle leapt from the road. If they weren't wearing seatbelts, someone may have died.

After ten minutes, they found a paved road and followed it west to a little town called Aloys. It wasn't listed in the atlas, so the teens continued west. They crossed County Highway 15 and eventually made it to Madison on Highway 81. They jogged south on 81 and then turned back to the west on another county highway. They decided it was better to stay off the main highways, and 91 had no major towns on it. They planned to head south on Highway 281 when they met up with it, and that would take them all the way into Grand Island.

Christian was amused by the small towns they passed through or near during the trip: Humphrey, Cornlea, Lindsay, Albion,

Spaulding, Greeley, Brayton, Wolbach, and Cushing. They were all tiny villages with darkened windows, and Christian knew he would never pass through them again.

The small towns were simply quiet, little blips on the radar, and then they were gone. Christian wondered if he was going to be just a blip, hunted tonight only to disappear from the government radar by tomorrow. Were they going to be able to stay hidden? If so, how would he ever find a way to be with his family again? Christian's hope, which had gotten him this far, was wavering. Where would they go from here? And what had happened to his grandfather? Those questions were swirling in Christian's head as the Buick crossed a bridge over railroad tracks at three in the morning and entered the city limits of Grand Island.

Since it was the largest city west of Lincoln, Grand Island had life to it, even though it was late. They drove past Wal-Mart, which had a number of cars parked in the diagonal stalls. Christian spotted a gas station with the lights still on and pointed to it.

"Does that place look open?" Christian asked.

Ray slowed and turned on his blinker but changed his mind.

"It's closed," Ray said, disappointedly.

"Hey, I see a 24 hour place up on the right," Sam said, excitedly, from the back seat.

"Why do we need to stop?" Alexis huffed. "Do you guys need to use the bathroom again?"

Christian sensed the eye roll from Alexis, and then he said, "No, but we need to find a city map so we can find where the street is located."

"A city map?" Sam said, confused.

"Yeah, a phone book should have a city map," Ray answered.

"Why don't you just ask the guy working inside?" Sam questioned.

There was a pause as Ray and Christian exchanged glances.

"I guess we just want to make things more difficult," Christian said, as he smiled and turned around. "That's a good idea."

Ray turned onto Thirteenth Street and made a quick right onto the frontage road. He pulled into a parking stall away from the front windows of a BYCO convenience store. Christian pulled out the scrap of paper with the address on it.

"Sam, go in and get directions to Capital Avenue," Christian said, remembering what his grandfather had told him before they left from Red Oak. The government agents did not have a picture of Sam.

"Are you sure you want Sam getting directions?" Alexis asked. "She is a little directionally challenged."

"Hey, I got lost one time in a mall, and you guys won't let me live it down," Sam whined her discontent.

"Just have him draw you a map," Ray said with a chuckle.

Sam exited the car, and she gave the door a pretty good slam before stomping to the front door of the convenience store. Christian marveled at how cute she looked even when she was mad.

Ray, Alexis, and Christian waited in the car for only a minute before Sam reappeared through the door. She had a grin on her face and a little swagger in her step.

"Hey geniuses, we already passed it," Sam said. "Capital Avenue is the first road we came to when we drove into town."

Ray laughed and put the Buick in reverse. Soon, they were back on Highway 281 headed back the way they came. Sure enough, Capital Avenue was only two miles up the road, next to the Wal-Mart Supercenter they had passed on the way into town.

"I guess we were all surprised to see cars outside a store at this late hour," Ray chuckled. "We totally missed the road."

"The address is 5420 West Capital, so I am guessing we go left," Christian said when they got close to the intersection.

"Left it is," Ray said.

They drove past a closed Dairy Queen, and Christian felt pangs of hunger. A row of gnarled trees lined Capital Avenue on the right, and a cornfield sat to the south.

"Maybe there aren't any houses out this way," Sam said, disappointedly.

"Nope, I see some houses on the left up there," Christian said, pointing excitedly.

Ray coasted past the first couple of homes.

"Anybody make out a house number?" Ray asked.

"It's too dark," Sam complained.

A street light marked a four-way stop ahead of them, and Ray braked at the intersection.

"North Road," Sam said. "Now, that's a strange name for a street."

"4001 is the number on that house," Alexis said, as she pointed over Ray's shoulder.

"Then we're headed the right direction," Ray said. "The numbers should get bigger."

"Yep, 4007 is on that mailbox," Christian said. "Keep going this way."

"So, is there a North and South North Road?" Sam asked the group. "Or is it just North Road?"

"What are you talking about?" Ray asked.

"Well," Sam said, confusedly. "That sign back there said 'North Road.' It runs north-south, so I was wondering if the southern part of that road would be called South North Road. It would be kind of funny if it did."

"Oh, brother," Alexis sighed.

"Hey, we are on West Capital," Sam pleaded her case. "Was that North North Road, or South North Road?"

"You are so strange sometimes," Alexis said.

"Do you live on South North Road?" Sam said, amusing herself. "I wonder if they have an East Road."

Christian saw Alexis roll her eyes again.

Sam continued, "What if I lived on the corner of West East Avenue and South North Road? Man, that would be confusing."

Christian just chuckled to himself in the front seat, as Alexis added a sigh to Sam's query. Even though it appeared to drive Alexis nuts, Christian thought it really was an interesting question that Sam was asking, and he would have to make sure he told her that later. Right now, he just wanted to find Uncle Mick's house.

They drove past a small church with an illuminated sign out front that read, "Our sign guy is on vacation, so come inside for the message," and then more houses before reaching the edge of town.

"Did we miss it?" Sam asked.

"No, we haven't reached 5420, yet," Christian replied. "It must be out in the country."

The path turned from pavement to gravel.

"Hopefully, his mailbox has the number on it," Ray said, "or we're going to have to guess."

They had traveled a mile on the gravel, when they passed through an intersection. A large mailbox reflected in the high beams of the Buick, and Ray slowed.

"5420," Christian said with pride. "We found it."

"Doesn't look like anyone's home," Sam added.

"Well, it's three in the morning," Christian responded, as he opened the door before Ray had the car fully stopped. "We can't sleep out here tonight."

Christian jogged to the front porch and rang the doorbell. After ten seconds, he rang it a second time. He was about to ring it a third time, when Alexis grabbed his hand.

"Someone is coming," she said, quietly, and they all backed away from the door.

A light flipped on inside the house, and then Christian sensed movement behind the clouded glass window of the door. A soft yellow light buzzed to life above them, and the sound of unlocking followed. The screen door shuttered as the wooden door behind it swung open to the inside.

"Who in the heck is comin' to my door at this hour?" an older man coughed, trying to drive the sleep from his voice. "What do you kids want?"

Christian recognized the voice, but he was guessing Uncle Mick didn't have his glasses on.

"Uncle Mick, it's Christian. We're sorry to show up like this," Christian said, apologetically. "We didn't have anywhere else to go."

"Holy crap! Is that Christian Pearson?" the man responded.

Uncle Mick quickly opened the screen door.

"Come in! Come in!" Uncle Mick shouted. "Boy, you've filled out. I haven't seen you in about a year. Not since the last time I made it to Omaha."

Christian entered the living room of the house, and The Three followed behind him.

"What in the world are you doin' at my front door at this hour?" Uncle Mick asked. "Is your dad with you?"

"Uncle Mick," Christian started, "we need a place to hide for a while. It's a long story, and honestly, I am too tired to go through everything that has happened to us in the last couple of days. We need a place to crash."

"Well, just give me the important stuff," Mick said, seriously.

"First, we need to hide that car," Christian said, pointing out the front door. "Don't worry! It's Grandma's, so it's not stolen, but people are going to be looking for it."

"What kind of trouble are you in?" Mick asked.

Ray answered, "We are on the run from the state patrol."

"Hold on a second," Mick interrupted. "Let me turn on a light so I can see who I'm talkin' to."

Mick turned and walked toward the light in the hallway. He fumbled in the dark and flicked the switch, illuminating the living room in a soft glow. Uncle Mick looked the same as he did when Christian saw him last, even though it was probably more like three years ago. His hair was unkempt because he had been sleeping, but he still wore it in a ponytail. It was mostly gray with a couple black streaks through it. His face was thin with a pointed chin and a narrow nose. Mick grabbed a pair of black, wire-rimmed glasses from an end table and put them on, making his dark brown eyes grow a bit larger.

"Who have you brought with you?" Mick asked, as his eyes darted to Sam, Alexis, and then Ray.

Christian made introductions, and then Mick asked if they wanted something cold to drink. He led them to the dining room before he disappeared into the kitchen. A moment later, he returned.

"State Patrol, huh?" Mick said, getting the conversation back to the problem at hand.

"More like every law enforcement agency in the country by now," Christian clarified. "Like I said, it's a long story, but we need to hide that car outside and lay low for a while."

Uncle Mick studied Christian's face and then looked at the others. There was a long pause.

"Let's get that car into the garage and put a tarp over it," Mick said, finally. "Then I'll make you some food, before you go to bed. But tomorrow… well, tomorrow you tell me everything when I get done with school."

Christian looked at Ray, and Ray nodded.

"Deal," Christian said.

"You go to the car, and I'll open the garage. Then we'll eat something," Uncle Mick said as he got up.

"One more thing, Mick," Christian said.

"Yeah," Mick responded.

"You can't call anyone in my family about this," Christian said, seriously. "Nobody."

"Boy, you must be in some serious stuff," only Uncle Mick didn't use the word stuff.

Mick paused for a second and then smiled.

"Hey, who covered for you when you caught the bush on fire on the Fourth of July," Mick said with a laugh. "You have always been my favorite nephew, even though I am not technically part of the family."

Christian laughed, "You'll always be family."

Ray pulled the keys from his pocket and Christian and Mick walked to the garage. Christian helped Mick pull a tarp over Grandma's Buick, they ate some sandwiches, and then they went to sleep. It felt good to sleep in clean sheets and air conditioning, but most of all, it felt good to go to bed knowing that there would be no capture tonight. They had slipped off the radar for the moment, and Christian hoped that Grandma's idea of hiding at Uncle Mick's house would pay off. They were due for something to go right for a change. Christian was sure that tomorrow would be a good day, and for the first time in a week, nothing would go wrong. But tomorrow would be another typical day on the run as a Phenomenon Child, and the problems were only beginning for Christian and The Three.

The sun had already risen quite high in the sky when Christian finally woke up. Even though it was late morning, nothing else stirred in the house, so Christian quietly crept across the hall to the bathroom. The door didn't have a lock, but he wasn't too concerned. Sam, Alexis, and Ray were probably still sleeping, and Uncle Mick had told them last night that he had school the next day. Once the shower was running, people would be able to hear that it was occupied, so Christian figured no one would come in.

Christian sat on the lid of the toilet before he moved the shower curtain and turned the knob. The old pipes in the wall grunted once; the water fizzed and then flowed steadily. He pulled his t-shirt off and stood to look in the mirror. Streaks of dirt were still on his face, and his hair was greasy. He moved the shirt closer to his nose and took a whiff of its rank odor. He balled up the shirt and chucked it to the floor near the door.

His back ached, and Christian turned to take another look in the mirror. Twisting his head allowed him to see the bruises that had formed. He still had scratch marks from the incident with Stratton's truck at the pond. It was only a few days ago that he was forced to dive off the road to avoid getting run over by Johnny Stratton, so little scabs had formed along the fault lines of the cuts. Christian shivered at the memory of Stratton's dead eyes above a mutilated jaw-line.

He moved back to the shower and checked the water temperature. It was too hot, so he adjusted the knob once more before taking off his shorts and underwear. Again, he wadded them into a ball and tossed them onto the sweat-stained shirt.

The water of the shower needed one more adjustment when he entered the tub, and it only took a few seconds for the stream to drop a few degrees lower. Christian put his head into the flow and the warm water washed over him. With his face down, he allowed the spray to beat against the back of his head and neck, cascading down his body.

After five minutes, Christian decided he probably should save some hot water, so he located the shampoo and quickly washed his hair. The lather of soap rejuvenated Christian, as he scrubbed the grime from his muscles. It was amazing how refreshed he felt with a clean body.

Christian turned off the water and then remembered he had not grabbed a towel.

"Crap," he said aloud.

"Forget something," a female voice with a mouth full of toothpaste said from the other side of the curtain.

Christian froze. It was Alexis.

"Don't worry," Alexis giggled, and Christian heard her spit into the sink. "I didn't peek."

She extended her hand through the curtain. A blue bath towel hung from her fingers.

"Thanks," Christian said nervously as he grabbed the towel.

Then he made sure the small opening of the curtain was closed again. Alexis chuckled.

"Relax," she stated, "I'm already involved in a relationship."

"Geez, a little privacy would be nice," Christian fired back.

"Only one bathroom, so deal with it," Alexis retorted. "I had to brush the last couple days off my teeth. I'm almost done. I just need to rinse one more time, and I'll be gone."

"Anyone else up?" Christian asked.

"I think Sam is," Alexis answered. "But Ray was still sawing logs when I got out of bed."

Christian felt a little weird about Ray and Alexis sleeping in the same bed, but their defense was that they were practically married. He wondered if it would end up being that way with Sam, if they would live their entire lives together in hiding. The Phenomenon Child way was sort of an arranged marriage situation. Mr. Banner paired up Phenomenon Children to send them off together. There weren't a whole lot of choices, so a Phenomenon Child couldn't be picky. Christian liked Sam, but was he really ready for that kind of commitment at fourteen or fifteen years old?

"All done," Alexis said, and the door opened and closed.

Christian peeked out to make sure she was gone. With the coast clear, he toweled off and wrapped it around his waist. Then he realized that he failed to bring clothes with him into the bathroom. Christian would have to make a break for it across the hall before he could get dressed. He did a quick double-check to make sure nothing was showing in the front or the rear before opening the door to hurry back to his room.

In a rush to cross the hall, he didn't look both ways before crossing. He looked right, as he turned left and bumped squarely into Sam, almost knocking her over. Christian reflexively reached to keep her from falling backwards, and when he did, the towel he was wearing loosened and fell to the floor.

Christian was standing completely naked in the hallway facing directly toward Sam, and he froze. His hands were clamped to Sam's arms at her shoulders, as he stood like a deer in the headlights of an oncoming car. Sam's blue eyes met Christian's and then darted to the towel on the floor. At least, Christian hoped it was the towel she was looking at. Sam's eyes moved quickly back to meet Christian's look of terror.

Even though he was horrified, Christian still couldn't move; he was frozen in place. Sam's lips curled into a grin.

"This is quite the predicament," Sam whispered.

"Looks good from behind!" Alexis hooted from the kitchen.

Alexis's words sprung Christian from his frozen state, and he dashed into his room. He quickly slammed the door behind him and frantically searched for a change of clothes.

"Why didn't I take clothes with me?" he muttered to himself.

"To give us a show!" cackled Alexis from down the hall.

How was he going to face them after this? Buck naked in the hallway in front of them both. Obviously Alexis had seen him from the rear, and he guessed Sam had not peeked at the towel on the floor when her eyes wandered down. Christian quickly put on his clothes, and then he sat down on the bed. He put his head in his hands.

There was a knock at the door.

"Christian," Sam called, "Are you dressed?"

"Yeah," he responded with his head still in his hands.

"Can I come in?" she asked.

"Be careful," Alexis hollered. "The flasher might still be in his birthday suit."

"Shut up, Alexis!" Sam chastised her.

"You can come in," Christian said, looking up from the bed.

The door opened and Sam peeked around the corner.

"You sure?" Sam asked.

"Yeah, I'm sure," he responded. "Just totally freakin' embarrassed."

Sam smiled and walked over to sit next to him.

"I can't believe that happened," Christian said, dejectedly.

"If it makes you feel better, Alexis said you're pretty cute from behind," Sam whispered.

"No, that really doesn't make me feel better," Christian replied, still mortified by what had just happened.

"Don't be embarrassed," Sam said quietly. "It happens."

"Really?" Christian responded. "How many former boyfriends have you seen totally naked? Wait, please don't answer that."

"None," Sam said, ignoring Christian's request. "You're the first. Not quite how I imagined it would be the first time."

She turned away from him.

"Actually, I thought it would be more romantic," she continued. "I didn't think it would be in the hallway of a strange man's house in Nebraska. It was an accident, so don't worry about it."

"Easy for you to say," Christian said in disgust. "You weren't the one standing naked in the hallway of a strange man's house in Nebraska."

Sam laughed and turned to put her arms around Christian.

"Sorry," Sam said.

"For what?" he asked.

"I think I accidentally knocked your towel loose," she said, sheepishly, as she released him from the hug.

Alexis cackled a second time from the kitchen.

"Alexis is making breakfast," Sam said. "Are you hungry?"

"I'll be there in a second," Christian said.

He wasn't quite ready to face Alexis, and he thought that maybe he could just stay in his room for another couple days.

Sam stood up, and then she leaned over to kiss Christian's forehead. She opened the door and walked into the hallway.

"Seriously, Alexis, can you turn your ears off every once in a while?" Sam called as she closed the door to the bedroom.

Christian waited a couple of minutes before he had enough courage to make the trip to the kitchen. If it wasn't for his hunger, Christian might have stayed put on the bed for another hour, but the pangs in his stomach forced him to face Alexis. Expecting the worst, he was pleasantly surprised that she made no comments to him about what had just transpired. Christian guessed that it was only due to a request from Sam.

Alexis was preparing scrambled eggs and bacon, and the aroma made Christian's stomach growl. The smell of breakfast also had awakened Ray, who appeared in the doorway to the kitchen shortly after Christian sat down.

"What did I miss?" Ray asked, rubbing sleep from his eyes.

"Nothing," Sam said, quickly looking to Alexis.

"Not much," Alexis answered, "just Christian leaving his towel in the hallway."

Ray looked puzzled. Fortunately, he was more interested in food than figuring out what Alexis was talking about. Christian was sure Alexis would tell Ray later, but at least she wasn't going into detail about it now.

"Does your uncle get the newspaper?" Ray asked.

"I don't know," Christian said. "I'll go check."

Christian wanted any reason to avoid Alexis, so he headed for the door. A plastic orange bag was lying in the driveway, so Christian darted out the door to get it. The air was hot and muggy outside, and the sun beat down from a cloudless sky. The ground appeared to be dry, and Christian wondered what had happened to the storm clouds from the night before. They must have stayed north of them all evening.

Christian returned to the kitchen and dropped the paper on the table before sitting down in front of a full plate. Sam finished eating and said she was going to take a shower. Alexis giggled, and Sam told her to shut up.

"Be careful with the towel," Ray said. "I've heard they have been malfunctioning around here."

"You already told him!" Christian cried. "I can't look at any of you for the rest of my life."

He grabbed his plate and got up from the table in the kitchen. He decided to walk into the dining room so he could eat alone.

"Come on, Christian," Ray pleaded. "It is pretty funny. You have to admit that."

It was totally embarrassing and Christian saw no humor in it. He didn't answer Ray. As Christian finished his noontime breakfast, he heard Ray unfolding the newspaper. Christian leaned forward to look into the kitchen.

"When you're done with the sports page, I would like to look at it," Christian stated. "I haven't been able to keep up on the standings in baseball."

"Keep your pants on," Ray replied, and Alexis roared in laughter.

Christian slammed his fork onto his plate at the table and stalked off to his room. Sam was coming out of her bedroom, the one next door to his, and she had clothes in her hands.

"Do you need a toothbrush?" she asked. "I just finished with mine, so you can use it if you need to."

"No, I have one," Christian said.

"I'll wait, so you can brush yours," she said, sweetly. "Man, did it feel good to brush mine; it's been a while."

"Thanks," Christian said.

He quickly grabbed his toothbrush and walked into the bathroom.

"Would you close the door?" Sam asked. "I'll turn the water on, so maybe Alexis won't be able to overhear us talking."

Christian closed the door, and Sam handed him a tube of toothpaste.

"Thanks, again," Christian said.

Sam had a knack for making him feel better. Christian turned on the faucet, and Sam started the water in the shower. Christian bent over the sink and worked feverishly to get his mouth refreshed. He cupped water into his hands to rinse out his mouth and grabbed a hand towel to wipe up some splatters of water.

"Can you help me with this?" Sam asked.

Christian turned and froze. Sam Banner was standing with her back toward Christian with just her bra and panties on. She had pulled the curls of blonde and brown hair up over her right shoulder, as she peeked over her left shoulder at Christian.

"I just need you to unsnap me," she whispered before turning her head back toward the shower curtain.

Christian had feelings he had never experienced. His heart pounded in his chest, and the weight of his body lightened. His eyes wandered up and down the contours of Sam's body, as he slowly moved toward her.

"Uh, you don't have to do this," Christian's voice cracked.

Sam giggled.

"Don't worry," she whispered, calmly. "I'm saving myself, but I thought I owed you a little look. It's basically a bathing suit."

But it wasn't a bathing suit. It was more than that. Christian's hands trembled as he moved closer to her. He knew this wasn't right, but he wanted so badly to touch her soft skin, kiss the back of her neck, and run his hands along her body.

"Just unhitch it here," Sam said, as she moved her finger to point to the two hooks keeping it on.

Christian reached forward and then hesitated. Instead of unhitching her, he put his hands on her shoulders. She leaned her head back and reached a hand back to caress the back of his neck.

He whispered, "We don't know each other that well. I really like you, but we can't do this. It isn't right."

"Oh, this is as close as you get," Sam said, with an embarrassed laugh.

Christian wrapped a towel around her and said, "I better go."

She turned and pressed against him, burying her cheek in his chest. Christian put his arms around her.

"I think I love you," Sam whispered.

Christian didn't answer. He liked Sam, and his father had tried to explain love to him once, but Christian wasn't sure that was what he felt right now.

"I know we haven't known each other that long," Sam said in a hushed tone. "But I love you."

Christian squeezed her tightly, but he did not say the words back to her. He wanted to, but he wasn't sure that what he was experiencing was love.

"Will I ever see my parents again?" she said with a sniffle. "Will we ever be free to live normal lives?"

"I don't know," Christian said, and his pounding heart slowed its beats.

Sam sobbed into his shirt.

"I'm sorry," she said.

"Sorry for what?" Christian asked.

"Well, I put you in another awkward situation, and then I start bawling," Sam said, as she wiped her eyes.

"We're going to be okay," Christian whispered. "Now, I better go so I don't ruin this moment."

"Ruin it?" she asked, looking up at him.

"You kind of stink," Christian said with a grin.

Sam laughed and hugged him tightly.

"Thanks, for being one of the good guys," she said.

"Okay, you can look," she whispered.

Christian opened his eyes.

"This better," Sam said, as she held the towel with one hand and put her other hand in the air to spin around like a model.

"Nope, you still look good, but I can handle it," Christian answered. "Hey, the shower is probably out of hot water now."

"Oh, I had it running cold," Sam replied.

"Good, I may need a cold shower after being in here with you," Christian said with a wry smile.

Sam leaned forward and pecked him on the lips.

"Let me wash the stink off," she whispered. "Then I can give you a better kiss."

"Can't wait," Christian said, before grabbing his toothbrush and turning to leave the bathroom.

He made a pit stop in his bedroom to put it away, and then he walked to the kitchen to see if Alexis and Ray were still there.

"Take a look at this," Ray said, as Christian stepped onto the linoleum.

"Sports page?" Christian asked, as he took the folded paper.

"Nope, front page," Alexis answered him, and she had a serious look on her face.

Christian unfolded the paper and laid it on the kitchen counter, wondering what was so important. The headline read, "Four fugitives foil federal and state authorities." A four-square of pictures accompanied the article. Artist drawings of three teenagers filled three of the boxes of the front page with the fourth picture being a snapshot of Christian.

"We're up a creek," Ray stated, seriously.

The pictures of Ray and Alexis were sort of close to the real thing, but they were somewhat vague. Sam's picture was way off, but Christian's was a photograph that he remembered had been hanging in the living room of his house in Red Oak.

"Why don't they have snapshots of anyone else but me?" Christian said, confusedly.

"Not sure," Alexis said. "I thought the same thing."

"And Sam's picture is way off," Ray added.

"Can we trust Uncle Mick?" Alexis asked.

"Definitely," Christian said, confidently. "Why?"

"There's a reward," Ray said. "Two hundred and fifty thousand dollars."

"What?" Christian responded.

"For each of us," Alexis added.

"Oh my," Christian said as he sat down.

Christian looked back at the newspaper. That was a lot of money, and Christian knew that money made people do strange things. He was pretty sure Uncle Mick wouldn't turn them in, but that was a million dollars for the capture of all four of them and a million reasons for Mick to do it. Christian started reading the article.

After a couple sentences, Christian felt like he was being watched. When he looked up, Ray and Alexis were staring at Christian.

"Maybe we should leave now," Ray said, seriously.

"Someone's here," Alexis said, turning her gaze away from Christian.

The water to the shower turned off, and Christian could hear the whine of the garage door. Uncle Mick had returned from school.

"We'll be okay," Christian said, reassuringly, but he was struggling with his own words. What if a million was enough for Mick?

The door to the garage opened in the living room, and Uncle Mick appeared in the hallway. He had a newspaper in his hands, and he walked directly to the kitchen where the teens were standing.

He put the Lincoln Journal Star on the counter on top of the Grand Island Independent that Christian had just been looking at. Mick's paper was opened to the front page.

"We need to talk," Uncle Mick said, seriously, and Ray and Alexis started to creep behind Mick toward the hallway.

CHAPTER 13

"Stop right there, you two!" Mick commanded without turning to look at Alexis and Ray.

Uncle Mick continued to look down at Christian. Behind his wire-rimmed glasses, Mick's large eyes glared, as if Mick was trying to burn a hole into Christian's forehead.

"You have fifteen minutes to discuss with your friends," Mick ordered, and Christian could imagine what misbehaving in Mr. McCarney's classroom felt like. "Then you are going to tell me everything, or your butts are out on the gravel road, and I don't know you!"

Christian peered around Mick's head and caught a glimpse of Ray and Alexis. Ray nodded, and Christian looked back at Uncle Mick.

Sam strolled into the kitchen, still drying her damp hair with a towel. Mick never took his eyes off Christian, but Sam stopped cold.

"Uncle Mick," Sam said, quietly. "Why are you so scared? What happened?"

Christian saw Mick's face contort, and Christian wondered if he was surprised that Sam had known how Mick felt the moment she walked into the room, and Mick hadn't even made eye contact with her.

After a pause, Mick turned toward Sam and said, "You have fifteen minutes." Then he walked out of the room and down the hallway to his bedroom.

"Fifteen minutes?" Sam questioned.

"Take a look at the papers," Ray explained. "Two different papers, and they both have pictures of us on the front page."

"What?" Sam said, in disbelief. "How?"

"Christian's uncle wants answers," Ray said. "If we don't tell him, then we can't stay here."

"Then let's tell him," Sam said. "If Christian trusts him, then we should, too."

"But tell him how much?" Alexis asked.

Mick returned from down the hallway, but he didn't come into the kitchen.

"You have twelve minutes," Mick ordered from the living room.

"All of it," Sam said, confidently.

"But he may not even believe it all," Alexis grumbled in a whisper.

"Well, we owe him the complete truth," Christian said, in a hushed voice. "He's risking a lot by letting us stay here."

"If we leave today," Ray said, "then we are going to have four pictures fresh in people's minds. We wouldn't even be able to stop for gas or food. How far could we get?"

No one spoke, because Ray was right. Their chances on the road were not good, and all four of them knew that.

"I say we tell him everything," Christian said.

Uncle Mick paced in the living room, while the four teens discussed how much they should tell him. Christian agreed with his uncle that he needed to be told the truth, but Christian also wanted to make sure the other three were united with him.

"Eight minutes," Uncle Mick called.

"We can't tell him everything," Alexis said, quietly. "The less he knows, the better off we are."

"He might not believe most of it anyway," Ray said. "Especially our abilities."

"He would if we showed him an example," Christian replied.

"Who?" Sam asked.

They all looked at each other.

"Well, I can't really show him what I can do, but I could tell him," Christian said, trying to get someone to buy into his idea.

Sam peeked around the corner to look at Mick, who had stopped wearing out the fibers of the carpet and had decided to sit on the couch.

"Sure, you want to volunteer someone else," Alexis said, furrowing her brow and pointing an accusing finger at Christian. "Do you want us to boil some water and have Ray put his hand in it?"

"Remember what you did after the fight with Eaton at the pond. Maybe you could show him like you showed me in the field that night," Christian pleaded with Alexis. "It made me a believer. Show him your super hearing."

"Oh, why does he need to know anything?" Alexis fired back, trying to keep her voice low.

"Well, our faces are plastered all over town," Christian answered in irritation. "We can't travel with our pictures on every doorstep."

"Maybe we just need to make a run for the safe house in Arizona," Alexis said. "If we leave tonight, we could travel all night and stop at a hotel in the morning."

Christian responded, "I am sure those pictures aren't just in the Lincoln and Grand Island papers. I bet they are all over this part of the country. We are fugitives, and we are running out of options. Those guys back at the farm were willing to shoot us."

They all stood quietly. Alexis's arms were crossed, and she was glaring at Christian. Christian recognized the look from Alexis; she was digging in her heels on this one, and Christian needed support from Ray to get Alexis thinking straight. Ray sat with his elbow resting on the table and his chin resting in his hand. He stared at the wall across from his seat, and he looked like he was deep in thought. Sam continued to watch Uncle Mick in the living room from her position next to the doorway.

"If Mick is going to risk everything to keep us hidden, we owe it to him to tell him the whole story," Christian said, calmly.

"Owe him?" Alexis said.

"Yes, we owe him. He is a teacher who has just aided teenage fugitives of the federal government," Christian explained. "This could cost him his career if he hides us, knowing we are wanted."

Ray sucked in a deep breath and turned toward Alexis.

"Alexis," he said, calmly, "Maybe Christian is right."

Alexis turned in shock. Her jaw dropped open, but no words came out. She stared at Ray in disbelief, as if Ray had slapped her across the face.

"Listen, Christian has known this guy his whole life," Ray explained. "He considers him his uncle. We may need to stay here for a long time. If these pictures of us are in the local paper in Grand Island, you can bet they're circulating the nation. Trying to travel anywhere will be dangerous."

"But what if he turns us in?" Alexis whispered.

"It's a risk," Ray answered, "but it's a risk we need to take. We can't go anywhere right now. We might have to hang around here for a week or more until the story fades from everyone's minds. People will forget about this in a couple days or so, and then we can make run for it."

"He won't turn us in," Sam whispered.

"How do you know?" Alexis fired back, quietly but harshly.

"I can tell," Sam answered, calmly as she turned toward Alexis. Alexis's shoulders slumped as she rolled her eyes.

"Alexis, when Uncle Mick first came through that door, his colors were agitated with anger and fear, and I could tell he was scared and upset," Sam explained. "But I have been watching him while you guys have been debating. He has calmed, and I remember when he first saw Christian yesterday. Uncle Mick looks at Christian like his own son. He won't turn us in."

Ray and Sam had both sided with Christian, and Alexis looked defeated.

"I hope you're right," Alexis said to Sam.

"You know I am," Sam said with a smile. "When it comes to reading people, I am pretty good."

"I know, Sam," Alexis responded. "I know."

"Christian, you take the lead, and we will fill in the blanks you leave out," Ray stated. "We are all good with this then?"

Alexis nodded her approval.

"Sorry to get so excited," she said, apologetically.

"I would expect nothing less," Christian answered with a smile, trying to show that he wasn't angry with her and that he understood who she was.

"I can't believe you took his side," Alexis said, playfully pushing Ray, as the teens headed for the living room.

"You know I wouldn't go against you if I thought you were right," Ray whispered.

"Even though I was arguing with him," Alexis said, "I knew what he said made sense. I'm just scared."

"We all are," Christian said.

"We still love you," Sam added.

"Let's go tell him," Alexis smiled, leading them out of the kitchen.

The four teenagers walked into the living room. Christian took a seat next to Uncle Mick on the couch by the window to the front yard, and Sam decided to sit on the floor next to Christian. Ray and Alexis sat down next to each other on a love seat on the opposite side of the couch. A coffee table separated them from Uncle Mick.

"I am sorry we are putting you in this position," Christian started. "And we are going to tell you everything."

"I have all day," Mick said calmly. "I didn't have any afternoon classes today, and I cancelled the computer club meeting after school."

"I am not sure where to begin," Christian said, "so I'll start with me. I went on a fishing trip with Grandpa about a month ago. There was an accident, and I was changed. Somehow, my body radically changed. It's a long story, but I have a special ability. In fact, we all do."

Christian's words hung in the air, as he checked his uncle's reaction. Christian looked at Sam, who was studying Mick's face. She nodded, and Christian proceeded.

Christian continued, "That is why the government is after us."

In a hushed tone, Sam said, "We are called Phenomenon Children. The three of us had been in hiding from the government, when we came upon Christian in Red Oak. That's when this mess all started."

"Abilities?" Mick asked, puzzled. "What kind of abilities?"

"I have extremely acute hearing," Alexis answered, quickly. "In fact, there is a car coming down the road from that direction."

Alexis pointed toward the door leading to the garage. After ten seconds, a car roared past on the gravel.

"You're telling me you heard that car coming?" Mick said in disbelief. "What can you do big guy?" He pointed at Ray.

Ray answered, "I can withstand extreme temperatures. Freezing or boiling water has no effect on me. I can go outside in subzero weather without a coat and be perfectly comfortable."

"Really?" Mick said, as a smile erupted on his serious face. "What can you do, Christian?"

Sam said, "He thinks we're amusing."

"Can you walk through walls?" Mick asked, mockingly.

"What do you see?" Christian asked, glancing at Sam.

Sam said, "He doesn't believe us."

"Oh, are you a mind reader?" Mick grinned at Sam. "Why don't you tell me what is really going on? I think you guys have been watching too many of those superhero movies. Christian, you know I wouldn't really kick you guys out, but I just had to figure out what was happening when I saw those pictures in the paper. You don't have to make up a bunch of hog wash."

Ray got up and walked into the garage. He quickly returned with two five-gallon buckets, before he moved on to the kitchen. The suction of the freezer door opening preceded the rattling of ice cubes into the buckets. The faucet came on, and soon Ray returned with two buckets of ice water.

Ray set one in front of Mick before putting one on the floor in front of his spot on the loveseat. He pulled the coffee table off toward the dining room, so Uncle Mick could see Ray's bucket of ice water.

"Take your socks and shoes off," Ray said, as he sat down and pulled off a sock.

Ray stuck his foot in the ice water in front of him.

"What the…?" Mick said.

"Let's see how long you can last in that cold water," Ray said with a smile.

"Oh, I like a challenge," Mick replied, excitedly. "I am part of the Concordia Polar Bear Club. Christian, your dad and I are charter members. Bring it on, big guy."

Mick pointed to Ray as he slid his own foot into the frigid water. Then he winced a little.

"Woo!" he exclaimed in a laugh. "That is freakin' cold!"

"You man enough?" Ray said, goading Mick a little.

Alexis said, "Mick, while you cool off, I'm going to go into my room and close the door. You say something to Christian so that no one else can hear it, and I'll be back to tell you what you said."

Mick grimaced a bit from the cold water before answering, "Whatever, doll."

Alexis retreated to her room and closed the door.

Ray leaned back and put his hands behind his head like he was relaxing in a hammock in the back yard on cool summer night.

"Is she ready?" Mick whispered to Christian.

"Yeah, I'm ready!" Alexis's muffled voice hollered from behind the door at the end of the hallway.

Mick whipped his head toward the hallway to show his surprise at her response.

"You're probably going to have to be a little softer than that," Ray said with a grin. "I could hear you."

Mick motioned for Christian to come closer.

"Uncle Mick," Sam interrupted. "You really are enjoying this aren't you? Your colors are quite nice."

Mick furrowed his brow at her statement, and Sam snickered, as she watched the scene unfolding.

"Christian, your uncle is getting quite a kick out of this little show," Sam added.

"How's the water?" Ray asked, calmly.

"Freakin' freezing," Mick whispered with a grin, as he leaned to answer Ray.

"Of course it's freezing!" Alexis hollered again. "It's a bucket of ice water, genius! Quit talking so loud; you're making this way too easy."

"What the hell?" Mick said in a quiet voice, as he looked back toward the hallway.

"She's good," Christian said to his uncle. "You ready?"

Mick leaned over toward Christian and whispered, "Funky Winker Bean," and then he adjusted his foot in the ice.

"Christian, did he give you a word?" Ray asked.

Christian nodded.

"Did you hear him?" Ray whispered to Sam.

"Yes!" Alexis stated as she opened the door.

Alexis strode down the hallway and walked into the kitchen.

"I don't want you to think I was cheating by having someone mouth it to me," Alexis announced. "I'm going to write it down and bring it out to you."

"Paper and pens are in the drawer by the m-m-microwave," Mick said, as his teeth chattered a little bit.

"Cold isn't it?" Ray said, smiling.

Alexis returned from the kitchen and handed Mick a piece of paper.

"I'll be damned," he said. "How did you do that?"

"Do you believe us now?" Sam asked.

"Someone get me a towel," Uncle Mick requested. "My foot is about to fall off, and I don't want to get water all over my new carpeting."

Ray laughed as Sam got to her feet.

"They're in the closet in the hallway," Mick explained.

Sam returned with two towels, handing one to Ray and the other to Mick. Mick quickly pulled his foot from the water to reveal reddened skin from midway up his shin to his toes. He wrapped the towel around his foot and rubbed it.

"I might not be able to feel anything for a while," Mick said, looking to Ray.

Ray kept his foot in the water.

"I'll leave it in here another ten minutes just to prove my point," Ray said, confidently.

"I can see emotions," Sam stated. "I see colors around a person and that tells me how they feel."

Mick looked at Christian with questioning eyes.

"Is she for real?" Mick asked.

Christian nodded his head.

"And I can breathe under water," Christian stated, matter-of-factly.

"No kidding?" Mick answered. "And what is it you call yourselves?"

"Phenomenon Children," Alexis replied. "Actually, that's what the government calls us."

"Phenomenon Children," Mick said, the words rolling off his tongue with an awe-filled reverence. "I can guess why the government would be after you. Your abilities would come in handy to them."

"So, now you believe us?" Alexis questioned.

"Yes," Mick answered.

Ray explained, "Alexis, Sam, and I have been in hiding for years. Mr. Banner found out about Christian's ability, and that was how we ended up in Red Oak."

"Mr. Banner?" Mick asked.

"He used to work for the government," Sam said. "Now, he tries to find Phenomenon Children before the government does."

"That's his story," Christian grumbled. "I don't trust him."

"But you don't know him like we do," Sam responded.

Ray interrupted, "The government found us in Red Oak, and we had to leave there in a hurry. We have been on the run ever since."

"Wait a second," Mick said. "How did they find you?"

"We're not sure," Ray replied. "We think the accident may have led them to us."

"What accident?" Mick asked.

"A boy on my football team was killed in an accident," Christian explained. "I tried to pull him from his truck to save him, but it was no use; he had been killed instantly. Another player had seen me on the road after the accident, and he sent a note saying he was going to go to the police."

"Did he?" Mick questioned, trying to keep up with the changing discussion.

Sam answered, "I don't know," and then she looked quizzically at Christian.

Christian wondered if the same thought that entered his mind was the same question that seemed to come to Sam.

"How did they find out about us, then?" Christian thought aloud.

"What do you mean, 'How did they find out?'" Alexis asked. "Calvin must have told them."

"No," Christian answered flatly. "There is no possible way that Calvin told anyone what he knew."

"Then why did agents show up at your house?" Ray asked.

"Agents at your house?" Mick questioned.

"Yeah, agents came to my house," Christian explained. "But Grandpa and I were returning from the store. He dropped me off in the country, so I could warn these guys, and then he went back to the house."

"Then you came here?" Mick asked.

"No," Christian said. "We ended up at David's farm outside Wisner."

"Why didn't you stay there?" Mick said, puzzled.

"They found us, again," Alexis said. "But we got away."

"How do you know they won't track you to my place?" Mick said.

"Mick, it's okay," Sam said calmly. "There is no way they followed us here. You can calm down."

"She's good," Mick said.

Mick didn't look agitated when Sam said that, but she had a better idea of his emotions than anyone else did.

"How can you be sure?" Mick asked, and his cracking voice gave away his concerns.

"They crashed," Ray explained.

"I thought we were going to get caught," Christian added. "Then they didn't make the turn on the west end of Grandpa's farm. Their rig crashed into that alfalfa field and rolled a couple times. That was when we came here."

"I almost lost it on that curve once," Mick said solemnly. "That is a nasty turn, especially when you've been drinking. But that's a story for a different day."

Mick smiled.

"Well, that curve saved us last night," Ray said.

"And there's no way they followed you," Mick said.

"I'm positive we gave them the slip," Ray said. "Now, we need to lay low for a while until our names and faces aren't in the paper anymore."

"So, I'm aiding and abetting four teenage fugitives?" Mick asked, and the words hung in the living room.

Ray pulled his foot from the icy water and set it on the towel lying beside the bucket.

"Feel how cold it is," Ray said as he lifted his leg toward Mick.

Mick put his hand on Ray's leg.

"Holy crap!" Mick said. "It doesn't feel cold at all. It ain't red, and it actually feels like it's normal body temperature."

"Sorry to put you in this spot," Christian said, apologetically.

"Hey, you're family," Mick said, as he returned to his seat. "Besides, your dad and I had plenty of run-ins with the law when we were in college."

"Really?" Christian responded, intrigued by the possibilities. "Dad always said you were a bad influence on him."

"Me?" Mick answered, sharply. "It's the other way around. Your dad and I did some crazy things when we were younger, and most of them were his idea."

"So we can stay here?" Sam asked.

"I suppose," Mick replied, "But you guys have got to stay out of sight. Don't even go outside to get the paper anymore. My neighbors are sort of nosey, and if they see a bunch of high school kids at my house, well, they're going to be suspicious. High school kids at a teacher's house late at night. That wouldn't be good."

"We can pay you," Ray offered.

"Hell, no!" Mick fired. "You are my guests. Besides, I'm not hurtin' for money. I made a good investment a while back, so actually, I could retire from teaching all together, but I like kids too much, I guess."

"Thanks, Mick," Christian said.

"Did your father ever tell you about the manure spreader we put in the chapel on campus?" Mick asked with a grin.

Christian shook his head, and Mick let out a bellow of a laugh. Mick regaled the teens with the story. Mick and Christian's father had taken apart a manure spreader for Grandpa Pearson, instead of taking it to the dumping ground for worn out farm equipment. They hauled it back to campus on a trailer and took it piece by piece into the campus church. Mick and Christian's father welded it back together in the chapel on a Saturday night, so when they showed up for church the next day, there was a manure spreader in the sanctuary. One of their professors was giving the sermon on that Sunday, and Mick said they thought he was full of crap anyway, so they decided to help him spread it for service that morning.

Mick almost doubled over when he told the teens that the manure spreader was too wide to fit through the double doors of the church, so the professor preached with the contraption sitting in front of him.

Uncle Mick drove into town to pick up some hamburgers, and the five of them ate well that evening before Mick settled in front of the television for the six o'clock news.

"This is a Lincoln station," Mick explained. "There is another one in Kearney and one out of Hastings, but I like this Lincoln station the best. The weather guy is always spot-on with his forecast."

The teens cleaned up the table and put the leftovers in the fridge. Alexis was still laughing, repeating a punch line from a joke Mick told at supper, when he called from the living room.

"Get in here!" Mick hollered.

They all raced into the living room, and Mick was cranking the volume with the television remote.

"Melody Peebles is at the site of this horrible accident," the news anchor said, seriously.

The scene changed to a gravel road that looked familiar to Christian, and the reporter stood next to a road sign.

"This sign did not help government agents last night, when their SUV missed this dangerous bend in the road, killing two FBI agents, and sending two more to the hospital," the reporter said.

The scene changed to footage that Christian guessed had been shot earlier, as the reporter's voice continued to tell the story. The angle of the sun was different.

"Agents for the FBI were pursuing four teens when their Tahoe missed the turn and rolled over the embankment into a farmer's field. Now, two men are dead, and two others remain in critical condition, and police have no leads on where the four teens have gone."

The shot went back to the live feed from near Grandpa Pearson's farm.

"Agents told us that the teens are wanted for questioning in the death of a senior football player from Iowa. What started as a routine search for answers has ended in tragedy. This is Melody Peebles reporting for 10/11 News. Back to you, John."

The anchor reappeared, "Thank you for that report, Melody. The four teens are wanted for questioning in the death of John Stratton of Red Oak, Iowa. Stratton was killed in a single-vehicle accident outside of Red Oak last week." The scene showed a school photo of Stratton next to a map of where Red Oak was located in proximity to Omaha. "In addition to that, these four teens," the same four pictures from the paper appeared on the screen, "are also believed to have stolen an SUV in Iowa before leading state troopers on a high speed chase through Onawa, Iowa two nights ago. If you have any information about the whereabouts of any of these kids, you need to contact the number at the bottom of the screen. A reward of $250,000 will be shared with anyone who assists in the apprehension of these young criminals. Ken is sitting in our weather center, and he is about to tell us about the beautiful weather coming our way. Ken, what do you have for us?"

Mick muted the television.

"You guys can stay here as long as you need to," Mick said before rising from his chair to go to the kitchen.

"Thanks," Alexis responded, and Sam echoed her sentiment.

"So, how long do we wait, and where is our next move?" Christian asked.

Alexis and Sam shrugged, so Christian looked to Ray.

"Well," Christian said to Ray. "What do you think?"

Ray paused for a moment before responding, "Arizona."

"The safe house?" Sam asked.

"Yeah, the safe house," Ray responded.

Christian knew a little about the safe house outside of Flagstaff, Arizona, but he wasn't sure if that was the best place for them to go.

"How long should we wait before going there?" Alexis asked.

"I don't know," Ray replied. "We want to wait long enough for this story to go away."

"A week?" Alexis questioned.

"Maybe longer," Ray answered. "We may have to travel by night."

Sam called toward the kitchen, "Mick, how long of a drive is it from here to Arizona?"

"Phoenix is about fourteen hundred miles," he replied. "Grand Canyon is probably closer, why?"

Uncle Mick returned to the living room with a tall glass of ice water and found his original seat.

"I think that will be our next destination," Ray answered. "How long does it take to drive there?"

"Straight through," Mick explained, "I guess it would take you about a day. Twenty-four hours, give or take. It would depend on how fast you drive and how many stops you make. I drove down there a couple years ago over spring break to take in some spring training baseball games. There were three of us driving, so we didn't stop to stay in a hotel. We went down through Kansas and the Panhandles of Oklahoma and Texas and crossed the mountains in New Mexico. Colorado has a lot of winding roads and steep grades, so we decided to take the southern route."

"That's a long time on the road," Sam said.

"And a lot of stops with the risk of being spotted," Alexis added.

"Are we sure we want to go to Arizona?" Christian said, seeing this as an opportunity to steer the trip away from the safe house. "That is a lot of risk to take, when we don't even know if that is a safe place to go."

"Why wouldn't it be safe?" Sam said, puzzled. "Mr. Banner has always told us to go there when things go bad. I don't think things could be worse."

Christian hesitated. Grandpa Pearson did not trust Mr. Banner, and Christian's grandfather had seen images that lead him to that conclusion.

"Grandpa saw things," Christian finally reminded them. "Remember, when the agents were at my house in Red Oak, Grandpa saw images. He told me they had photos of each of us."

Christian pointed to each of them and then himself.

"Yes, the government already had files on us," Alexis stated, motioning to Ray and herself. "That's why we have to keep our pictures out of the local newspapers."

"That's why we can't play sports," Ray added.

"Grandpa also saw a file on Sam and on me," Christian said. "How would they have a file on me? I had only known you guys for a few days. It doesn't make sense to me. Grandpa did NOT trust Mr. Banner, and I don't think we should either."

"But he has taken care of us for a long time," Sam pleaded. "We have no reason to NOT trust him."

Alexis stood up and began pacing, but Ray stayed motionless and silent.

"Mr. Banner has kept us safe and hidden forever," Alexis said. "He is the reason we haven't been caught."

Christian interrupted, "He also may be the reason why I was almost caught in Red Oak. Things just don't add up!"

"What do you mean?" Sam asked, as Alexis continued to pace.

"Okay, in Red Oak," Christian explained, "I told you that I had solved the problem with Calvin. That he wasn't going to go to the police; that we didn't have to leave. But Mr. Banner was gung-ho that you guys were leaving with or without me, right away. Doesn't that seem odd to you? The timing of it! He wants to leave, and oh, by the way, agents show up at my doorstep. Come on!"

Ray didn't move, and Sam and Alexis looked at one another, neither of them sure how to respond.

Christian continued, agitatedly, "The government has pictures of each of us. Why would that agent have a photo of me in his memory when the only one who knew about me was Mr. Banner? There was no reason for those agents to show up at my house, unless someone told them! I'll tell you who the rat is! It's Mr. Banner!"

Christian was not yelling, yet, but he was teetering on the edge of it, as his anger toward his situation grew in intensity. He saw a hurt look in Sam's eyes, so he stopped before saying more.

Alexis looked questioningly at Ray, who had remained silent and still through Christian's entire tirade.

"Is he right?" Alexis whispered to Ray.

For a moment, no one in the room moved. Then Ray looked up from his thoughts.

"Why don't the papers have photos instead of those artist's drawings?" Ray said, calmly.

Ray must have seen confusion in Christian's face, because he repeated the question, only slower.

"Why… don't… the papers… have photos?"

Ray paused for it to sink in.

Ray spoke again, "Christian, if the agents have photos, why don't they put those in the newspapers and on television? Why is the only photo of you? I agree with you that it's odd that the agents showed up at your house, and I was beginning to wonder if Mr. Banner's involvement is not what we think it is. But then those pictures came out, and honestly, wouldn't they be a bit more detailed if Mr. Banner was behind it?"

"No names," Sam added. "I can't believe we didn't notice it sooner. No names with the pictures, either."

"Are you sure?" Alexis said, as she ran to the kitchen to retrieve a newspaper. "She's right!"

Alexis returned to the living room and tossed a paper at Christian.

"No names are listed below the pictures," Alexis said. "And those pictures aren't very detailed, well, except for your photo, Christian."

Christian didn't know what to think. His grandfather's distrust of Mr. Banner had made it an airtight decision for Christian. Sometimes, it's easy to keep thinking one way because all the proof seems to keep pointing in that direction. Christian had missed some crucial things because he was so convinced that Mr. Banner was the bad guy. Now, Christian wasn't sure.

"I still don't trust him," Christian muttered.

"Do you trust us?" Sam asked.

"Yes," he answered, quickly. "Of course I trust you guys."

Christian did trust all three of them, even though he had known them for only a short period of time. They all had the same things to lose, their freedom, but Mr. Banner was not one of them.

Christian continued, "I trust all three of you, but I don't trust Mr. Banner. Things just don't add up, and I still think Arizona is a big gamble."

"I agree," Ray said. "It is a gamble, but I don't know where else to go. We can't live here forever. I say we wait a week, and then we drive to the safe house."

"It's pretty secluded around that house," Alexis added. "We could hike in and stake it out, see if anyone is keeping tabs on it."

"We could go to Phoenix," Sam interjected.

Ray and Alexis turned toward her with questioning looks.

"We could check in with my parents in Phoenix," Sam said. "They could drive to the safe house just in case it's being watched. Then we aren't in danger of capture. They could make up some story that they took a wrong turn if it turns out to be a trap."

No one spoke.

"It's just an idea," Sam said uncomfortably as everyone stared at her.

"It might be our best option," Ray said, and Alexis nodded in approval.

"If the safe house is compromised, then that will shed a little more light on Mr. Banner's allegiances," Alexis added.

"At least we will know where we stand with him," Ray stated.

"I am not looking forward to that trip," Sam said with a sigh. "That's a long time in a car."

"Me either," Alexis huffed.

Uncle Mick had remained quiet through the entire debate. For a minute, Christian had forgotten he was there, until Uncle Mick raised his hands behind his head and leaned back in the lounger he was sitting in.

"How long can we stay here?" Christian asked.

"As long as you need to," Mick responded with an odd grin, like he had a good joke to share.

"What are you smiling about?" Sam asked, and Christian was thinking the same question.

"About your trip," Mick answered. "I can get you down there a lot faster."

"How?" Sam asked.

"Got my pilot's license two years ago," Mick said. "I bought a little six-seater. Like I said, I made some smart investments a few years back. I could take you down to Phoenix over the weekend."

CHAPTER 14

As the little airplane dropped in altitude, Christian's stomach crawled up into his neck. The trip had not been too bad, but Uncle Mick was having a little fun coming out of the mountains.

"It's amazing how maneuverable this small aircraft is compared to a big airliner," Mick had said, but Christian thought the ride was a lot bumpier.

They had stopped only once to refuel in Dalhart, Texas, but the teens never got off the aircraft.

"When I fly back," Mick had said, "it will be a direct flight, since the wind will be at my back."

Their altitude gradually dropped, and Christian marveled at the close proximity there appeared to be from the mountains to the plane. Whenever Christian traveled on one of the major airlines, the plane was so high in the air that there wasn't much detail to the ground below, or he had not been able to see much because his seat always seemed to be in the aisle and over a wing. A smaller plane meant a lower flight path, and Christian had kind of enjoyed it, even though it meant an occasional dip or bump. Mick pointed out the Salt River Canyon as they approached the Phoenix area. The winding river below was dotted white in a few areas, and Christian assumed it was rapids of some sort. Most of the Salt River was a deep blue surrounded by rock walls.

"We will be flying into Mesa," Mick explained. "It is one of the largest airports in the United States for small aircraft."

Like when they first left the ground, Christian just closed his eyes and prayed during the landing. Alexis had made fun of him during takeoff, and she picked up where she left off during the touchdown. Sam squeezed Christian's hand with the same force he wanted to squeeze hers, but he chose to grip the opposite armrest instead, so he wouldn't hurt her. Sam had the same displeasure with the takeoffs and landings.

"You two are meant for each other," Alexis laughed from in front of them.

Once the wheels touched down, Christian opened his eyes. The airport was a flurry of activity, and small airplanes lined up to take their turn on another runway. A tiny plane at the end of a line of twelve checked its rudder as a panel on the tail flipped to the right and then the left.

"Now, let's get you to your ride," Mick said.

Uncle Mick had called ahead to arrange for a car to pick them up and take them to Peoria, where Sam's parents lived. Mick guided the plane to get it refueled, and once he cut the engine, they climbed down a small ladder to the asphalt.

Mick pulled their bags from a storage compartment, and Christian slung the strap of his bag over his shoulder and looked into the sky. The heat in Arizona was nothing like the Midwest. There was little humidity, but with the concrete surrounding them, Christian felt like he was in an oven. Mick led the teens past a couple of buildings to a pilot hospitality room. From there, they wound through a pair of hallways to a set of glass doors that led to the outside. The oppressive heat met them head on again as they pushed through the door into a covered area where cars could drop people off or pick them up.

"If I remember right, they should be waiting for us over here," Mick said, as he led them to the right.

Everything around Christian was rock, except for a couple prickly pear cacti and one palm tree. There was no grass anywhere, and where grass should be, gravel took its place.

"Phoenix, I have missed you," Sam said, taking a deep breath.

"Is it always this brown?" Christian asked.

"Pretty much," Ray frowned. "No seasonal change, and very little rain, so it's always like this."

"It's a desert," Alexis said.

"There's some green," Sam said, defending her hometown.

"Christian," Ray said. "You'll see some green, but only if the rocks in the yard are painted that color."

Sam rolled her eyes, "Oh, there's green here. You just have to look a little harder to find it."

"There's your car," Mick said, pointing to a sedan parked near a palm tree. "I told them to take you wherever you need to go, and then they will bill my card directly."

"How much do we owe you?" Christian asked.

"Not a cent," Mick said. "Not even one thin dime."

"We can't thank you enough," Christian said.

"No thanks needed," Mick replied. "Your family has done so much for me over the years. It's the least I could do to start repaying them for all their hospitality."

Christian gave Mick a hug.

"I plan to call your dad tonight and see if he will meet me for dinner in Omaha. Then I can bring him up to speed on what is going on. You call me if you want any information, and I can contact your father."

Christian nodded and Mick shook hands with Ray and Alexis.

"It was nice to meet all of you," Mick said.

Sam decided another hug was in order, and she thanked Mick numerous times while squeezing.

"You kids take care of each other," Mick said.

Mick returned through the doors they had exited minutes before, and he was gone. The teens loaded their bags into the trunk of the waiting car before escaping the heat by climbing into the air conditioned vehicle.

The female driver slammed the trunk shut before joining the foursome in the car. Sam rode up front to help guide the trip, while Alexis selected the middle portion of the back seat.

"It should give you boys more leg room," she said with a smile.

They were on the move again, but this time there was no looming risk of pursuit. There was just desert sky and cacti.

"So where am I takin' you kids?" the driver asked, a hint of the East Coast in her voice.

"You know where the Peoria Sports Complex is?" Sam questioned.

"Sure," the lady replied. "Drove a bunch of people there during Spring Training last year. I'll make more trips there when the winter leagues are in full swing in a couple months. Name's Daisy."

She sure didn't look like a Daisy to Christian. That name conjured up the image of a southern gal, and she didn't seem like a southern belle. She was well-tanned, but her black hair, broad shoulders, and New York/New Jersey accent, although not very noticeable, made Christian think she should have a tougher name than Daisy.

"Daisy's more of a nickname," she continued when no one spoke. "Shortened from Danielle Isabella Cerrananno. My family calls me DC, but most of my friends call me Daisy."

"I'm Sandy," said Sam, "and this is Annabelle, Robert, and Chad."

At first, Christian was surprised at the fake names Sam had given, but then he realized how smart it was to cover their trail.

Daisy repeated the names to memory, "Sandy, Annabelle, Robert, and Chad," as she peered in the rearview mirror for the last three names, locking them to memory. Christian did the same.

It was a long trip, even though they never traveled outside the city. They drove on a road with three wide lanes before hopping onto Loop 202. Even though it was a weekend, a lot of traffic filled the lanes. When they merged onto Highway 60, the number of lanes grew to five and the amount of cars matched the extra space. Daisy talked for most of the trip, which made it easier on the teens. Christian was having a hard enough time remembering all their fictitious names.

"Phoenix can't build roads fast enough to keep up with the traffic. During rush hour, sixty turns into a giant parking lot," Daisy said as they left Highway 60 to get onto Loop 101. "They built Loops 202 and 101 to help with the congestion, but if you are in a hurry during rush hour, forget-about-it." Her accent seeped out. "Loop 101 will take us all the way around the north end of the metro to the Peoria Sports Complex."

Daisy noted landmarks as she drove. She pointed in the direction of Sun Devil Stadium, but it was quite a ways off to the west. Camelback Mountain was much easier to spot, rising high from the flat basin of the city. In the distance, Christian noticed other humps of rock towering high in the brown haze of Phoenix.

"There's all sorts of mountains in the Valley," Daisy explained. "Squaw Peak, Lookout, Shadow Mountain, Thunderbird, but my favorite mountains are the Superstitions. It's like God was playing in the desert sand and decided to build some hills for his people to play on."

As they reached the northern part of the metropolitan area, Christian noticed row upon row of mountains bordering the Valley of the Sun. He guessed those were the same mountains they had flown over earlier in the day, and he was amazed at what a change in view did to the picture. The mountains looked large from above, but nothing compared to the view from the ground.

Even though they had driven on highways and Interstates the entire time, the trip took over an hour. Finally, Sam sat up in her seat as the sign for the Peoria Sports Complex appeared on the right.

"Take the Bell Road Exit and head back to the east," Sam said, cheerfully.

Bell Road, near the sports complex, was teeming with restaurants that Christian had never seen before. Anything you could imagine was located on the first two miles of that street, and the traffic was horrible, even though it was four lanes in each direction. Daisy weaved through the maze of turning cars and merged with ease, adding her critiques of a few eateries on the way. She did pause to lay on the horn and fly a New York-style finger gesture at a Buick with North Dakota plates.

"Damn snow birds!" she yelled to punctuate the finger she had awarded to the elderly couple with the "I Love Fargo" bumper sticker. Then she promptly cut them off to get into the right turn lane at 67th Street.

The quaint, little Fargo tandem changed lanes and pulled up next to Daisy as she waited for the "No Right On Red" sign to turn off. The cute old woman in the passenger seat promptly fired up her bony middle finger to give the "bird" right back to Daisy before the light changed to green and the two cars parted company.

A few uneventful miles passed, before Sam led them onto Greenway for a short jog before turning south into a residential area.

"This is my neighborhood," Sam stated, proudly.

The homes were large but not completely ridiculous. Most of the homes had three-car garages, and some had a three-car garage with a covered slab of concrete where a fourth garage space would have been. What caught Christian's eye was the landscaping.

"It's mostly rocks and trees," he said, puzzled.

"Tough to grow grass here," Daisy commented. "Not a lot of rain, so it's easier to keep a rock lawn than a grass one."

"We have grass in the backyard at my house," Sam said. "You can let us out here."

Daisy pulled to the right side of the street where Sam was pointing.

"Do you need me to help carry the bags in?" she asked.

Sam responded quickly, "Nah, we packed light."

Daisy popped the trunk and handed the bags to the waiting arms of the four teens.

"Gotta run," Daisy said with a smile. "You guys are my last passengers of the day, and I got me a hot date with my New York Yankees this afternoon. Rubber game of a three game set with the cursed Sox. Man, I hate those boys from bean town."

She told them to enjoy the Valley of the Sun before she jumped in her car and sped off down the street.

Christian started walking up the driveway, but Sam stopped him.

"This isn't my house," Sam explained, surprising her three friends. "My house is around the block a ways."

"Nice thinking," Ray said, amused. "Just in case…"

"Yeah, just in case Daisy thinks she recognizes us as the four fugitives when she gets down the road a ways," Sam whispered. "And she wants to cash in. Follow me."

Sam quickly led them up the street and turned right, in front of a beautifully landscaped yard. Hedges blocked the view of the sidewalk from the front windows, and a large ficus tree shielded the house across the way from the sun and most of the street.

"Unlike the Midwest," Sam explained, "this heat keeps people indoors or in their cars until the sun goes down. If anyone is enjoying the outdoors at this time of day, they're doing it by their pools in the backyard."

Sam turned up the driveway of the second house on the right. The rock yard accented the light-brown stucco of the two-story home. A bed of lighter colored river rock flowed from a brown block wall, meandering through a landscape of desert plants. A saguaro loomed over small bushes and desert flowers in the focal-point island of green in the sea of brown rock. A prickly pear spread its spike-covered arms along a wooden fence that reminded Christian of an old Western movie set where cowboys would tie up their horses before heading into the saloon. Two barrel cacti flanked an iron gate that led into a small corridor to the front of the house.

Sam quickly led them through the gate. She seemed nervous and excited at the same time as she peeked into the street in both directions, before gently closing the gate behind her.

Alexis, Ray, and Christian waited near the entrance. No one had to say anything; they all knew Sam had to ring the doorbell. After all, it was her house that she was returning to after almost two years on the run.

Christian sensed Sam's jitters, so he placed his hand in hers. She gripped his sweaty palm in a vise, and together they walked two steps closer to Sam being reunited with her parents.

Sam reached her finger to the button to the right of the security door, but before she could press it, a lock clicked from inside the house.

Instinctively, the teens took a step backwards, wary of what could be on the other side. Sam gripped Christian's hand tightly.

The wooden door whooshed open, and a voice similar to Sam's cried out from behind the metal bars of the screened security door, "Samantha, is that really you?!"

CHAPTER
15

Sam's mother unlocked the security door and rushed to push it open, almost knocking Christian over. She wrapped her arms around Sam and squeezed tightly. Then she stepped back and cupped Sam's face in her hands before repeating the hug a second time.

"I can't believe it's you," Sam's mother sniffled, as she wiped her eyes.

She glanced at the other three teens, and then her face became serious, "Inside, all of you, quickly!"

She ushered the four teens into the house and nimbly locked the metal security door and then closed and did the same to the main door. Sam's mom quickly grabbed her daughter again and wrapped her arms around her.

"Oh, honey, I never thought I would see you again," her mother whispered, as she released her.

"Where's Daddy?" Sam asked, as she scanned the living room before peeking down a hallway.

"He had to run to the store," her mom replied, wiping her eyes a second time.

Christian, Alexis, and Ray had been standing only a couple feet from the entrance to the house during the emotional reunion of mother and daughter. Christian felt uneasy with the way Sam's mother seemed nervous about getting them into the house right away. Her eyes turned to him as she kept an arm around Sam's shoulders.

"Now, who have you brought with you?" she asked as she nodded to the three teens in front of her, acting as if there was no need to worry anymore.

"Vicki Kirgan, meet Alexis, Ray, and Christian," Sam said, introducing them from closest to furthest.

"Kirgan, huh?" Christian said in a quiet voice, mulling over Sam's real name. "Sam Kirgan."

Sam giggled and nodded.

"That's right," she said.

Christian marveled at the similarities between Sam and her mother, now that he had a better look at Mrs. Kirgan. Her hair was a little lighter in color than Sam's, and it was straight compared to Sam's curly locks, but that was the end of the differences. Mrs. Kirgan stood maybe a half inch taller, but the body build was identical.

"Pleased to meet all of you," Mrs. Kirgan said, smiling.

With Sam grinning next to her, Christian thought the pair could pass for being sisters. Each of them shared the cute dimple that accentuated perfect rows of teeth.

"Let's get your bags out of the way, and then we can go downstairs," Sam's mom said, cheerfully, as she picked up Sam's duffle bag and led them down a hallway.

They followed Mrs. Kirgan and Sam out of the quaint little foyer into a large living room. The sand-colored tile gleamed and Christian hesitated a moment.

"Mrs. Kirgan, should we take off our shoes?" he said, not wanting to be rude.

"Not necessary," she responded, "and please, call me Vicki."

Christian peered out a long set of bay windows to a breathtaking view of the backyard. The greenery hid most of the brown block wall that encircled the Kirgan's property. They walked through the living room and an adjoining dining area. Two large glass doors led from the small dining area to a stone patio. On Christian's right, a long granite countertop separated him from a spacious kitchen.

They moved into a hallway and turned left down a short corridor. Light splashed into the narrow space from yet another door that exited to the patio. As Mrs. Kirgan took the group into a room, Christian paused to peek into the backyard once more. Steps led from the stone patio to a swimming pool. The water glistened in the afternoon sun, and Christian marveled at the secluded oasis in the backyard. It appeared that each tree, bush, and vine had been strategically placed to ensure no one from the outside world would be able to catch a glimpse of the Kirgans' life.

"Did we lose you, Christian?" Sam called.

"Coming," he responded turning to catch up with the others.

Christian passed through another door into a small living room adorned with a couch and coffee table. A kitchenette gave the room the feel of an apartment.

"In here," Alexis said, leaning back into the kitchenette from a doorway.

"It only has the one bedroom," Vicki explained, as Christian entered. "But at least it gives you your own spot to call home for a while. We have other rooms that you can use, but I thought maybe you guys wanted to have a separate place to stay, so you could all be together."

"It's wonderful," Alexis said.

"Yes, thanks so much," Christian added.

Ray and Alexis had set their bags on the bed, so Christian retreated to the couch and sat down. Sam and her mother exited the bedroom arm in arm, and Christian wondered if Mrs. Kirgan would ever let go of her daughter again.

"I can sleep on this couch," Christian commented. "It feels pretty comfortable."

He patted the soft cushions with his hands.

"Sometimes, Dan comes down here to nap," Sam's mom said with a grin. "He thinks it's the quietest spot in the house. Sam, you can sleep in your room; it's just as you left it."

With those final words, Vicki Kirgan broke into sobbing tears.

"It's just that we have missed you so much, and we weren't sure we would see you again," Vicki said. "And then you just appear on our doorstep."

Sam hugged her mother, and they both cried.

"Mom, I am so sorry to have put you through all of this," Sam responded in hushed words. "We will explain everything when Dad gets home. It's long and complicated, so I want both of you to hear the same thing."

Mrs. Kirgan nodded and wiped her tears again, smudging more mascara.

"Oh, I'm a wreck," she said, laughing and sobbing at the same time. "I need to freshen up before you father gets home. Sam can show you guys to the basement. I'll be down in a few minutes."

With that, Mrs. Kirgan released her hand from Sam's and left the room. Christian moved his bag to the floor to make room for Sam next to him.

"How much do we tell them?" Alexis asked as she leaned on the high counter of the kitchenette.

"I don't know," Sam sighed. "Maybe everything."

"The more they know, the more they can help us," Ray added, as he put his arm around Alexis's waist.

Christian responded, "The more they know, the more danger we are in. It could also put them in danger."

"You're right, Christian," Alexis said in agreement. "Anyone who knows about us could end up like your Grandpa."

Alexis winced, "Sorry, Christian. I didn't mean for it to sound so harsh."

"But you're right," Christian stated.

He did worry about the people who had helped them, like Grandpa Pearson, David, and Uncle Mick. Grandpa had already been hauled in by the government. Would the same thing happen to David?

"My parents are willing to risk it," Sam said. "Just like Grandpa Pearson would do anything for you, Christian. My parents would do anything to help us."

"Then we tell them everything?" Ray asked.

Alexis nodded and Christian said, "Yep."

"Well, let's go downstairs," Sam said, as she rose from the couch.

The teens walked back down the hall and through the dining area into the living room. Christian had not seen the stairs leading to the second level on the way in, but he noticed them this time. They curled along the wall and over the foyer, emptying into a large open space on the left. A catwalk-like area led back across the upstairs to the right, and Christian assumed bedrooms were somewhere in that direction. He hoped for a tour later.

To the right of the stairs leading up, Sam led them through a short corridor to the basement steps. The stairwell split into two directions as they reached the halfway point to the lowest level of the house.

"Doesn't matter which way you turn," Sam explained. "Right and left both lead to the same area."

"Now, this is a man cave," Ray said in approval. Christian went the opposite direction.

The basement was wide open except for a few columns spread evenly in a row across the middle. Sports memorabilia and scenic pictures covered the walls. Christian had entered on the side with the pool table, while Ray and Alexis had taken the route past the poker table. The lights were bright above both game tables, but the rest of the great room was bathed in a soft glow from cutouts in the ceiling. The bulbs didn't hang down like they did in Christian's basement at home. The space was large enough for two sectional sofas and a couple recliners to fit easily with plenty of room to spare.

"Basements aren't common in Phoenix," Sam said. "Too much rock to move, but Dad spent extra to have it dug out."

She pointed to the ceiling along the right wall.

"That is where the kitchen and dining room is located," Sam explained. "Directly above where I am standing is the living room and along the left wall is where the master bedroom sits. The upper floor is quite a bit smaller than the main floor and the basement. Dad figured that the extra money for a basement would almost double our living space."

"I think it was a great decision," Ray commented as he plopped onto one of the sectionals. "I could hang out here for weeks."

"He has added quite a bit since the last time I was here," Sam commented depressed, looking at some of the pictures on one wall, Christian guessed she was wondering about what else she missed out on.

"What's with the big white area?" Alexis asked, pointing to the far wall.

"Oh, that's the T.V. screen," Sam said with a proud smile. "I am not sure how to turn everything on, but I'm sure my dad will want to show you. He was pretty proud of it when it was installed."

Christian picked a brown leather recliner on the far end of Ray's couch, while Sam and Alexis chose to sit on the floor. The furniture was all brown, earth tones, while the carpeting appeared to be a darker shade of green. The walls matched the furniture.

"This carpeting is so soft," Alexis said, as she grabbed a throw pillow and returned to the floor. "I could fall asleep down here."

"Dad wanted it to be like a ballpark," Sam explained. "Mom doesn't really like the carpeting, but Dad said she gets everything upstairs, so he gets to have his spot in the basement, and she can't touch it. I kind of like it down here, too."

"He's home," Alexis said, as she tilted her head upward to listen. "I hear the garage door."

A few moments later, a door slammed shut inside the house. They could hear Mrs. Kirgan talking from the top of the stairs.

"Dan, I have a surprise for you in the basement," she said, excitedly. "No, it can't wait. Just put the groceries on the counter."

"Let me at least put the cold stuff away," a man's voice answered.

"Okay, but you have to close your eyes when you come down the stairs," she replied, and Christian could hear the anticipation in Mrs. Kirgan's voice.

"You better not have replaced my carpeting," Mr. Kirgan said with a laugh as the steps creaked to announce their impending arrival.

The couple turned the corner on the poker table side and Mr. Kirgan had both hands covering his eyes.

"Can I look yet?" he asked impatiently.

"Not yet," Mrs. Kirgan said, motioning for Sam to get up and come over to him. "Wait just a second… Okay, you can open your eyes."

Sam stood only three feet from her father, and Christian knew it was difficult for her to not grab hold of him immediately. Instead, Mr. Kirgan slowly moved his hands and paused for his eyes to adjust to the dim lighting. Then a reaction of pure elation took a hold of him as he crossed the short distance in a blink and lifted his little girl off the ground.

"Oh, good Lord, it's really you!" he shouted at the top of his lungs. "We have missed you so much!"

Christian could see Mr. Kirgan's eyes watering as he set Sam down and took a step back to get a second look. Her father's dark eyes stared in disbelief, as he slowly shook his head from side to side.

"Where have you been?" he asked, still dumbstruck by the person standing in front of him. "The last letter we got was postmarked in St. Louis."

"Ugh, St. Louis," Alexis said, interrupting Mr. Kirgan's focus.

"And who are you?" he asked, puzzled.

"Daddy, that's Alexis on the floor, Ray on the couch, and Christian in the recliner," Sam said. "Alexis and Ray have been on the run with me ever since I left Phoenix."

Christian stood up as Sam made the introductions.

"Christian, he just joined up with us in the last couple weeks," Sam explained.

Mr. Kirgan walked around his daughter to get a closer look at her travel companions. Christian moved forward and extended his hand to Sam's father.

"All three of them are the reason we have made it this far," Sam said.

Dan Kirgan brushed Christian's hand aside and grabbed him in a bear hug.

"Thank you," he sobbed. "I can't thank you guys enough for helping my daughter make it home."

He let Christian down and grabbed both Alexis and Ray with the same force to show his gratitude.

"You kids have no idea how much this little girl means to us," Mr. Kirgan said, enthusiastically.

"After those hugs, I think we have a pretty good idea," Ray said, laughing and rubbing a rib.

Sam's father was not what Christian had pictured. His frame was lean like Sam but sinewy, and he was quite tall. Christian guessed he was at least six-three. Mr. Kirgan had no problem lifting Christian off his feet when he had grabbed him, and he had almost squeezed all the air from Christian's lungs.

If age had no hold of Vicki Kirgan's appearance, it had gripped tightly on Dan Kirgan's looks. His face was tanned but worn with wrinkles of age around his eyes, and his gray hair probably made him appear older than he really was. The gray continued across his upper lip and down the sides of his mouth in a thick Fu Manchu moustache that surrounded his wide grin.

Instantly, the grin wilted, and Mr. Kirgan began scrutinizing Christian's face.

"You look familiar," he said, pointing to Christian.

Christian began to get an uncomfortable feeling, as Mr. Kirgan's dark eyes squinted and moved closer.

"Where have I seen your face?" he asked, rhetorically, as he thought aloud. "Hey Vick, doesn't he look familiar, like you've seen him before?"

Mrs. Kirgan shook her head, "Nope, doesn't ring a bell."

"The paper!" Alexis cried, "Do you read the newspaper?"

"Every day," Mr. Kirgan answered, turning his head to look at Alexis. "Why?"

"Do you have any of your old newspapers?" Sam asked.

"Sure, I don't think we put them in the recycling bin this week," he answered. "They should still be in the box in the laundry room."

Sam shot up the stairs, leaving the rest of them in uncomfortable silence. She returned a minute later with a brown grocery bag full of newspapers, spreading them on the poker table. As Sam sifted through them, Ray and Christian quickly took positions on each side.

"Don't check the front page," Alexis said. "I bet it would be in the national news sections, since Nebraska isn't local."

The three teens at the table went back through the stack more carefully, scanning each page. Finally, Sam located what they were after.

"This!" she exclaimed. "This is where you saw him!"

Sam handed the section of the Arizona Republic to her father.

"It's from three days ago," Sam said, disgusted that the pictures had beat them to Phoenix.

"But it's buried on the sixth page," Ray said, calmly, trying to ease Sam's concerns.

"Yeah, but it's still there!" Sam responded in agitation.

"But no one knows we're here," Christian said, putting a hand on Sam's shoulder. "Even the driver thinks we were dropped off up the street."

"Okay, okay," Mr. Kirgan interrupted. "Let's all sit down on the couches, and you guys can explain everything."

As they shared their story, Christian found it interesting that Mr. and Mrs. Kirgan didn't even flinch when Sam explained the special abilities of Ray, Alexis, and Christian, but he did notice them look knowingly at each other when Sam explained what she could do.

When Christian relived the Red Oak nightmare, Mr. Kirgan started interrupting with questions.

"So government agents came to your house, but they didn't come to Mr. Banner's place?" Mr. Kirgan asked.

"Yes," Christian replied. "But that's not the only strange thing. If Mr. Banner was involved, we think the pictures in the paper would be better than what they are. Mine is the only photo, and Sam's doesn't have any resemblance at all. Alexis and Ray's drawings are vague, at best. In fact, the written description that the troopers in Iowa had was much better than those in the paper."

"What troopers in Iowa?" Mr. Kirgan asked.

"We were spotted by the State Patrol in Iowa," Ray answered. "They chased us for a short time before we lost them."

"Then those agents found us at the farm," Alexis added.

"Agents at what farm?" Mr. Kirgan asked.

"Christian's extended family owns a couple farms in Nebraska," Sam explained. "Late one night, we were on our way back to a house hidden in the trees, but agents were waiting for us."

"We got away when they wrecked their SUV on the gravel roads," Ray said. "The next day, it was all over the news."

"Well, we haven't had any agents or police officers come around here," Mr. Kirgan said, confidently. "I would say you're pretty safe to hide out here as long as you need to."

"Hey, he's right," Ray said to Samantha, excitedly. "Wouldn't it make sense that if Mr. Banner had a hand in this that he would have sent someone to check on your house? Your parents haven't moved since you left, so he would know exactly where to look."

"Sure," Christian said, "But I don't think Mr. Banner would have expected us to be able to get a flight down here."

"Knowing Mr. Banner," Alexis commented, "I bet he would have all bases covered. Besides, we could've driven down here in the last three days."

"We should go to the safe house," Ray said confidently. "If Mr. Banner was the bad guy in all of this, he would have been here already. At least, he would have been watching this place."

"You kids have got to be getting hungry," Mrs. Kirgan interrupted. "When was the last time you ate?"

"Breakfast," Ray replied.

"I am hungry," Christian added.

"Starving," Alexis and Sam responded in unison.

"Let's get you guys something to eat and we can finish the stories during supper," Mr. Kirgan said. "The Diamondbacks are on tonight, so we can eat down here."

"I'll grab some chips to tide you over until the pizza arrives," Mrs. Kirgan said. "We'll order Grande's Pizza."

"It's New York style, and it is good," Mr. Kirgan added as he rubbed his hands together in excitement. "We better get two and an order of wings. I'm famished, and by the looks of these two boys, I bet they plow through one pizza by themselves."

Sam followed her mother up the stairs and returned with a couple bags of chips and a bag of pretzels.

"Mom's going to pick up the pizzas," Sam announced. "She said they will be done by the time she gets there."

"There are some Cokes in the fridge over there," Mr. Kirgan said, pointing to what looked like a dresser.

Alexis walked over and called back, "What fridge?"

"That wooden thing in front of you," Mr. Kirgan laughed. "It looks like a piece of furniture, but just pull on one of the middle knobs."

"That is totally cool," Alexis commented, as the door swung open. "What do you guys want?"

"Coke is fine," Ray answered.

"Um, there is no Coke," Alexis responded.

"What?" Mr. Kirgan shouted. "I just refilled that thing yesterday."

"Nope, just Dr. Pepper, Pepsi, and some diet," Alexis said.

Sam rolled with laughter.

"What is so funny?" her father asked.

Sam explained, as she put a loving hand on Mr. Kirgan's shoulder, "My wonderful father calls any kind of soda a 'Coke' even though he can't stand drinking Coca Cola. It is some kind of Canadian thing, I think. When you order a coke in Canada, you have to tell them what kind of 'coke' you want. Pepsi, Dr. Pepper, it's so funny."

With the first parts of their adventure told, Christian relaxed on one of the couches. The pretzels and Dr. Pepper satisfied his hunger pangs for the time being, and he closed his eyes to relax. The break of pool balls interrupted his rest, and he looked up over the edge of the sectional to see that Ray and Mr. Kirgan had gravitated to the bright lights of the table. Sam and Alexis were each reading a section of today's paper at the poker table on the other side of the stairs.

Christian got up and walked over to the boys.

"How about a game of cut throat?" Mr. Kirgan said. "Ray, toss me the rack."

"I've never played cut throat," Christian commented.

"Oh, it's simple," Mr. Kirgan responded. "First shooter has balls one through five, second has six through ten, and third has eleven through fifteen. The goal of the game is to knock all of your opponents balls into the pockets before yours go down. It's pretty basic."

"Dad, go easy on them," Sam chimed from the other side of the stairs. "Be careful boys, he's kind of a shark."

"What if you scratch?" Christian asked.

"Good question," Mr. Kirgan said excitedly.

"Then your opponents get to take one of theirs out of a pocket and put it on the table," Ray answered for him.

"Last man standing wins," Mr. Kirgan said with a smile. "I'll let you boys go first."

Ray knocked in two off the break, one of Christian's and one of Mr. Kirgan's. He accidentally put one of his own in next.

"You still shoot, Ray," Mr. Kirgan explained. "As long as you knock one in, you keep shooting, even if you knock in your last ball."

Ray dropped two more of Mr. Kirgan's before he finally missed.

"Not bad, Ray," Mr. Kirgan said. "Your turn, Christian."

Christian knocked in two of Mr. Kirgan's balls on one shot, putting him out of the game. One was on purpose, and the other was accidental. But on the following shot, Christian scratched, giving Mr. Kirgan new life in the game. The two boys never saw the table again, as Mr. Kirgan dropped every ball on the table except his own.

"Hey, an old friend of yours stopped by a couple days ago, Sam," her father hollered as he set up the rack for the next game.

"Oh, who?" she responded.

"I can't remember the name," her dad replied, shaking his head, as if it would jog his memory.

"Boy or girl?" Sam asked.

"Boy," he said. "Your mother will know. You'll have to ask her when she gets home."

Sam walked around the corner with her brow wrinkled in puzzlement.

"What did he look like?" Sam asked, as Alexis came from the stairs and surprised Ray with a hug while he was lining up the break.

"I don't know," Mr. Kirgan responded. "Your mother answered the door."

Alexis kissed Ray and nudged him playfully.

"Christian, you could have some competition," Alexis taunted.

"Competition?" Mr. Kirgan questioned.

"Dad, Christian and I are dating," Sam said, nonchalantly. "Is that a problem?"

"Christian?" Mr. Kirgan said, seriously, furrowing his brow. "You're dating my daughter?"

"Yes, sir," Christian responded, uneasily, and his voice cracked.

"Have you seen my backyard?" Mr. Kirgan asked.

"Yes, it's very nice," Christian said nervously, not knowing where this was leading.

"And very secluded," Mr. Kirgan added, quickly. "I could bury a body back there and no one would ever know."

Mr. Kirgan stared harshly at Christian.

"Daddy, stop it!" Sam chided. "You'll scare him."

Mr. Kirgan's death stare morphed into a grin, and then a bellow of laughter. Soon everyone was laughing but Christian.

"Sorry, Christian, I couldn't resist," Sam's father said, still laughing, as he slapped Christian on the back. "Everyone needs a good chuckle now and then. Sorry that it was at your expense. You seem like a good kid, but make sure you take good care of my daughter."

"Dad shows his evil side every once in a while," Sam said, as she pulled Christian close and kissed him on the cheek.

"Hey, now, your father is standing right here," Mr. Kirgan said, acting cross.

"Then my father should turn his back," Sam retorted before turning away from her father.

"Kids these days," Sam's dad fired back.

"Everyone needs a good chuckle," Sam said, mockingly.

"Hey, I remember that kid's name now," Mr. Kirgan responded, eagerly.

Everyone turned to look in Mr. Kirgan's direction.

"Charlie, the kid's name was Charlie."

The laughter stopped immediately, and the four teens all looked at each other. Christian remembered the story about Charlie. The last time The Three had seen Charlie was the night he was abducted from the convenience store by government agents. That was the night that Samantha decided to leave with Mr. Banner, Alexis, and Ray. The last night The Three saw Charlie was the last night that Dan and Vicki Kirgan saw their daughter.

CHAPTER 16

The four teens were quite subdued when Vicki Kirgan returned home with the pizza. During the meal, Sam's father insisted that they fill in some holes in the story. He wanted to know how they found a car to steal in the middle of the night in Iowa. He asked about what led up to the chase near Grandpa Pearson's farm in Nebraska. In addition, Dan Kirgan was interested in how Christian and Sam had met and how serious they were. Everyone but Christian got a kick out of his probing question about how good of a kisser Christian was. Most importantly though, Mr. Kirgan wanted to know why they reacted so shocked by the visit from Charlie.

"I didn't really care for that boy much," Mrs. Kirgan stated coldly when the topic of Charlie came up at the end of supper.

"You never told me that," Mr. Kirgan said, surprised by his wife's words.

"What didn't you like about him?" Sam asked. Christian wondered if she still had feelings for Charlie.

"He seemed nice enough, I guess," Mrs. Kirgan responded. "I guess it was the way he constantly looked over my shoulder, like he was casing our house like a bank robber would before planning a heist."

Christian noticed Ray and Alexis glance at each other and nod like there was meaning in what Mrs. Kirgan had shared about Charlie.

"And the questions he asked were so strange," Mrs. Kirgan said.

"Like what?" Sam asked her mother.

Mrs. Kirgan took a deep breath before answering, "He wanted to know if I had spoken to you, recently, and I told him I hadn't. When I told him that you had disappeared over a year ago, he seemed puzzled. He asked what had happened, and I told him that you just vanished. Charlie appeared to be very perplexed by your disappearance, Sam. He must have repeated the phrase, 'She just vanished?' at least four or five times, like the words didn't make sense to him.

"After a while, he asked if I had noticed anything strange about you before you had disappeared. I told him that I hadn't, but he didn't seem to buy it. He hinted about special abilities."

"How?" Alexis asked. "How did he hint at it?"

Mrs. Kirgan turned away from Sam and spoke to the entire group.

"Let me see if I can remember his wording," Mrs. Kirgan said, as she paused to think. "He said, 'Did you know your daughter was special?' and I told him that she has always been special to me. That flustered him, and he tried to reword his question, but I had no idea what he was getting at until you guys explained your gifts to us earlier."

"How does Charlie fit into all of this?" Mr. Kirgan asked. "And be quick about it, the Diamondbacks are on in half an hour."

Sam grinned, "You and your stupid game of baseball."

"Hey now," Christian said, stiffening his back. "Greatest show on dirt."

Mr. Kirgan reached to high-five Christian, which shocked him considering the kissing questions that had been asked earlier. But Mr. Kirgan seemed to be pretty cool about things.

"I like your new boyfriend," Sam's dad said with a smile. "Better than any of those junior high kids you hung out with. Now tell us about Charlie."

"We knew he was a Phenomenon Child," Alexis stated.

"What is his ability?" Christian asked.

"Vision," Ray said. "He can read a newspaper from a hundred feet away."

Christian nodded, realizing why that was important earlier.

"Mrs. Kirgan," Ray started.

"Please, Vicki," she interrupted with a wave of her hand. "Mrs. makes me feel so old."

Ray continued, "Vicki, Charlie wasn't casing your house. He was probably looking for clues. It is amazing what his eyes can spot from a distance. He may have been trying to locate some proof that Sam was back home. That guy could see a contact lens on the floor like you or I would spot a hundred dollar bill lying on the sidewalk."

"We had approached Charlie about coming with Mr. Banner and the two of us," Alexis said. "While we were getting him to trust us, we found Sam. Well, she sort of found us."

"So you took Sam, too?" Mr. Kirgan interrupted.

"No, Dad," Sam said, rolling her eyes. "Will you let them finish the story? I didn't want to go with them, at first."

"So they forced you?" her father said, agitated.

Vicki intervened, "Dan, you're jumping to conclusions. Let the kids finish."

"Sorry," Mr. Kirgan said, apologetically. "I do that on occasion."

Vicki rolled her eyes, and Christian noticed it was practically identical to the way Sam had done it moments before.

Alexis continued, "Sam and Charlie were at a convenience store getting a soda, when agents grabbed Charlie and threw him into a van."

"I was afraid I would be next," Sam explained. "I hadn't believed the danger Mr. Banner said I was in, but seeing how Charlie disappeared from society with no one in law enforcement lifting a finger to search for answers, I knew I couldn't risk it. I had to leave with them, or I was worried that I would be gone from you forever."

"So why is Charlie back?" Mr. Kirgan asked.

"That is a good question," Ray said, puzzled. "I've been wondering about that myself."

"If agents took him the same time you left," Vicki questioned, "why would he be free to visit this house? Would the government just let him go?"

"I doubt that happened," Ray said. "From what Mr. Banner has told us, once a Phenomenon Child is captured, they are never released on back on their own."

"Could he have escaped?" Alexis asked.

"Possibly," Ray said, calmly, "but highly unlikely. And why would he come here if he escaped?"

"And the timing of his arrival is odd," Sam added.

"Do you think he is working for the government?" Christian wondered aloud. "Is he looking for all four of us?"

"How would he know about all four of us?" Ray asked. "He wouldn't know about you, Christian."

"Charlie knew about me before he was taken," Sam commented. "The only other people who knew about my ability are in this room."

"Except Mr. Banner," Christian stated, coldly. "Mr. Banner was the only other person who knew about you, Sam."

"Is it possible that this Mr. Banner is still working for the government?" Mr. Kirgan asked. No one answered.

That question had loomed over Christian for days, and he had swayed back and forth like the pendulum of a clock about which side to take. Was he still working for the government or not?

Christian broke the silence, "He could be. Mr. Banner conveniently left your farmhouse in Red Oak," he pointed at Ray, "right after agents moved in on my house, so I was sure he was the bad guy in all of this. On top of that, my grandfather didn't trust him from square one."

Christian was thinking out loud, so he let the pendulum swing again, "On the other hand, if he was still working for the government, I think he would have posted better pictures of Alexis, Ray, and Sam in the newspapers. It just doesn't make sense, either way."

"And remember, he also would have access to Charlie if he's still working for the government," Ray sighed. "Maybe we shouldn't risk going to the safe house."

"I'm so tired of this; I'm to the point where I think we need to take the initiative," Alexis said in irritation. "I am tired of being on the run. We know the terrain around that house in Flagstaff better than anyone. Why don't we do some surveillance of our own?"

Sam asked, contorting her face into a questioning look, "What do you mean?"

Alexis explained, "There are plenty of hiding spots around that old place. We can hike up there and scope the house out. I can hear anyone coming from a mile off in those woods, and we have plenty of trails to follow to get away."

"But what will we gain from it?" Ray asked.

"Information," Alexis said, confidently. "Maybe Mr. Banner has left a note for us to help us make our next move."

"Or maybe we find government agents when they find us!" Ray retorted, punctuating the last word.

"At least we would know which side Mr. Banner is on," Sam said meekly. "If agents capture us, that is."

"We could go in first," Mr. Kirgan stated coolly. "Vicki and I could get lost in those woods and stumble upon the house by accident. If agents swarm, we're just two lost lovers trying to recapture our youth."

"Oh, brother," Sam said, crossing her arms.

Christian liked the idea and added, "We could hide in the back of your parents' vehicle and they could drop us off. If agents swarm, we take one of those hidden trails and hike to safety."

"Your mom and dad could call us when they're in the clear," Alexis said.

"Or we could leave a second car up there, a few miles from the house," Vicki commented. "You guys could use that car to get away."

"We need to know where we stand with Mr. Banner," Alexis stated. "That is the best option for us to find out."

"I am tired of running," Ray sighed, and Christian realized he was starting to buy into the plan as well.

"Let's sleep on it," Mr. Kirgan said. "It's time to watch some baseball."

Mr. Kirgan bounced from his seat and opened a cabinet hanging on the wall of the backside of the stairwell. He pushed a couple buttons and grabbed a remote from a shelf before closing the door.

The wall slowly illuminated into a fuzzy picture as the sounds of a ball game floated from speakers hidden in every corner of the room. In seconds, the screen focused as Diamondbacks Baseball was on the air.

Mr. Kirgan darted to another hidden fridge on the other side of the room before he plopped down on the couch and announced the start of the game with the opening of a beer.

"I'd offer you one, but I don't think you're old enough," he said with a smile before turning back toward the game.

"Your father and his sports," Vicki said, lifting her hands in a sign of surrender. "Who are they playing tonight, honey?"

"The battery chucks from San Francisco," Mr. Kirgan hollered in anticipation.

"Battery chucks?" Ray questioned.

Christian just shrugged his shoulders and walked to the other couch. He had no idea what Mr. Kirgan meant by battery chucks.

"I thought you were a baseball fan," Ray said, as he followed Christian.

"That doesn't mean I know what battery chucks means," Christian replied.

Mr. Kirgan stated, "It's a term we used to use for the Giants when I was playing. The fans have been known to chuck small batteries at opposing players."

"When you played?" Christian said in surprise.

"Dan used to pitch," Vicki said, proudly. "Didn't Sam tell you that?"

"Probably too busy kissin' to talk about the father she missed so much," Mr. Kirgan laughed.

"Dad!" Sam whined.

"Who'd you play for?" Christian asked.

"Oh, I bounced around to a couple of different teams," he explained. "All National League, so I never had the luxury of having a designated hitter. Let's see, I spent most of my time with the Expos in Montreal, but I pitched for St. Louis and the Cubs."

"How long did you play?" Ray asked.

"Three years in the majors with a couple of minor league stints mixed in, mostly to rehab my arm," he explained.

"Danny K. Kirgan, the specialist," Vicki crooned from the table. "He was the guy they called on to get the big lefties out."

"Oh brother," Sam sighed.

Christian turned to look at Sam, who mouthed the words as her father said them.

"The K is for killer," Mr. Kirgan hooted.

Alexis and Sam hung out with Sam's mom while the boys spent the evening watching the Diamondbacks pound out twelve hits en route to a seven to one beat down of the Giants. They shot pool for an hour after the game before the yawning started.

"I don't think you need to go to church with us in the morning," Vicki said, as the teens walked to their room. "Probably not a good idea to make public appearances."

Christian stopped to help tidy up the kitchen.

"Mr. and Mrs. Kirgan, thanks for letting us stay here," Christian said as he threw away some trash.

"It's Vicki and Dan," Mrs. Kirgan said. "I feel like a grandma when you guys are so formal."

"You can call me Killer if you want," Mr. Kirgan said with a grin. "It will totally bug your girlfriend."

Christian smiled in return, "Thanks, Dan and Vicki."

As Christian walked down the hallway to his room, he overheard Vicki say, "They really are good kids."

"And sharp, too," Killer added.

Christian knew he wouldn't have to listen in on the rest of their conversation; he was sure Alexis would fill him in on any other important items the Kirgans would be sharing with each other in the kitchen.

When Christian entered his room, the door to the bedroom was closed. One of Ray's socks was hanging on the knob. Christian wasn't sure what that meant, but he was positive he didn't want to know. He crept to the bathroom to brush his teeth, and he heard giggling from behind the bedroom door when he turned the faucet off.

He changed into a pair of athletic shorts and pulled his T-shirt off. Christian searched through his bag to see if, by chance, he had packed anything to read. He hadn't. Christian was pretty sure he wouldn't be able to sleep for a while even with the door to the bedroom closed, so he looked for something to occupy his mind until he was truly tired.

Christian opened the drawers of the coffee table, but he didn't locate any reading material. He did, however, find a television remote. He found that odd, considering he didn't see a T.V. in the room. He pressed the power button, and to his amazement, a flat screen popped to life on the wall near the door to the hallway. Christian hadn't noticed it there earlier.

"Must have looked like a picture frame when I came in," Christian muttered to himself.

He relaxed on the couch with his head propped up on the armrest, and he flipped through channels until he found the end credits of a movie scrolling the screen. Thinking that another movie would surely follow, he set the remote down on the back of the couch against the wall and listened to the theme music playing.

There was a knock on the door, and Christian hopped up quickly, hoping it was Sam paying him a visit. When he opened the door, he saw Sam standing before him, holding neatly folded sheets, a blanket, and two pillows.

"Hey," Christian said.

"Hey," she replied. "Mom figured you needed some sheets and blankets. It might get cold over night with nothing to cover up with."

"Thanks," Christian said, taking the pile off her hands. "Come on in."

Sam had changed into a button-down, flannel pajama top and Umbro shorts.

"Dad told me to be good,\ when Mom handed me that stuff," Sam huffed. "He can be so irritating."

"He loves you," Christian said. "I like your parents."

"Mom can be a worrier at times," Sam whispered. "Dad is pretty open about things, and he knows I am growing up, so he doesn't get worked up about boys and stuff."

"Yeah, I thought he was going to kill me when the kissing comments came from Alexis," Christian laughed. "But it really didn't seem to bother him at all."

"Well, he's always wanted me to be open about everything," she replied. "He won't go all crazy on me, if I am willing to talk about everything with him. He says that open communication is the key to being a great kid and a great parent, so I am almost always honest with him."

"That's pretty cool," Christian responded.

"The only secret I ever kept was my ability," Sam said. "I just thought it was something quirky, and I didn't think it was that important."

He spread one sheet over the couch, but Sam reached around Christian and pulled it off.

"The cushions on the back take up a lot of room," she explained. "You'll have more space if you take them off. The back is just as comfortable without the cushions on."

Sam and Christian removed the three back cushions and placed them against the wall below the counter to the kitchenette. Sam spread a sheet out and tucked it under the seat cushions on all four sides. Then she laid another sheet over the first one and the blanket on top of that. Christian tossed the two pillows toward the far armrest.

"Looks pretty comfy," he said.

"What're you watching?" Sam asked, pointing to the wall mounted television.

"Shooter, I guess," Christian replied, as the current commercial ended and the screen flashed to a blurred action scene with the words "Now Showing – Shooter" in bold letters.

"Can I join you?" Sam asked, sheepishly.

"I guess," Christian answered, his voice cracking embarrassingly.

"Unless you're too tired," Sam said. "I can leave."

"No, no," Christian responded, quickly. "I would love to have you hang out with me for a late night movie."

Christian sat down on the couch, and Sam whispered, "Do you want to lie down? It might be easier to watch the movie in that position."

Then she walked over to turn off the lights.

"Better movie atmosphere with them off," she said softly.

Sam pulled the blankets back, and Christian repositioned his legs up so he could stretch out on the back half of the couch. There was plenty of room for both of them.

"Do you want me to put my shirt back on?" Christian whispered nervously.

"Are you cold?" Sam giggled as she moved close to him and kissed him. "That's what the blankets are for."

Sam pulled the covers up as she snuggled close to Christian. He could feel the heat radiating from his body as she nestled in close and kissed him again. This time, it was a deeper kiss than before. Christian could feel the rate of his heart pound faster with each passing second. Samantha pulled back a few inches.

"Is the movie starting yet?" she whispered.

"Um, yes," Christian stuttered.

In a slow turn, Sam moved her light frame around so she could see the screen. Christian stayed motionless as she repositioned her body to fit perfectly with his. Under the covers, Sam moved her hand underneath of Christian's hand, interlocking her fingers in his. She gently pulled his hand up across her legs and slowly across her midriff to the middle of her chest. Even though his hand rested on top of hers, Christian could feel that Sam's heart was pounding as hard as his was.

They stayed in that position for the entirety of the movie, minus the occasional jump by Sam every time the action startled her or the tight squeeze of her hand when the scene was too intense. When the main character, played by Mark Wahlberg, finally achieved justice, Sam released Christian's hand and turned back toward him. She kissed him once more.

"Thanks for taking me to the movies," Sam whispered sweetly.

"Any time," Christian said with a smile. Sam moved her head below his chin and pulled her body tightly against his.

"Are we going to be okay up in Flagstaff?" she said quietly. "I mean, are we taking too big of a risk?"

"I don't know," Christian sighed as he stroked Sam's back. "I don't know."

At some point in the early hours, Sam had wiggled out of their sleepy embrace and gone back upstairs. When Christian awoke, the sun was creeping in from the edges of the window's blinds above the couch. The bedroom door was still closed with the sock hanging on the knob. This time, Christian made sure he took a change of clothes with him when he went into the bathroom to shower. He also made sure he locked the door.

CHAPTER 17

Christian took his time getting dressed in the bathroom, even though he heard muffled voices from the bedroom, and he knew Alexis and Ray would also want their turns in the shower. The aches in his muscles from the previous week's adventures were all but gone, but the remnants of some scratches and bruises dotted potions of his back and sides.

Even with the fan on, the mirror had clouded, so Christian used a hand towel to wipe down the center. His mother hated when he did it at home, and he laughed.

"Christian, it leaves streaks when it dries," she would chastise.

He missed her.

Christian donned his gray Red Oak Football t-shirt and peered at his reflection. He felt much older than the worn freshman looking back at him appeared to be. He was too young to be dealing with what life had thrown him in the last couple weeks.

Instead of chasing down wide receivers and going to pep rallies, he had spent his time running from government agents and avoiding people he didn't know.

"My high school years are going to suck," Christian muttered to himself.

"Hey, are you done in there?" Ray's asked. "We would like to use the shower."

"Gimme a second," Christian answered, turning toward the door. "Then it's all yours."

Christian heard Alexis make a high-pitched, half-second scream, like when a person gets a surprise tickle, and then the bedroom door slammed shut. Christian chuckled to himself and shook his head before he looked into the mirror a second time. Still half-smiling, he saw a different person. He was amazed at how the hint of a smile changed his appearance. Actually, his grin reminded him of his father.

"Life can be tough for everyone," Christian's father had told him after he survived the tornado in South Dakota but couldn't start football right away. "When bad things happen, you have a choice to make. Either you can feel sorry for yourself and get bogged down in a 'poor me' attitude, or you can make the decision to deal with it positively and move on. It's easy to be a good teammate and love life when everything is going your way. It's the rough periods in your life that define what kind of person you are. It's not about what happened to you; it's about what you are going to do from this point forward."

Christian chuckled to himself as he remembered that discussion because that injury only kept him out of a few days of football. What he faced now was more long term. He had to keep a positive attitude about his situation.

Christian finally opened the door to relinquish the bathroom to Ray.

He knocked on Ray's bedroom door. "All yours," he said.

Christian sat on the couch to put his socks on. He looked up to see Ray poke his head out from the bedroom before opening the door wide. In his boxers, the pale, bare-chested teen exited the bedroom with Alexis clinging to his back in a sports bra and tight shorts with her arms wrapped around his neck. Alexis's dark skin pressed against Ray's pasty-white body was quite a sight. Her black locks of hair and his white crew cut contrasted as much as the pigments of their skin.

Christian hastily left his living quarters and walked down the hall to the kitchen. As he turned the corner, he was greeted by the smell of bacon and eggs. Sam was up, and she tended a couple of frying pans on the stove top.

"Morning, sunshine," Sam smiled as she turned a piece of bacon with a fork, causing a quick rush of sizzles and pops.

"Good morning," Christian responded with a grin. "Are your parents up?"

"Just left for church," she said. "They like going to the early service at CCV."

"CCV?" Christian asked, puzzled.

"Christ's Church of the Valley," Sam answered.

"Oh," Christian said. "What denomination is that?"

"It's non-denominational," she replied.

"Oh," Christian said, confused by the term non-denominational. "My parents are Lutheran, so I guess I am too. Is CCV Christian?"

"Yes, silly," Sam grinned. "Want a couple of eggs and some bacon?"

"Please," Christian answered.

She scooped up two eggs and placed them on a plate.

"You Midwesterners are so funny," Sam said. "Non-denominational doesn't mean it's some cult. It just means we aren't Lutheran or Methodist or Baptist. We're still a Christian church; we just don't have a specific affiliation or denomination."

"Did you go to church a lot, I mean, did you go before you went into hiding?" Christian asked.

"Yeah, I really enjoyed it," Sam said. "In fact, I miss it. We had a service that was just for teens."

"Really?" Christian said in disbelief.

"Yeah, and it was on Sunday night, so I could sleep in on Sunday mornings," Sam said. She seemed excited to share.

"And you liked it?" Christian asked quizzically.

"Loved it," Sam answered quickly. "The music rocked, and we would do different actions with different songs, and we would jump and shout. It was a blast."

That was not the type of church Christian had grown up with. His experiences weren't as bad as getting a shot in your mouth at the dentist, but church was not something Christian would have called "a blast."

"What is your church like?" Sam asked as she forked a couple pieces of bacon.

"My parents' church is Lutheran," Christian said. "We go every Sunday."

"But what about youth stuff?" Sam questioned. "What did you do?"

"Well, the church in Red Oak really didn't have much for the high school group," Christian replied. "But my church in Omaha had youth classes. We'd sing some hymns and have a sermon in the service on Sunday. Our youth stuff was on Wednesday nights, but I hated it."

Sam looked confused.

"Wednesdays?" she said, wrinkling her nose like she smelled something awful.

"Confirmation," Christian said with disgust in his voice. "For two years, we had to take classes during the school year on Wednesday nights. We learned prayers and had to memorize the books of the Bible. We even had a test over it. Then in the spring of my last year in Confirmation, I had to give a speech to the whole church about my faith."

Sam must have sensed the distaste for his experience in Christian's voice, because she put her hand on his knee.

"I'm sorry you didn't enjoy it," she said.

Christian reminded himself to be more positive.

"I'm making it sound all bad," Christian said with a sigh. "There was a lot of good, too."

"Like what?" Sam smiled.

Her eyes focused intently on his face, and the tension in Christian eased a bit.

"I met a lot of other kids; that was fun," Christian said, forcing himself to perk up. "What I liked best was the discussion groups. Most of the Confirmation stuff was done by our head pastor, but our youth pastor led the discussion groups. Pastor Z was what we all called him. He would direct us to pieces of scripture, and we would read them."

Christian smiled as he thought about Pastor Z.

"Then he would ask some tough questions," Christian continued. "I mean tough questions, like respecting parents and temptation kinds of questions."

Christian laughed at the memory before finishing his thought, "And he always would say, 'That was a great Sunday School answer, but what is your real answer?' when he knew we were just telling him what we thought he wanted to hear."

Sam cocked her head sideways and said, "Explain to me what a Sunday School answer would be."

"Well, he might ask us about what temptations we face," Christian said. "Of course, everyone mentions stealing or cheating on a test. But Pastor Z would call it a Sunday School answer and then he would ask for what our real temptations were. We all would look uncomfortably at one another, or we would look at the floor. Then he would say something like… 'What about thinking your parents are idiots?' and we would laugh. Then he would say one word and get serious with us. Those discussions got interesting."

"What one word?" Sam asked.

"Sex," Christian whispered, embarrassed about saying it aloud. "And he wouldn't say it once; he repeated it five or six times. Pastor Z was the bright spot in my Confirmation experience. I learned more from him about God than anyone else, besides my father. You know, I almost failed Confirmation."

"Failed?" Sam laughed. "How can you fail at church?"

"I am a solid student," Christian explained. "I take advanced classes, and I do my work. School is easy for me, but Confirmation was from six to eight at night on Wednesdays. I didn't want to be in school for two more hours. I wanted to be outside playing baseball or basketball. Wednesdays meant coming straight home from school to do my homework and then off to church to eat a meal before two more hours of school. I usually had a homework assignment for Confirmation as well."

"So you didn't want to be there," Sam commented.

"You know, I cheated on my books of the Bible test," Christian laughed at the thought. "I cheated in church."

"Probably not the right choice," Sam chuckled. "How did you cheat?"

"I wrote the first letter of each book in order on the edge of my folder," Christian said. "I could remember the names of the books of the Bible but not the order. Pastor Z saw my folder on the way out that night."

"What did he say?" Sam asked, leaning closer in anticipation.

"He told me that he didn't want to hear a Sunday School answer when the topic came up in our next discussion group, but I never got in trouble for it."

"Sounds like Pastor Z gets it," Sam said as she stabbed a couple pieces of bacon in the pan and placed them on a plate covered with a paper towel.

"What do you mean?" Christian asked.

"Your Pastor Z understands what's important," she explained. "It isn't about how many prayers you know or if you can memorize the books of the Bible. It's about knowing God. It's about reading scripture and applying it to your life. At your church, why do you go through confirmation?"

"Well, once you complete it, you are a member of the church and you can take communion," Christian responded.

"Really, what about baptism?" Sam cocked her head again.

"Oh, I was baptized as a baby," Christian answered.

Sam looked confused again.

"So do you have something like Confirmation?" Christian quizzed. "When are you considered a member of your church?"

"Baptism, I guess," Sam said. "We don't have anything like Confirmation."

"You're lucky," he sighed. "Member from birth, huh?"

"No, I was baptized when I was thirteen," Sam said, surprising Christian. "I did it at a youth camp."

Christian was baffled.

"You were baptized at a youth camp at thirteen?" he said in shock. "Was there a church at this camp?"

"Not really, I was baptized in a river in Washington state by our youth group leader," Sam replied.

Christian had never heard of someone getting baptized as a teen, especially in a river at some kooky youth camp.

"Was he a pastor?" Christian asked, hoping to find some sense to her story.

"Nope, I think she was an attorney or accountant or something," Sam said.

"Does that count?" Christian asked.

"For a good guy, you sure don't know much about the God I know," Sam joked. "Of course, it counted. You don't have to be a pastor to baptize someone. Actually, my dad was disappointed that he didn't get to do it, but he was still excited about my choice."

"Choice?" Christian said, confused again.

"Choice to follow God," Sam replied. "It's a choice, and I decided during my week at camp that I was going to follow God."

Sam had rocked Christian's world. He did not know God the same way Sam did. To Christian, God was paperwork. Go to church, pay attention, and be a good person. No one ever told Christian he had a choice to make. He started thinking that maybe Sam's idea of believing in God was different from his own.

"So what does it take to get to heaven?" Christian asked.

"You have to believe that Jesus died for your sins," Sam stated.

After a brief silence, Christian said, "That's it?"

"Well, baptism is good, but not necessary," she said. "Going to church is good but not necessary. Making good choices, being a good person, all good but not necessary. Isn't that what you believe?"

Christian had never really thought about what he believed.

"Well," he said, and then he paused to think through everything.

It was the same, but the way Sam had put it made it sound so easy. Just believe. The more he mulled it over, that was really the heart of it all.

"Yes," he answered, finally. "I guess, I never really thought about it."

"Well, sometimes I forget about it, too," she smiled.

Christian ate the eggs and bacon, even though the eggs had gone cold during their conversation. He glanced over at Sam, who was looking out the back windows. She really was beautiful, but Sam's beauty was really amplified by what was inside. The feelings Christian experienced around her were foreign to him, and he was sailing uncharted waters in his heart. He got up and rinsed his plate in the sink and Sam followed. She opened the dishwasher and put her hand out for his plate. Instead of handing her his dirty dishes, he placed the plate on the counter and pulled her close.

Looking into her eyes, Christian whispered, "I think I love you, too."

She wrapped her arms around him, and turned her head sideways against his chest.

"I knew you'd come around to my way of thinking," Sam whispered. "Now, I can tell my father that we're in love."

Christian laughed and squeezed her tightly. He was confident that Mr. Kirgan would actually be okay with it.

*****

Dan and Vicki Kirgan returned home from church before noon, and Dan fired up the gas grill on the back patio. They ate burgers for lunch before they all retreated to the basement to discuss the plan for the trip to the safe house in Flagstaff.

"First of all, I think we need to do some shopping," Vicki stated.

"You always want to shop," Dan laughed. "In times of emergency, Super Vicki uses her shopping powers to stave off disaster."

"I am serious, Dan," Vicki huffed. "Look at Christian's shirt."

Christian looked down at the words "Red Oak Football" in big letters.

"Do the rest of you have shirts like this one?" Vicki said, pointing to Christian.

Alexis nodded and Ray shrugged, and Christian wasn't sure what Sam's mom meant.

"I think we need solid colors with no emblems and definitely no school shirts," Vicki declared. "And if that means I have to do a little shopping, then that is the price I will have to pay."

Vicki smiled and Sam laughed.

Christian hadn't thought about the shirt he had on. He was wearing a billboard for Red Oak.

"Mom is a power shopper," Sam chuckled.

Vicki quickly stood up and checked each teen's collar.

"I just need sizes, and I will be off," Vicki said as she nimbly danced around the table.

"Be careful when she checks your pant sizes, boys," Dan whispered before he roared at his own joke. "She might yank up your briefs for a wedgie."

"Oh, Dan Kirgan, that is totally inappropriate," Vicki chastised. "You boys can just tell me your waist sizes. I might as well get you some shorts. Actually, I should get each of you a pair of jeans, too, if you are going to be crashing around in the forest up north."

"I wish I could go with you, Mom," Sam said dejectedly.

"I know," Vicki replied disappointedly. "But I don't think that would be safe. Besides, you guys can plan the trip without me getting in the way with all my questions."

Alexis laughed, "So that's who you get it from, Sam."

Ray and Christian chuckled, as well.

In just a few minutes, Vicki had all the needed measurements. Excitedly, she rushed upstairs.

The four teens and Dan discussed the trip to Flagstaff and the safe house. They used the Internet to give Dan an idea of where the house was situated in proximity to Flagstaff.

"Basically, there is only one road, but you almost need four-wheel drive," Ray explained. "If it rains, you definitely need four-wheel drive."

"My truck can handle it," Dan responded, confidently.

"There is another road, here," Ray said, pointing to a black line north of the red X marking the house's location. "I have hiked up to that road a number of times. It's rough terrain to get there, but with Alexis listening, we will be able to hear anyone in that forest after you drop us off. Has it been pretty dry up there?"

"They had a wet spring and summer," Dan replied. "But it has been really dry the last month. They are concerned about forest fires with the lack of rainfall for the last four or five weeks."

"You'll have to backtrack to the highway and drive down to this road." Ray pointed to the black line on the map that led to the red X. "That road is about four miles from the one up north, but where you drop us off, it's only about a mile and a half from the safe house. And it's mostly downhill."

"That's when I drive to the safe house?" Dan asked.

"As soon as you drop us off, you can head out to the highway and wait," Ray said. "When Alexis thinks the forest is clear, we will call you. That's when you go down to the safe house road and check it out. With you driving through there, if anyone is keeping tabs on that house, you'll at least spook them. Alexis will be able to hear anyone outside the house. And as we get closer, she will be able to tell if someone is inside."

"People just can't seem to stay quiet all the time," Alexis said, smugly.

"You can stop at the house and ask directions," Ray continued. "If no one answers, we can be assured the house is safe."

"What if they don't answer because it's not us?" Sam asked.

"With four fugitives on the run," Ray smiled. "They'll answer. They will want to know who is coming to the safe house."

Alexis said, "Then if the house is empty and I can't hear anyone in the forest, we will go to the house and check it out. See if we can find out more about what is going on, or see if there is a message."

"Do I need to wait around for you?" Dan asked.

"No," Ray answered quickly. "You can turn around at the house and go back the way you came. That road does continue down to the south, but it's about ten miles until you get back to a paved road if you go that way. You're better off going out the way you come in."

"When we're done in the safe house," Christian added. "We can call for you to pick us up on that northern road."

"Or," Ray said. "We can meet you out closer to the highway. It might be a long walk for us, but if we have to leave the safe house in a hurry, we may not want to have you driving on that northern road."

"What do we do then?" Sam asked. "If we have to leave in a hurry."

"Punt," Ray said, flatly. "If things go FUBAR, then we will have to improvise. We may have to hike a couple more miles north to meet your parents. There is a cozy little hotel on the highway about five miles up from that northern road."

Sam looked confused, "FUBAR?

Her dad laughed, "F'd Up Beyond All Recognition."

"Oh, I don't like the idea of FUBAR," Sam said, shaking her head.

"What if someone is at the house when the Kirgans drop by?" Christian asked. "I bet those agents will make sure they follow your truck, Dan."

"I don't know," Ray said.

They all looked at each other, mulling over that conundrum.

"We could take two cars up there," Christian said. "Park one at that little hotel."

"Vicki and I could get a room at that hotel," Dan said. "Just in case we need to hang out for your call."

"You're already doing so much," Christian said. "I don't want us to be a burden."

"Burden?" Mr. Kirgan said. "We're talking about the safety of my daughter and her friends. Besides, wait until you see what Vicki comes back with from her shopping trip. You'll need suitcases to haul it all with you when you go home."

Sam and Christian laughed, but Ray and Alexis both slumped their shoulders. They didn't have homes to go back to, and Dan didn't know that.

"Someday, we'll have a home," Alexis said, curling her fingers into Ray's hand on the table.

"Don't you guys have a home to go back to?" Dan asked.

"No, they don't, Dad," Sam said sadly, with a slight scolding to her voice.

"Both my parents died in a car accident," Ray said quietly.

"And I don't know where my parents are," Alexis commented. "But that's all water under the bridge. Ray and I are going to be together forever."

Alexis feigned a smile, but Christian could still sense pain in her words.

"Well, I know Vicki would agree with me on this," Dan said. "We will help you guys financially, in any way that we can. At least, until you guys can get on your feet."

"Let's just get to and from the safe house first," Ray said. "Then we can talk about that other stuff."

"No problem," Dan said. "We can discuss it later."

"Any questions?" Ray said, looking squarely at Sam before turning to Alexis. "Any problems with what we've come up with? Any other concerns?"

They were all silent.

"We go tomorrow," Dan said excitedly. "Diamondbacks have a travel day, anyway."

Sam rolled her eyes, and Christian laughed.

The doorbell rang, and everyone paused.

"You guys stay quiet until I come back downstairs," Dan said seriously. "Not a peep."

The teens huddled at the bottom of the stairs with Alexis next to the rail, closest to the voices. She relayed the conversation to the rest of them.

"It's Charlie," she whispered. "He wants to know if Sam is home. Your dad said that she hasn't been home for years. She disappeared over a year ago. Charlie said that he had heard that, and he spoke to Sam's mom a couple days ago, but he heard that she might be back in town. Your dad asked who told him that. Charlie said that he got a call from a friend."

There was a pause and then Alexis got up and walked back over to the table.

"Your dad is coming back down," Alexis said in a hushed tone.

Sam's father thumped down the steps.

He started to say, "You won't believe…"

"Charlie, we know," Sam interrupted. "Alexis gave us the play-by-play."

"That is so cool," Mr. Kirgan marveled.

"Comes in handy, sometimes," Alexis said coolly.

The boys watched baseball with Dan, and the girls spent their time reading on pillows they had stacked near the poker table. Sam curled up with a Michael Crichton novel that she said she had read before. Alexis found a worn copy of The Outsiders on one of the bookshelves in the upstairs living room. When Christian mentioned that he thought she hated reading fiction, Alexis had answered with, "It started pretty good, so I'll give it a try. Besides it's short. I can finish it before we leave tomorrow."

Everything was quiet until Vicki arrived. She called downstairs that she needed help bringing in the bags. Sam and Alexis raced up the stairs to help her. In moments, the three women returned with Vicki's haul. Christian couldn't believe it when he turned to look at a pile of plastic bags with the names Aeropostle, Banana Republic, Hollister, and Vanity, all stores he had never entered. Sam and Alexis were already searching for their items when the boys got up from their seats on the couch.

"Geez, I can't hear the game with all that plastic rustling," Dan complained to no avail.

Vicki had purchased enough outfits to last them a week, and she even bought socks and underwear, which made Christian feel just a bit uncomfortable.

Then Sam's mother held up a large green Cabela's bag, as she gleamed with pride. That was one store Christian was familiar with.

"I am most proud of this purchase," she announced, spreading the contents onto the poker table. "I bought you all matching camouflage outfits. For your trip into the woods. Don't you just love them?"

Sam held up a camouflage shirt and Ray grabbed the largest pair of pants. Christian noticed the quality of the material, and he guessed each pair was at least a hundred dollars. Mrs. Kirgan must have spent thousands on the clothes.

"Your mother loves a shopping assignment," Dan said as he joined the group and wrapped his arms around his wife, kissing her on the neck.

Vicki giggled and shook her shoulders like a cool breeze had just chilled her body.

"I even got you camo baseball hats," she cooed. "Aren't they just darling?"

"Honey, boys don't want darling," Dan interrupted. "They want tough."

"Well, aren't they tough?" Vicki commented. "And just darling to boot."

"They're perfect," Sam said. "Thank you, so much."

"My pleasure," Vicki replied, proudly watching everyone look through the clothes and stack them into neat piles like it was Christmas morning at the Kirgan house.

"Charlie stopped by again, but I gave him the same story you did," Dan said to his wife. "He did tell me that a friend told him that Sam might be back in town."

"A friend," Vicki said, concerned.

"No worries, though," Sam said. "We are planning to leave for the safe house tomorrow. Dad can explain everything to you later."

"Your mother and I are going out for supper tonight," Dan announced. "So you guys will have to fend for yourselves."

"Really?" Vicki responded. "Shouldn't we stay here and hang out with the kids? We haven't seen Samantha for a long time."

"Nope," Dan said seriously. "We have some things we need to discuss, and there are too many ears around here for our discussion."

Everyone around the table snuck a glance toward Alexis, who ignored the comment and held up a blouse in front of her body.

"What do we need to talk about?" Vicki said, looking up at her husband.

He widened his eyes and nodded as if to say, "Remember what we talked about last night?"

"Oh, that," Vicki said, nodding her head like she just recalled what her husband was referring to. "Yes, we do need to discuss that."

Vicki and Dan hustled upstairs, since it was already close to five o'clock. When the other three approached her, Alexis claimed to have no knowledge of any discussions in the house that evening.

"Your parents have been pretty tight-lipped about everything," Alexis said, unconcerned. "It's like they have had practice dealing with someone like me. They haven't slipped up once since I've been here. Not even a whisper of secrets, so what they have to discuss is unknown to me." She paused, "Maybe they're planning a little getaway at a hotel to shack up."

"Alexis!" Sam cried. "You're talking about my parents! Gross!"

Ray and Christian chuckled, and then Christian put his arm around Sam and hugged her.

"Don't listen to Alexis," Christian whispered. "I'm sure it's no big deal."

The four teens made sandwiches and Christian and Ray had a Dr. Pepper chugging contest after the meal. Christian beat him by a split-second, but Ray won the burp-off that followed. They were watching a movie when Sam's parents came home.

"Down here!" Sam called.

Vicki and Dan were in good spirits when they came down the stairs laughing. At first, Christian thought maybe they had shared a couple drinks. Then he realized they weren't tipsy; they always acted that way. Christian could tell that Sam's parents had a good marriage and they truly loved each other. It reminded him a little of his own parents, how they joked with each other but never with mean intentions. They were like best friends.

The movie ended, and Sam grabbed the remote to scan the menu for another flick to watch.

"Okay, turn the TV off," Dan said, his voice going from jovial to serious. "We have something to tell all of you."

"We weren't sure if we should just tell Sam," Vicki added. "But we talked it out, and we think all of you should know."

"That way, Sam has people she can talk to about it," Dan said. "She doesn't have to think it's a secret."

"Oh, crap!" Sam said, her face going pale. "Mom, are you pregnant?"

Christian saw Vicki's eyes widened in horror as she gasped, and Dan almost blew a gasket laughing.

"No, honey," Vicki said, regaining her composure. "I am NOT pregnant!"

"And you think I jump to conclusions," Sam's dad roared as he struggled to catch his breath. "Please, everyone sit down on the couches so we can talk to you."

Dan wiped tears from his eyes as he tried to regain his composure.

"Your father and I had been discussing this since the day you left," Vicki said to Sam. "We should have shared it with you right away, but the whole event happened so fast."

"So, we want to tell you we're sorry," Dan said. "We should have told you this when you were old enough to understand; we just didn't know the appropriate age."

"We have a theory about how you got your ability," Sam's mom said nervously.

"How?" Sam asked.

"Yesterday, you told us about your abilities," her father explained. "Then you shared all that stuff about the Phenomenon Child Program."

"What does that have to do with how I got my ability?" Sam asked.

"Well, you didn't have a traumatic event, like these other three did," he answered.

"Yeah, so?" Sam responded.

"And your ability is very different from their physical talents," he continued.

"So how did I get my different ability?" Sam replied.

"From us," her father replied. "Your mother and I are both what you called 'Phenomenon Children.' Each of us has a special ability of our own."

The room was silent. Ray leaned back in his chair, and Christian leaned forward. Sam sat with her mouth open, as if she wanted to utter something, but the words would not come out.

Finally, Sam whispered, "How?"

"Your mother and I have always wondered how we happened to get these gifts," Dan said. "When you guys explained the government's theory of traumatic events triggering phenomenon abilities, the one that Mr. Banner told you, it made complete sense. Each of us endured serious events when we were younger."

"So, what can you do?" Sam asked.

"Well, your mother has a nose like no other," her father said, smiling. "No only is it cute, but she can catch a whiff of something a mile away and know what it is."

"Really?" Sam said in disbelief.

"She's like a hound dog," her dad whispered as he leaned close to Sam, "on the trail of the scent."

Vicki elbowed her husband hard in the ribs and whispered harshly, "I hate when you call me that."

"Sorry, honey," he responded, rubbing his ribcage in the location of the blow. "I was just making a point."

"But you were grinning when you said it," she chided. "I didn't mean for it to hurt that much… you wimp."

Sam's mom smiled.

"What about Dad?" Sam questioned. "What can he do?"

"It's all in his head," Vicki pointed to her husband's gray hair.

"Numbers," Dan explained. "I can compute equations and keep all kinds of stats in my head. It's really freakish, and I still don't know how it works. It sure came in handy as a pitcher though. I knew the numbers for all the hitters I faced. I could tell you what pitch had a higher success, percentage-wise, for every hitter in the big leagues."

"But you couldn't remember Charlie's name when I asked you the first day we were here," Sam said, and Christian could sense she didn't quite believe what her father was telling her.

"Not a number," her father replied, matter-of-factly. "But if your mother told me what she spent in each store, I could give you a total. I could also tell you how much she paid in tax, the average price per item, rank the stores in order of most money spent to least, or anything else you wanted to know."

"That is so cool!" Alexis said.

"Never helped me in English class, though," Dan said, smirking in response.

"So that's why I am the way I am," Sam said. "Both of my parents are Phenomenon Children, so I didn't need a catastrophic event to trigger my DNA. I was just born this way."

"That's what your mom and I think," Sam's father replied.

"But why can I see your emotions?" Sam asked. "With other Phenomenon Children, I can't see their emotions."

"I don't know," her dad said. "It might have something to do with the fact that you are from us, but that's only a guess."

Sam sat digesting the new information.

"So you two better be careful," Vicki said to Ray and Alexis. "If you have a little one, he or she will probably be a Phenomenon Child from day one."

Ray turned bright red from embarrassment. It was less noticeable on Alexis's face, but it was there.

"You would be surprised what I can smell," Vicki said, smiling ruefully at the two reddening teens across the table.

"Now, this is uncomfortable," Christian said quietly.

"Not for you," Vicki said, turning toward Christian. "You and Sam have been playing nice."

Alexis uncomfortably adjusted her body in the chair.

"What you guys do is your own business," Vicki said, looking back at Alexis and Ray. "But I would like to request that you don't do it in my house."

Then Vicki got up from the table and walked around to behind Alexis and Ray. Her voice was not angry or even irritated. Sam's mom was talking to Alexis and Ray calmly, but her maternal tone even made Christian feel guilty, and he hadn't done anything wrong.

"Okay, now stand up," Vicki ordered gently.

Both teens stood up with their heads bowed like they were about to get reprimanded. Instead of a butt-chewing, Vicki put her arms around Alexis.

"Alexis, you have been my daughter's best friend for the last year, and you took care of her when we weren't around. I love you, and I will do anything I can to help you out. If you will allow me, I will play the part of your mother for the rest of your life, but only if you want me to. You are a special girl, and I promise you that I would never let you down."

Then Vicki released Alexis and turned to Ray.

"Ray, you saved my daughter's life with your skillful driving, and I can tell that you have been the leader of this group through extreme peril. You are strong, both in muscle and coolheaded thinking. I'm trusting your judgment when it comes to my daughter's safety. I could never replace your parents, and I don't want to try. Whatever you and Alexis need from us down the road, simply ask and it will be given."

Then she let go and put a hand on the shoulder of Ray and one on Alexis.

"I love my daughter, and I want you to know that I love each of you," Vicki said.

"I'm sorry," Alexis answered.

"There is no need for you to be sorry," Sam's mother responded. "You are teens, and you don't always think through the repercussions of your actions. You could end up pregnant and on the run. Not a great situation for a teenager or a fugitive. And you're both."

Alexis and Ray nodded.

"I love each of you," Vicki reiterated. "I am telling you these things because I care for you."

"Thank you," Alexis responded, her voice sounding choked up.

Ray echoed Alexis.

"I don't know if you have a religious belief," Vicki said, "but I would like to pray for you if that is okay."

Ray and Alexis nodded.

Sam and her father each moved to opposite sides of the teenage couple.

"Lord, I ask for your favor on these kids," Vicki started. "Please open their hearts to you."

Christian had been sitting down, so he quietly stood up and moved to Sam's side and bowed his head.

Vicki continued, "Please extend your protection over these four kids as they deal with what life has given them, but help them to avoid blaming you. We don't know why you have allowed these special gifts to be bestowed upon these four teens, but I do know that you are in control, and that we can't fathom the plan you have for them. You have created each of us to serve a greater purpose."

Christian had not experienced a prayer quite like the one Vicki was saying, and as she continued to speak, his eyes began to water.

"God, you have blessed us with so much, and for the last year, we have prayed that you would send our daughter back to us."

Sam's shoulders shuddered, and Christian felt her quiet sobs.

"Not only have you brought Sam back home, but you have also brought us three other teens that are in need of your guidance and strength. The task before them is daunting, and Dan and I understand that we need to do whatever we can to help them. You have blessed us beyond imagination, and we humbly ask that you allow us to bless these four.

"I pray that you watch over them tomorrow. Please keep those bent on capturing them at bay. Lord, please give us all the wisdom and courage to face what lies ahead. Most of all, Lord, bring them all back safe to us when this trial of life is over, if that is your will. Let us trust in you. Let us trust that whatever happens tomorrow is for the greater good of your kingdom. Give us hope for tomorrow. In Jesus name, we pray."

"Amen," said Sam and her father.

"Amen," Christian whispered.

Christian lifted his bleary eyes and saw that there wasn't a dry eye in the room. Sam had completely ruined her makeup, and Vicki's face matched that of her daughter. Sam's father wiped his eyes on his shirt sleeve as he released his hand from Alexis's shoulder.

Ray and Alexis still had their heads bowed, and Vicki leaned in to hug Alexis again. As she did, Christian could see Alexis's shoulders shudder as she bawled into Vicki's chest. When Ray turned around, he wiped his eyes, and Christian could see the redness encircling them.

Christian was surprised that he was not the only one moved by Vicki's prayer.

CHAPTER
18

The teens were awakened early the next morning by gentle shakes from Sam's mother. Last night, they had loaded the back of Dan's pickup with a couple of backpacks supplied with water and snacks in zip-lock bags, just in case the stay in the woods was an extended one.

Ray had said, "Let's plan for the worst-case scenario and take some food and water, in the event that we have to spend the night in the forest."

A couple of sleeping bags had been placed in the back of the truck as well. Dan wanted the ride to be comfortable for the four teens. All of them had tried it out by lying in the back of the pickup the night before to make sure it wasn't too cramped, and they barely had enough room. Dan had told them that it might get cold as they climbed higher into the mountains, but the first part of the trip would be quite hot.

Dan's Toyota came equipped with a hard cover over the back end that opened like a cooler lid. It would assure that no one saw the teens in the vehicle when they left the house, just in case Charlie was watching from a distance. Vicki's Forerunner had been packed with two suitcases, so if Sam's parents were stopped, it would appear that they really were traveling on a little vacation.

Dan looked at some maps he had printed from his computer while the teens quietly ate breakfast. Christian noticed how subdued everyone appeared to be. Not much was said during the pre-trip meal. Christian was thinking about the possibility that this was the last time they would be at this house, and he wondered if anyone else had the same thought. He hoped they would be able to return to Phoenix, but he had learned over the last couple weeks that the life of a Phenomenon Child on the run was very fluid.

Originally, he had planned to leave with the Banners in Red Oak, but his grandfather helped solve the original problem.

Then the government got involved, and he was forced into the role of fugitive. Christian thought they would be safe for a while on David's place, but only one night of respite was their reward. Then they were off to Grand Island, which wasn't even part of the original plan, and a plane ride had led them here. Now, Christian and three other kids, who should be enjoying high school, were leaving once more, hoping to find answers and return to Phoenix. Christian knew the plan was solid: wait in the woods for the phone call from Sam's parents, make their way to the safe house when it's all clear, search for messages or clues to what is going on, get out unseen, and come back to Phoenix. Most importantly, don't get caught in the process.

To Christian, it seemed like a good plan, but concern nagged at the back of Christian's mind. He chalked it up to jitters and reminded himself to stay calm and be positive. It was just nerves.

"Everyone had enough to eat?" Vicki asked quietly.

The four teens each nodded.

"Good," Dan said. "Let's get you guys into the back of my rig and head north."

Sam's father tossed the printouts on the dash and opened the lid on the bed of the truck. Vicki kissed each of them on the forehead and wished them good luck. Christian had an inkling that she was saying a brief prayer for each of them. She hugged Sam for a little longer than everyone else. Christian truly felt loved by Vicki, even though he had only known her for a couple of days. The teens got themselves situated and the metallic cover was lowered.

The Kirgans decided they would meet at the little hotel south of Flagstaff after Dan dropped the four teens off in the forest. He planned to go back to the hotel and switch to the SUV for the approach to the house.

"That will give us time to listen for anyone else who might be in the forest," Ray had explained.

The ride north was rather warm for the first half of the trip. Even though the sun was just rising in the east as the pickup backed out of the driveway, the Phoenix air was still and stifling, especially in the metal bed of a pickup with a metal top. Vicki had frozen a couple of dozen water bottles, and the teens used them to keep cool. Dan had raised the metal top an inch to allow some airflow without letting anyone see the human contents hiding underneath.

Alexis fitted ear plugs into her ears.

"What are those for?" Christian said loudly.

"I can hear you just fine with them in," Alexis answered.

"Sorry," Christian said, lowering his voice.

"It will be a loud ride for you guys," she explained. "Imagine what it will be like for me."

They all lay quietly as the truck's engine started and pulled out of the garage. Christian could see the garage door lower for a brief moment, and then they turned out of the driveway.

Christian spent the trip peering out the small space between the tailgate and the cover. He could only see a small, flattened view of the outside world, but there was nothing else to do. Driving on the interstate was loud, and the teens soon figured out that yelling was the only way to communicate unless they were talking to Alexis. Even with her ear plugs, she could still hear them pretty well. Trying to communicate grew tiresome as they traveled northward up the mountain, so they stopped trying to carry on any conversation. Every once in a while, Sam would elbow Christian and holler a comment over the growl of the motor and the wind, but Christian would only hear parts of Sam's statements.

Occasionally, the roar of a tractor trailer would resonate through the bed of the truck as Sam's father passed the slow-moving behemoths crawling up the steep grade of the Interstate. As the pickup wound up the inclines, the air became cooler. Soon, the ice bottles weren't needed, and they passed them back to Ray, who put them in a box near his head.

After a couple of hours and two cat naps, Christian noticed the wind howling less and less. The scenery outside was much greener and closer to them than the earlier portions of the ride on the freeway. Christian guessed they were exiting the Interstate. The truck slowed and came to a stop. A low rumble approached behind them and Christian lifted his head to see what it was. A Peterbuilt truck slowed as it rolled to a stop behind them. Christian could only see the front grill as the brakes coughed and squeaked from the big rig.

A few second later, the Peterbuilt engine growled to life again, and the front end jostled slightly, as the beast tried to inch forward. The lighter-weight pickup quickly picked up speed through the turn, causing the semi to lag behind. After another minute, they made another left-hand turn and the sun completely switched sides of the truck. Christian guessed they were headed south on the 89 Alternate that he had seen on Dan's map. The path of this road meandered back and forth through the mountainous terrain, popping up or dipping down from time to time.

Eventually, the truck slowed again, and the sharp right turn caused Christian's weight to shift against Sam, which caused Alexis to push against Ray's groaning body. The girls' giggling stopped as soon as the smooth ride changed into a bumpy nightmare. Without being able to see where they were headed, Christian couldn't anticipate the jolts to the pickup as it twisted along the mountain road. The first couple bounces jarred the metal top, and it slammed closed, tightly. They bounced like kernels of popcorn in heated oil until the pickup finally stopped.

Christian heard the door to the Toyota open and close and then the crunching of twigs underneath Dan's feet. The tailgate opened and Sam's dad leaned down to peer in.

"You kids okay?" he whispered. "I couldn't avoid the bumps."

"Yeah, we're alright, just a little beat up," Ray groaned as he slid his body toward the opening. "Alexis, make sure you grab those two backpacks."

Alexis followed Ray's sliding maneuver with one pack in tow while Sam rescued the other one as she did the same maneuver. When Alexis exited, the sleeping bag slid along with her, so Christian leaned off his side of the thin cushion when Sam followed suit. The weight of Sam's body pulled the sleeping bag with her.

"Do we have everything?" Christian called in a whisper.

"I think so," Ray answered quietly.

"These sleeping bags roll up into a pack," Sam's father explained. "So you can take them with you just in case you guys do spend the night out here."

Ray and Christian donned the heavier backpacks, while Alexis and Sam strapped the sleeping bags to their backs.

"Cell phone?" Ray whispered.

"Got it," Sam said.

"Make sure it's on silent," Alexis reminded her, and Sam nodded as she double-checked it.

Dan quietly closed the tailgate. The four teens slipped into the brush, as Dan hopped into the cab and pulled away. Ray told Sam's father that, besides this one, there was a second turnaround spot up the road a ways. A couple minutes after the drop off, the Toyota rolled back by their location.

There was no good luck honk or ceremonial wave from Dan when he drove by. It was all business today. The plan had been set, and with the help of the Kirgans, the four Phenomenon Children were putting it into motion.

After Alexis listened for five minutes, the teens moved up the road toward the second turnaround. Ray knew a deer trail crossed the road between the two turnabouts, but he wasn't sure of its exact location, so the best way to find it was to walk the half mile between the two spots.

Christian had a difficult time seeing any trails, but he had never hiked through woods like this. Ray knew what he was looking for, so he spotted it much more easily. They moved off the one-lane truck road onto the faint deer track, and in a matter of seconds, the road behind them disappeared from view.

They crouched on the ground as Alexis listened for sounds. A light breeze from the south rustled branches, and ancient boughs creaked around them. Smaller bushes, once full of vigorous growth, now showed the signs of lack of moisture. Pine needles and brown leaves littered the ground where vines crawled across the worn dirt waiting to trip up the hoof of an unsuspecting animal.

After almost fifteen minutes of the soft sounds of nature, Alexis whispered, "I think we can move closer, but we need to avoid any noise at all."

"What is it?" Ray said in an almost inaudible tone.

"Not sure. I don't hear people, but something is out there," Alexis answered.

Alexis took point, but Ray followed closely behind her since he had the best knowledge of the terrain. Alexis's black ponytail poked out from the back of her camouflage baseball hat and swung side-to-side as they moved down the trail. Ray's large frame stepped lightly behind her, and Christian laughed at the thin strip of white skin that showed between the collar of his shirt and the brown camo paint Alexis had smeared on his neck when they first exited Dan's pickup.

A curl of Sam's golden hair coiled below her hat, down the back of her neck. She had wrapped her hair into a bun, but a few strands had escaped. Christian followed the group with the pack slung over his shoulders. He laughed quietly to himself about what they looked like: a militant group of teens, outfitted in Cabela's finest camo gear, bent on staking out a safe house for Phenomenon Children, when they probably should be in hiding. The camouflage pants and shirts were a good match for the forest. As long as they stayed quiet, they would be tough to spot from a distance.

Alexis held up her hand, commanding them to stop. She crouched down, and the other three followed her lead. She motioned for Ray to move closer, and then Ray turned to wave Sam and Christian up. Christian tried to stay low as he approached Ray, who was huddled with Alexis in hushed conversation.

"Alexis thinks there may be a large animal on the trail up ahead," Ray whispered.

Alexis was leaning around a tree trunk with her ear pointed down the trail, which turned sharply to the right before leading downward.

"How large?" Sam asked, nervously, in a hushed voice.

"She hopes it is an elk and not…" Ray whispered, turning his head toward Alexis, who still hugged the tree, motionless.

"Not what?" Christian asked.

"A bear," Ray said as he held up his hand to stop the conversation.

Holy crap! Christian thought. A bear! How the heck are we going to deal with a bear? Throw some zip-lock baggies of crackers at it and run?

"We're okay," Alexis whispered as she moved back to the group. "Not a bear. There is a large deer on the trail about two-hundred feet ahead. I can't believe we got this close. I guess we've been really quiet."

"Do you hear anything else?" Sam asked nervously.

"No, just the deer," Alexis answered. "Otherwise, this forest is empty."

When the teens rounded the corner, the deer flushed up the mountain, bulling its way through the brush. After a minute, the snapping of twigs ceased, and the woods returned to nature's quiet sounds.

They walked another fifteen minutes down the trail, following the bends and curves until Ray motioned for them to stop.

"We're close," he whispered. "I can see the very top of a roofline."

Ray pointed to the left, through the trees, to where he spied the roof. Christian looked, but he could not see what Ray had noticed. All Christian saw was trees, but he knew Ray had been here before. Like the trail, Christian also knew Ray had an idea of what he was looking for.

They followed Ray a little further, until the trail turned toward the direction of the house. Christian peeked around the bend and down the natural corridor of the path. At the bottom of the hill, Christian spotted grass. When his eyes panned left, he noticed brief glimpses of a dark green house with wooden shingles. The house itself was camouflaged, and Christian realized that's why he couldn't spot it earlier. Sam pulled out the cell phone and sent a text to her parents that they were in position.

Alexis went into listening mode one more time, and everyone but her took a seat on the ground as they waited for the arrival of Sam's parents.

CHAPTER 19

Christian could not remember a time where he had to remain silent for so long, but considering the importance of it for their safety, silence was tolerable. He knew it was also driving Sam nuts because she kept adjusting her hat and fidgeting with her belt. Then it was her shirt sleeves that gave her fits. She couldn't decide whether to bunch them up by pushing them to her elbows or allow them to dangle just past her palms. The sleeves were a little too long for Sam's arms.

Alexis tensed up, and Christian and Ray sat upright at her tension. Sam stopped fussing with her clothing and perked her ears up. Three minutes passed before Christian heard what had grabbed Alexis's attention. A vehicle engine hummed in the distance.

Alexis's audio capabilities shifted into high alert, and the three teens on the ground tried to move as little as possible. They needed to give Alexis every opportunity to listen for any danger that might be lurking in the house or the forest.

Soon, the vehicle, which Christian assumed to be the Kirgans', rumbled in front of the house. The engine cut out, and two doors slammed shut.

"I think we should ask for directions," Vicki's familiar voice called out.

"Don't you think I know where we are going?" Dan fired back.

Christian smiled at the acting he was listening to. Sam's parents were really selling their roles.

"I'm going to check to see if anyone in this house knows how to find that road," Vicki huffed.

"Fine!" Dan yelled. "Maybe I'll just let you walk from here."

A car door slammed moments later, and Sam tapped Ray on the shoulder.

Checking it out, the text read.

After a few more minutes, Vicki shouted, "I guess we'll just keep driving around these woods until we find someone!"

Then a second car door slammed shut. The Kirgans' truck roared to life and headed back down the road.

"No one there," Sam whispered as she looked at the phone's screen.

Alexis crouched, smiling.

"Your mom rang the doorbell about 15 times and pounded on the door while doing it," she whispered. "If there is someone in that house, they would have to be dead to not hear her ringing or pounding."

"Or yelling," Ray added. "Let's go."

Ray led the teens quickly down the mountainside to the house. Christian was amazed by the size of the home hiding in the forest. It was two stories tall with dark green siding and dark brown accents with a wooden shingle roof. A large wooden porch spanned the back of the house, and small pines separated a grass-covered yard from the encroaching forest. As they walked around to the other side, Christian noticed the pines encircled almost the entire perimeter, except for the deer path they had come down on and the half-circle, earthen driveway in the front.

The mailbox also blended in with its surroundings, giving the entire set up the appearance of a camouflaged hide-a-way. The front door was locked, but Ray quickly shuffled off the front porch to the right and disappeared around the other side of the house. A minute later, he returned with a key in hand. He unlocked the door before quickly disappearing back around the side of the house. Christian assumed he was putting the key back.

"We all know where it is," Sam said.

They waited for Ray to return. The dark oak door creaked on its hinges as it swung open wide. There was no turning back now, so the four teens crept silently into the house. Ray quickly found the switches, and lights in the foyer and living room popped on.

"I'll check the answering machine," Sam said.

"Alexis, you stay by the door and listen," Ray ordered. "We need to make sure no one surprises us."

"This place is abandoned," Alexis answered. "No one is coming out here."

"Christian, with me," Ray said. "Alexis, please, stay at the door."

Alexis rolled her eyes, but she stayed put. Christian agreed with Ray that they needed to have her ears by the front door. Ray led Christian through the living room to a large oak door. Ray tried the knob.

"It's locked," he said in frustration.

"What's behind that door?" Christian asked.

"The only room we were never allowed to go into," Ray said, as he backed up and took a run at the door.

A solid thud, followed by Ray's groan, meant it was going to take more than brute force to open that door.

"Are there tools in the garage?" Christian asked. "Maybe we could use a crowbar to pop it open."

"Good idea," Ray said, as he led Christian back through the living room and into the kitchen.

Sam was reading a sheet of paper when the boys walked through.

"Hey, you need to see this," Sam said seriously as they passed her.

"In a minute," Ray huffed, and he pushed open the garage door.

"There's a truck here," Christian said nervously.

"It's always here," Ray answered, unconcerned. "Along with that ATV over there."

Christian looked in the direction of Ray's gesture to see a camouflaged four-wheeler along the far wall.

"This is what we need," Ray said as he pointed to the wall. "That will get me through that door."

"Won't Mr. Banner be a little upset about the destruction of his property?" Sam said, peering in from the doorway to the kitchen.

"At this point, I don't really care," Ray said, as he plucked the axe from its spot among the tools.

Christian noticed a sledge hammer resting in the corner, so he grabbed it just in case. When they passed back through the kitchen, Alexis was reading the sheet of paper Sam had been looking at earlier.

"You need to see this," Alexis said.

"You should be watching this door," Ray said, pointing the axe at the front entrance as he lumbered by.

Ray was on a mission.

Alexis and Sam followed the two boys through the living room.

"Stand back," Ray ordered, as he lined up his body for the first blow.

The gleaming finish of the oak wood was no match for the steel in Ray's hand, as the axe head came crashing down into the door. He wiggled the weapon to loosen it and pulled it back from the door, revealing a large gash of lighter colored wood where the pristine dark stain had once served as a protector from dust and grime. After a few more blows, the dark wood was riddled with similar gashes, but they were all over the place.

"I can't aim this darn thing," Ray said as the door shuddered from another slash.

"Ray!" Alexis shouted. "You really need to read this note."

"And you need to watch that door!" he commanded. "And did anyone check that answering machine? I saw the light was flashing."

Sam and Alexis immediately retreated to the kitchen.

"Women," Ray huffed as he unleashed another attack. "Damn! I can't seem get this thing to hit the same spot twice."

"Give me a try," Christian requested, and Ray offered the axe to him. "No thanks, I'll use this."

Ray smiled as Christian hauled the sledge hammer to his shoulder. His target was the door knob, but he underestimated the weight of the hammer and missed low. The door popped, but it held firm. On the second swing, the polished knob crumpled from the force and the door parted from the jamb. It was only an inch, but Christian thought it would be enough.

"Axe," he said, as Ray moved closer. "It's still locked, but I think it's enough to wedge that in there."

Ray pushed past Christian and said, "Great thinking!"

Ray positioned the axe between the jamb and the door, and he began to pry at it. Christian heard the wood pop and crack, but the door refused to give way.

"Hammer it one more time," Ray said as he backed away.

Christian tightly gripped the sledge hammer and widened his stance. This time, the door jumped open another inch, and Ray slipped the head of the axe all the way through. Christian could see shelves of books and a filing cabinet through the opening. The once-shiny oak door creaked one last time before a single, sharp pop, and the door opened.

The boys dropped their heavy tools and rushed into the room.

"What am I looking for?" Christian asked.

"Not sure," Ray shrugged. "Just start looking for anything with our names on it, Mr. Banner's, or the title PC."

"PC?" Christian asked.

"Phenomenon Children," Ray replied.

"Filing cabinet is locked," Christian said, as he tugged the drawers.

Ray rifled through a desk drawer.

"Try this," he said, tossing Christian a ring with three keys on it.

Sam and Alexis appeared in the doorway.

"Ray, you need to read this," Alexis said impatiently.

"What did the phone message say?" Ray asked.

"Same thing," Alexis replied.

"Read it to me," he fired back as he pulled open another drawer and fingered through files, pulling a couple out and placing them on the desk.

Christian unlocked the cabinet with the third key.

"It's always the last one," Christian mumbled to himself as he opened the top drawer.

Christian flipped through folders with names on them. They were alphabetized by last name. He plucked out one for Kirgan and one for Tines. There was no Pearson in the files.

Alexis started reading, "Welcome to my home. Please stay put."

Christian interrupted her, "Alexis, what's your last name?"

"Banner," she answered sarcastically.

"No! Your real last name," Christian responded agitatedly.

"Jundos, with a J," she said. "Why?"

"There are files in here on all of you," Christian responded as he found the "J" section. "There must be a hundred folders in this drawer. I can't take them all."

"Grab ours," Ray ordered. "Then just pull some others. Alexis, keep reading."

"There is plenty of food in the freezer and the refrigerator," she continued. "A friend of mine stops in to check on the place every Monday and Thursday. Make yourselves at home, but don't answer the door or the phone, and don't make any calls or leave for any reason. Your safety is important to me. My friend has a key to let himself in."

"Today is Monday, Ray!" Sam said, seriously.

"Why didn't you tell me about that message right away?" Ray growled.

"We did!" Alexis and Sam answered.

"Alexis, door, please," Ray pleaded, as he pulled his backpack off and emptied some of the food contents. His movements were quick and specific.

Ray shoved the three files he had pulled from the desk, and Christian handed him more files before shoving a couple in his own backpack when Ray's was full. Alexis raced in from the living room, and Christian looked up and noticed that the lights were off.

"Uh, guys," Alexis said in a quiet but worried voice. "We have company."

"How many?" Ray asked.

"It's an old car, not government," Alexis stated.

"Did you get all the lights?" Ray questioned.

Alexis nodded, and Ray moved to the window.

"It's Charlie," Ray said, disgustedly. "He will spot us out here if we make a run for it."

"But he's alone," Alexis said. "How did he find us?"

"Would he know about this house?" Sam asked.

"Only if he is working with Mr. Banner," Ray said.

"He must have followed your parents," Christian whispered.

"Stairs," Ray whispered, as he led them to the stairs that led to the second level. "You can't see this spot from any window."

"The front door," Alexis whispered. "It's unlocked."

"Follow me," Ray said to Christian, as he raced to the living room and snatched up the axe and sledge hammer.

He handed the hammer to Christian.

"Don't hurt him," Sam whined quietly as they made their way to the front door, too.

"I won't," Ray answered. "Unless he makes the wrong move."

Ray and Christian each took a side of the door and waited.

The doorbell rang, and Christian's body began to tremble. A pit formed in his stomach. The ring was followed by a knock, and then the knob twisted on the door. As soon as Charlie placed a foot inside, Ray jumped him and tossed him down onto the porch. In a flash, Ray was on top of Charlie with the handle of the axe pinned against Charlie's neck.

CHAPTER 20

"What the hell are you doing here?" Ray snarled through clenched teeth as he allowed his full weight to keep Charlie pressed firmly against the concrete of the front porch.

The red axe handle matched Charlie's color as he squirmed under Ray's grip, gasping for breath. Christian saw the way Charlie landed, and Christian had experienced what Charlie was feeling now. Charlie had the wind knocked out of him, like a football player who lands hard on his back. Charlie couldn't breathe. He flailed harder as he struggled for oxygen.

"Stop it!" Sam shouted. "You're killing him!"

Ray let off, and Christian leaned in and pulled up on Charlie's belt. Charlie sucked in oxygen like he had finally surfaced after being stuck with his head under water for too long.

"I ain't killin' him," Ray responded calmly. "I just knocked the wind out of him."

Charlie gasped more as Christian held Charlie's midsection off the ground a few inches by his belt. Christian had a coach do that with him, when he landed like Charlie did with an offensive lineman reinforcing the shock from the turf.

"Stop it!" Sam ordered again.

"I'm pulling up his waist line so he can get air back into his lungs," Christian said, calmly. "See, he's breathing easier, now."

Ray leaned down close to Charlie.

"If you so much as breathe wrong from here on out, I'll split your head with this axe," Ray whispered. "And he is pretty accurate with that sledge." Ray motioned his head toward Christian. "We gonna have any problems?"

Christian let go of Charlie's belt.

Sam had not heard the threat, but Christian did, and he was positive Alexis did, too. Charlie shook his head weakly, and Ray helped him up.

Charlie was not at all what Christian had pictured. Sam had told Christian that Charlie was from a rough home life, and that he was one of those kids who might end up turning to gangs. Christian had pictured a rugged looking inner-city kid with tattoos and a muscle shirt. The boy who stood in front of him, now, was not the tough-looking gangster Christian had imagined.

Charlie wore khaki shorts and a blue polo shirt. He was about Christian's height, but he was thin. Charlie looked like a stiff breeze could blow him over. Ray instructed Charlie to put his hands over his head to increase his lung capacity, and Charlie soon began to breathe more steadily. His short black hair was clean, and he looked more like a guy who worked on computers than a gangbanger. Charlie turned, and Christian could see his arms had very little muscle.

He's a nerd, Christian thought as Charlie knelt over and clutched his ribs.

"You big oaf!" Sam chastised Ray as she put a hand on Charlie's shoulder. "Are you okay?"

"Yeah, I'm fine," Charlie answered, looking warily at Ray's axe.

Charlie turned back to Sam.

"I can't believe I found you," he said, in disbelief. "I saw the map on the dash of your father's truck when he left the house, so I raced ahead and waited on the highway by the road with the red X. After he and your mom drove out, I decided to come up here and check it out. I didn't think I would actually find anyone."

"Why have you been looking for Sam?" Ray asked, tapping the axe handle and catching Charlie's attention once more.

"Um, well," Charlie stumbled over his words. "A friend told me to be on the lookout for you."

"What friend?" Alexis questioned harshly.

"I can't say," Charlie said, looking at the ground.

"Ray, he won't tell us," Alexis said calmly.

"Have Christian hold him down while I cut off one of his fingers with that axe," Ray responded, coldly. "If I clip two of them, oh, well."

Charlie stepped back, quickly.

"Stop it!" Sam shouted as she whirled to face Alexis. "We are not going to hurt him!"

"Then he better start talking," Alexis growled back. "I am tired of being on the run, and Charlie here can give us some answers."

"Like what?" Sam said, stepping between Charlie and the other teens.

"Like why is he free after government agents kidnapped him?" Christian fired. "How is it that he is roaming free?"

Sam's eyes flickered and Christian saw her eyes coolly harden like Alexis's had. She turned to face the accused.

"Charlie, how come you're free?" Sam asked as she stepped back toward Alexis, leaving Charlie alone to face them. "We have all been on the run, but you seem to be able to just show up on people's doorsteps."

"When I was taken by those agents, they eventually sent me to New Mexico," Charlie explained, his eyes averting theirs and looking toward the ground.

"What do you mean by eventually?" Christian asked.

"First, they put me in a little padded room and interrogated me," Charlie said. "They asked me a bunch of questions."

"Who did?" Alexis asked.

"I don't know," Charlie said meekly. "The questions came through the speaker in the ceiling. I never saw the person who was talking, and the voice was altered."

"What did they ask you?" Ray questioned.

"What had happened to me to cause my ability," Charlie replied. "They wanted to know what traumatic event had taken place in my life, and I told them to pick one since there were so many."

"What else?" Ray said.

"About my family," Charlie said. "My friends, my hobbies. They wanted to know if I had told anyone about my ability."

"Did you tell them about us?" Alexis asked.

Charlie didn't say anything.

"What did you tell them?" she ordered loudly, and when Charlie didn't answer she grabbed the axe from Ray. "I'll cut them off myself!"

"Okay, yes, I told them about you and Ray," Charlie said, flinching from Alexis's feigned attack. "But I didn't tell them about Sam."

"Why not?" Sam asked.

"Because I loved you," Charlie responded, looking up at her. "I still do."

Now, Christian really didn't like Charlie.

"See the guy with the sledge hammer?" Ray said, motioning to Christian. "You probably don't want to say that in front of him."

Charlie glanced at Christian, and Christian did his best to look intimidating. It must have worked, because Charlie stepped back, nervously. Christian figured the sledge hammer probably helped.

"What do you know about the Phenomenon Child program?" Alexis asked.

Charlie's poker face was not very good. Christian could tell Charlie knew about it, even though he tried to play dumb.

"The what?" Charlie asked, faking a puzzled expression.

The Three seemed to buy it, but Christian didn't.

"Never mind," Alexis said impatiently. "So how did you get out?"

"After what seemed like days in there," Charlie explained, "a man came into my holding cell and told me I was going to be given a special assignment. In exchange for my willingness to work for him, he would take care of me."

"How?" Sam asked.

"He would feed me and give me a place to live," Charlie said. "Take care of me, sort of like a father."

"What was your assignment?" Ray asked, gripping the axe handle.

"I spied for him," Charlie shrugged.

"Who did you spy on?" Ray asked.

"He never gave me names," Charlie explained. "I only had descriptions and locations, but I could figure out lots of things by scanning the rooms they were in."

"What rooms?" Ray asked.

"Mostly offices and conference rooms," Charlie replied. "Most of them weren't in Phoenix, but some were."

Now Charlie had an interested audience, and Christian noticed Charlie appeared to be excited by the questions. He liked talking about his special ability to spy.

Charlie continued without prompting, "I spied on a casino owner in Vegas, but most of my assignments were government agencies. Mostly I looked for names on files or addresses for persons of interest.

"Typically, I would be assigned to one of two places. Either I was in a building in close proximity to the office, or I became the hired help for the day, the guy cleaning up two or three glass windows away. I can read a newspaper from a hundred yards," Charlie said, as he looked directly at Christian like he was bragging.

Now, Christian hated him entirely.

"So, what do we do with him?" Ray asked.

"We can't let him go," Christian said. "But we can't take him with us, either."

"Let's tie him up and then decide," Ray whispered.

At those words, Charlie jumped the railing of the porch and fled to his car. Christian had seen Charlie's muscles tense, and he caught the fleeing victim three steps from the hood. Christian tackled him into the front fender, and Charlie's face caught most of the impact. Christian felt satisfied with the pain inflicted on Charlie, and he showed little mercy as he dragged Charlie back toward the porch. Ray grabbed his legs and helped carry a woozy Charlie into the house.

"Rope and tape is in the garage," Ray said.

Sam looked pleadingly at Ray and Christian, but even she knew the danger Charlie posed. Once Charlie decided to make a break for it, Sam was done trying to protect him.

"I am sorry, Charlie," she said, almost sobbing. "We just can't trust anyone."

Charlie's lip was bleeding, and the swelling was already setting in. Ray and Christian carried him to a wooden chair in the kitchen, avoiding the sight of the decimated door to the office. Charlie tried once to get free, but Ray delivered a fist to his midsection that ended the struggle as quickly as it had started.

They tied rope around Charlie's arms, legs, and waist. Then they reinforced it with duct tape. His hands were taped, palms down, to the armrests and his ankles to the legs. When Charlie screamed, they taped his mouth shut.

"We need to get out of here," Alexis hollered.

The teens wasted no time. They grabbed their bags and headed out the front door. Christian stopped to flip the switch off and lock the knob from the inside.

"See ya, Charlie," Christian said as he closed the door and followed The Three across the front lawn.

They ran through the row of pines that encircled the house and Alexis stopped them before they plunged into the brush of the forest.

"Wait!" she whispered, sharply. "False alarm. That vehicle must have been doing a U-turn. I don't hear anything else."

"Well, we aren't going back in that house," Ray whispered. "We need to get out of here."

"Then we need to go back up that hill to the other road and call my parents," Sam whispered harshly and turned to go back through the trees.

Alexis grabbed her shoulder and spun Sam around, pulling her to the ground. Sam opened her mouth to voice her discontent, but something in Alexis's eyes stopped her from uttering the words. Alexis turned toward Christian, and he saw a look of horror on Alexis's face.

"We need to go," Alexis whispered as she motioned for them to follow and broke into a full sprint when her feet touched the mountain road.

Christian, Ray, and Sam didn't wait to ask questions. They all understood that Alexis's ears had picked up a noise that meant danger, and Christian didn't think it was a bear.

CHAPTER 21

Alexis's pace slowed, but she continued a brisk jog for almost half a mile. Finally, she found what she was looking for, a depression in the forest for them to hide in. She slid into the ditch, and the other three teens followed her.

They all panted for breath before Ray asked, quietly, "What… did you… hear?"

Alexis breathed deeply before speaking.

"That vehicle," she said, quietly. "The one I heard on the road. It must have dropped men off. I heard the crackle of a headset."

Christian edged up the slope of the ditch to look back up the road. A headset meant they must be agents.

"Did they say anything?" Ray asked, still catching his breath.

"It's a surveillance team," she replied quietly. "They are setting up a high perimeter overlooking the house, and then road blocks on every county road for five miles."

Ray fired off a hushed S-bomb before turning back to Alexis.

"Anything else?" Ray asked.

"That's when I started running," she replied. "I knew we didn't have long to get away from that house."

"Do we need to keep going?" Christian asked.

"Give me a second," Ray said calmly. "Let's not make a rushed decision."

Ray thought for a moment. He pressed his hands together and put his thumbs to his chin with his fingers resting on his nose and forehead, and then he closed his eyes.

After thirty seconds of deep breaths, he said calmly, "Alexis, listen in on their chatter. You said they were surveillance, so maybe they don't know we're here. Christian, you move down the road a ways and see if there is a deer trail that leads south."

Ray pointed left.

"If we are going to have to make a run for it, we want to be going downhill," Ray explained. "Sam, text your parents 'Bad guys near, but we're safe. Wait for contact.' Anything, yet, Alexis?"

"If you would zip it," Alexis said in an irritated huff.

Sam's fingers pressed buttons on the phone, and Christian moved cautiously down the road. When he glanced back, Christian realized that they had run far enough away from the house that the mountain created a natural barrier from the surveillance team's line of sight. But he decided to continue to move quietly and crouched, almost like a gorilla.

After a few minutes, Christian found the type of trail he was looking for, and he scurried back to the ditch.

When he got there, Sam and Ray looked more relaxed. Christian found a spot next to Sam.

"The team is just waiting and watching," Ray said calmly. "They won't go into the house until they see movement, and unless Charlie has scissors for hands, they won't see movement in that house for a long time."

"So, we're leaving," Christian said.

"No, we're going to wait for Mr. Banner's friend to show up," Sam whispered. "Remember, it's Monday, and someone is supposed to be stopping by."

"Won't we run out of daylight?" Christian asked. "We won't be able to see where we are going at night."

"Did you find that deer trail?" Ray asked.

"Yeah," Christian replied.

"A mile down that trail, there is a little cut-out," Ray said. "We should be able to find our way to that spot as the sun is setting, if we have to. We can hold up there until morning, and then continue south as far as we have to."

"Anyone need water?" Christian asked. "This pack is getting heavy."

Ray and Alexis shared a bottle, as did Sam and Christian.

"Too bad I threw all that food out on the desk in the office," Ray said.

Realizing what had taken the place of the bags of crackers, Ray took off his pack and slowly opened the zipper. He pulled out three folders and handed a file labeled "P.C. – Eagle Eye" to Christian. He gave another one to Sam and kept one for himself.

Christian opened the file and saw a photo of Charlie walking out of a glass door. Next to the picture, scribbled notes listed

Charlie's address, phone number, and known aliases. The picture was paper-clipped to a document titled "Operation Eagle Eye." Christian read the text.

He was finishing the first page when Alexis broke the silence.

"Here comes Mr. Banner's friend," she said quietly. "And I think he is driving a big rig."

In a matter of minutes, even Christian could hear the rumbling of a large diesel engine, groaning to climb the hill to the safe house. Then the motor died and sputtered.

"They're moving in," Alexis whispered. "I wish I could see what's going on."

Alexis provided play-by-play as best she could, and Christian quickly flipped through five more pages before he returned the file back to his backpack. He caught a glimpse of the name at the bottom of the last page, but he decided to double-check it later. He needed to be ready to leave when Alexis gave the word.

"The team is moving in and one man is providing cover. I bet these guys are armed with more than pistols. They are approaching from behind the house, and the cover man is giving them the truck driver's location. Target is approaching the door. They have weapons drawn on target. The cover guy must be relaying what's happening to a control center somewhere. They have the target in custody."

Ray interrupted, "So, they don't know who the target is."

"I guess not," Alexis answered.

"Interesting," Ray said calmly.

Christian was amazed at Ray's demeanor. He seemed cool and collected as they sat and listened to Alexis spew information. Christian was ready to jump out of his skin and run for the deer trail, and Sam seemed as edgy as Christian. The file in her hand had been bent by her tense grip.

"They have I.D. on the target. Man's name is Samson King, and they are checking his record right now," Alexis said in a whisper.

"Have they entered the house?" Ray asked.

"No," Alexis replied. "They are searching the truck, but it's empty. Samson King of Tuscon, Arizona, no priors, served four years in the Air Force, Honorable Discharge."

Ray still sat calmly, his hands in the same position as earlier, thumbs to his chin and fingers resting on his nose and forehead.

"I can hear Samson talking through one of the headsets," Alexis said, and Ray opened his eyes and looked in her direction. "He is telling them that he is hired to check on this house twice a week. He doesn't know the man, but he gets paid well to make sure expired food is thrown out on Mondays and replenished when he returns on Thursday. Key is hidden near a hose on the east side of the house. Control says to release him and check the house; Samson is not who they are looking for."

"Good, we can get out of here," Christian said. "They're entering the house."

"Wait," Ray said, calmly. "Let's see what they say about Charlie."

Christian was in a hurry to leave, but he did have some interest in what happened to Charlie. He didn't trust Charlie at all, and he wanted to know if his gut instincts were right.

The semi roared to life, and Sam jumped to her feet.

"We need to go," she said impatiently. "We have waited long enough."

"Shh!" Alexis hissed. "It's hard enough to hear with that diesel engine going."

Ray rose to his feet and said, "Give Alexis another minute; then we move to the trail Christian found."

"They found Charlie," Alexis said. "We can go."

"What did they say?" Sam asked.

"We need to go!" Alexis repeated with a sharp edge to her whisper. "That truck is coming this way."

CHAPTER
22

"We won't make the trail in time," Christian said, as they raced down the dirt road. "That truck is probably going downhill by now."

"Move into the bushes," Ray ordered. "Pull branches over yourselves and wait for the truck to pass."

The four teens moved off the road to the right. Alexis and Sam climbed a slight incline with a large bush to hide behind. From Christian's location, he could see the two of them pulling a log over to their spot. Finally, the girls both lied flat, and Christian hoped they were concealed enough. Christian shoved his tennis shoes under some leaves and yanked some branches from the ground to cover his face.

The rumble of the big rig moved closer, and it growled more intensely as it reached a short incline near their position. Christian could see the red cab pull even with the girls' location as it shifted gears. The truck bounced on the rough road and Christian could feel the rumble slowly roll past him. Ray had bounded into the forest ten yards further down the road, and Christian hoped Ray had found good cover. Then the gears ground, and the truck stopped with the rear wheel only ten feet from Christian.

Christian heard the door open and the unmistakable grunt of someone dropping to the ground. The driver was outside his truck.

A deep voice spoke over the engine, just enough for anyone within earshot to hear, "If you want to get out of here, you need to come now."

Christian knew Alexis had heard the call, but neither of the girls moved. He didn't want to risk a look behind him, so he stayed as still as possible.

"I can see your pale white skin," a voice said, and then a laugh boomed.

Christian thought that maybe Ray had been spotted, but the voice came from closer than before, and Christian looked to his right. He saw a half-empty water bottle on the road a couple feet from where he hid, but he saw nothing else but forest. Christian swore the laugh had come from right next to him, but no man was standing in the road beside his hidden location. Then Christian saw the brown boots in the grass next to him and camouflaged shorts a couple feet higher, but to his amazement, there were no legs to hold the shorts up. It was just forest.

"We have little time," the voice called from above Christian. "Is there anyone else with you?"

The boots moved toward Christian, and suddenly, black legs filled the boots and shorts. A large black arm reached down and grabbed Christian by the shirt, pulling him off the ground from his hiding spot. Christian was face to face with Samson King, only Christian's feet were not touching the ground.

"Put him down," Ray called in a hushed voice, as he stepped from the trees to Christian's right.

"We have no time, little man," Samson answered. "It won't be long before those agents realize I've stopped."

Ray's puzzled expression matched Christian's confused fear.

"What are you talking about?" Christian asked.

"No time, no time, little man," Samson whispered. "Is it only two?"

"No," Alexis said as she and Sam stepped onto the road.

"Four will be tight, but look how skinny you all is," the black giant said. "No time, you must get in the cab. Explain later, no time."

With the only other option being a night in a cave and possible capture, Christian looked at Ray and shrugged.

"I guess we go with him," Ray said.

"Sounds good to me," Alexis said. "Charlie told them we were at the house, but he must have some good in him."

"Why is that?" Ray said as he opened the passenger door and helped the others into the cab.

"He sent them north," Alexis replied.

"Odd," Ray said.

"I still don't trust Charlie," Christian voiced his discontent.

"Me either," Ray added, as he closed the door of the cab.

Samson had already shifted the engine into first gear.

"We not out of the woods, yet," Samson said, laughing at his own pun. "You must hide. They probably check the cab again."

"Where can we hide?" Sam asked.

"Pull up the mattress back there," Samson said. "I a big man, so it a big mattress. Secret spot underneath."

Samson pointed to the floor of the sleeping compartment behind the front seat, and Christian repositioned himself so they could pull up the mattress. To Christian, it looked like an ordinary floor with metal screws along the edge, where the flooring was connected to the truck.

"Push on that metal button," Samson said, pointing to one of the screws.

Christian pressed firmly, and the washer ring around the metal screw popped up like a latch. Christian pulled on it, and a hidden door slowly opened.

"You got it on the first try," Samson laughed. "That a rare deed, indeed, little man. Now, you all squeeze in there and stays quiet. I get us past the road block to the south. I sees it on the way up here. It be a tight fit, but it won't be long and I gets you out."

Christian went first and moved to the far left of the box. Ray and Alexis switched spots, so Ray could shimmy into the far right.

Then Samson rolled down the window and in one motion he grabbed the two backpacks and two sleeping bags and threw them out the window.

"Hey, our bags," Sam cried.

"They suspicious," Samson said, calmly. "We don't need agents asking questions."

Alexis and Sam slid in as Ray and Christian held the lid up. It was extremely tight, but when they lowered the lid, it closed all the way. The cramped quarters went pitch black, when Samson tightened the latch. Christian heard the mattress flop down on the secret door.

"He's going to need a crowbar to get us all out of here," Sam whispered.

"I hope we made the right decision by going with him," Alexis said.

"It was the only option," Ray answered quietly in the dark. "By the sound of it, those agents would have found us in the woods."

The truck bounced along the trail, but the teens were packed in so tight, the jarring ride didn't have much effect on them. Christian felt as if an eternity had passed when Samson finally stopped the truck.

"You kids stay quiet, now," Samson called. "We at the road block. No sound 'til I get you out."

The driver door opened, and Samson said, "I already checked by them men with guns. Okay, okay, you the law."

No one breathed as doors were opened and closed, and even the mattress moved above them. Christian wanted to ask Alexis what was going on, but he knew he shouldn't. Christian's feet began tingling, since his knees were pinned against his chest. The truck shifted gears and pulled forward a ways before stopping again. Christian wanted to get out of the box, but he was afraid to say anything. Not one of them seemed to be breathing.

A door opened again, but still no one spoke.

Samson's voice boomed, "Thank you, officer," as the truck moved under his weight taking the driver's seat.

A door slammed and the truck shifted gears again.

"You done good, little ones," Samson sung. "Those agents tricky, but you stay quiet. I get you out in a minute."

After five minutes, the truck stopped, again. The mattress moved above them, and the lid popped open. Samson's white smile greeted them, as he reached a huge black paw and gently pulled Sam free.

"You all so light," Samson said as he gently extended a hand to Christian and easily lifted him out.

"Don't you mommas feed you?" the large man laughed.

With the extra room, Alexis climbed out and tried to help Ray, but the giant arm of Samson had to reach in to assist.

"You all so scrawny," Samson said, roaring with laughter.

He shifted the truck into first once more as Ray moved the mattress back into its original position. Alexis and Sam hopped back into the sleeping area, but Christian stayed up front.

"You too, little man," Samson said. "You needs to go back, too. Don't want anyone to see you."

Christian moved into the back.

"But I don't know how any could," Samson jeered. "You all so skinny. You turn sideways and just disappear from sight."

Samson shook his head and grinned as he turned his white smile toward them.

"You all so scraw-ny!" he repeated, shaking his head some more.

The mountainous man took up all of the driver's area and then some. His bald head glistened with sweat, and Christian marveled at his broad, muscular shoulders. Without a shirt on, Samson King's barrel chest was intimidating. Even though he was an imposing figure, when Samson smiled, Christian couldn't help but smile back. Those pearly whites made his face look much darker than it actually was, and it was a large toothy grin to boot.

"How come I couldn't see you on the road?" Christian asked him.

Samson laughed a booming laugh.

Ray questioned, "What do you mean you couldn't see him?"

Christian turned to Ray and said, "I could see his boots and his shorts but nothing else."

Ray made an odd face as if to say, what the heck are you talking about?

"Seriously, all of a sudden he materialized," Christian pleaded his case.

"Like he was invisible?" Alexis said, rolling her eyes.

"Yeah, like he was invisible," Christian said, repeating her words and not wanting to believe of his own vision.

"I saw him clearly come around the back of the truck," Ray said. "So, your mind must have been playing tricks on you."

"Play tricks!" Samson howled from the front seat. "Ole Samson, he trick little man."

"What the!" Alexis hollered as she pointed to the front and backed against the rear wall like she was trying to escape from something horrifying.

Ray cussed, wide-eyed, and Christian turned to see what had caused them to freak out. Samson was gone.

CHAPTER 23

He wasn't really gone; Christian just couldn't see him, not totally. As Christian focused more, he could see the rough outline of Samson, and he noticed the image that seemed to cover Samson's body was similar to the background of the woods out the window. Samson wasn't gone; he was camouflaged.

A raucous laugh let the passengers of the semi know their driver had not vanished. In an instant, the dark skin of Samson reappeared.

"You, you, turned invisible," Alexis said.

Samson boomed another laugh, and his shoulders shuddered with the tremor of humor.

"Invisible," Samson chuckled. "She said that I was invisible, little man. That funny."

"What is it, then?" Alexis asked, still backed against the wall.

"Camouflage," Christian said as he figured the mystery out.

"Little man right," Samson said, his deep voice calm. "Samson like chameleon."

"He must be able to change his skin to match his surroundings," Christian said excitedly. "He's a Phenomenon Child."

"Yeah, little man, you right," Samson bellowed. "I am P.C."

Samson's shoulders shuddered as he laughed again.

"Samson, where are you taking us?" Christian asked.

"I dropped the trailer," the booming voice responded. "Needs to pick it up."

"Where?" Christian responded.

"On forty, outside Flagstaff," Samson replied.

"Are you leaving us there?" Christian questioned.

"No, little man," Samson laughed. "I take you with me. I get you to a safe place."

"Thanks, Samson," Christian said.

"No prob, little man," Samson responded.

Christian closed the curtain between the front seat and the sleeping compartment so their conversation in the back did not easily drift to Samson's ears. When Christian did so, Samson turned on his radio. Now Christian was sure Samson wouldn't be able to hear their discussion.

"Where's forty?" Christian asked.

"It's the Interstate that runs east-west through Flagstaff," Ray replied. "It goes through New Mexico and Texas, all the way to the East Coast, I think."

Sam pulled open the curtain and asked, "Samson, what trailer do you have to pick up?"

Samson's large finger pressed the knob on the stereo, and the music cut off.

"I gots to get my trailer from the truck stop," he answered. "I needs to return it to the warehouse in Tucson, then I'm goin' home. I just stop by that house to check in on it, like I always do. Then those men come point guns in my face."

Samson appeared angered by the thought of the guns.

"Do you know the man who owns the house?" Sam asked.

"Yeah," Samson replied. "We old friends."

"What's his name?" Christian questioned, expecting to hear Mr. Banner's name as the answer.

"Mr. Tibbs," Samson said, surprising all of them. "He a good man."

"What does Mr. Tibbs look like?" Christian asked, wondering if Mr. Banner had many different names.

"He tall and scrawny," Samson said. "Like you, little man."

Samson pointed at Christian.

"Does he have a moustache?" Ray asked.

"Yeah, he do," Samson said, surprised. "Does you know Mr. Tibbs, too?"

"I think so," Ray said.

"Good, little man," Samson said to Ray. "By you's scared looks on the road back there, I thoughts maybe I was the first black man you seen in you's whole life, but Tibby, he darker than me."

Samson shook his head and smiled, as he looked into the rearview mirror.

"Tibby, he a dark, dark man," Samson said.

The teens all looked at each other, wide-eyed. Mr. Banner was not Mr. Tibbs because Mr. Banner definitely wasn't black.

CHAPTER 24

"Little ones, you stay in here, curtain closed," Samson commanded before opening the door. "I gonna hook up the trailer."

The door slammed shut, and the four teens were alone.

"Mr. Tibbs?" Alexis said, puzzled. "Who is that? I thought, for sure Samson was talking about Mr. Banner."

"I wish we had our backpacks," Ray said, disgusted. "I can't believe he just threw them out the window."

"They would have looked suspicious, and those agents would have checked them," Sam said.

"I know," Ray responded with a slump of his shoulders. "But they may have contained more clues to what was going on. I didn't get much of my files read."

"Me either," Sam added. "I was too busy worrying to read. I thought we would have time later."

"I read some of a file that I had," Christian said, and the others perked up. "Just the first page, though. It was something called Operation Eagle Eye. Ring any bells?"

Alexis, Ray, and Sam all shook their heads.

Christian continued, "I don't know if I can remember it word for word, but it involved your buddy Charlie."

Christian pointed to Sam, and she stiffened.

"Sorry," Christian said, feeling bad for stinging her with the comment.

"That's okay," she said, and then she smiled. "I know you don't like him."

"Anyway," Christian said, returning to the content of the file. "It was an explanation of Charlie's involvement in an operation to spy on government operatives from other agencies: CIA, FBI, Homeland Security, etc. They were concerned about double-agents working in the higher ranks of the Phenomenon Child program. That's pretty much it, but the most interesting part is who the letter was from."

"Who?" Ray asked.

"I flipped to the last page before I put the file away," Christian explained. "I was going to double-check it later, but I never had the chance. The letter was signed by Banner, I think it was."

"William," Alexis said, flatly.

Christian nodded.

"No way!" Sam cried. "Are you sure?"

"Not one-hundred percent," Christian answered. "I never got a second look, but I'm pretty sure. I do remember that the date at the top was from October of last year."

Christian had dropped a pretty big bomb on all of them. Up to this point, they were under the assumption that Mr. Banner no longer worked for the government. They all thought he had gone rogue, working against the government to find and protect Phenomenon Children.

"Why wouldn't he tell us that?" Sam asked, puzzled.

"Because he is working for the government, not for the Phenomenon kids," Ray said, angrily. "Think about it. Charlie shows up at Sam's parents' house days after we make our escape. Who else would know about Sam or where her parents live?"

"Banner," Alexis answered, acting like the word rolling off her tongue was gagging her.

"How else would Charlie have been freed? Banner must be pretty high up," Ray said. "I just can't figure out why he kept us on the run, when he could have just taken us in."

They all sat quietly, and Christian pondered what Ray had said.

"Maybe it's easier if he can get us to go willingly," Christian said. "Easier than trying to kidnap someone. Less press. If we don't go willingly, then agents show up to take you unwillingly."

"Possibly," Ray said, digesting Christian's theory. "So Charlie and Mr. Banner are working together."

"Charlie is working for Banner," Alexis said disgustedly. "We should have cut off a finger. They are the bad guys in this."

"We don't know that for sure," Sam said pleadingly.

"Maybe not, but it sure makes it look like they aren't the good guys," Ray said calmly.

"So who is Mr. Tibbs?" Alexis asked. "Could he be the double-agent that Mr. Banner is looking for?"

"I don't know," Ray commented. "But I hope Samson is one of the good guys, and I hope he takes us to this Mr. Tibbs."

"You're hoping, Ray," Christian said with a wry smile. "I thought you were against hope."

Ray smiled back, and Alexis said, "You're such a dork, Christian."

Christian agreed with Ray. He wanted to meet Mr. Tibbs, but Christian had a feeling that Samson was one of the good guys. He couldn't pinpoint why he felt that way, but deep down, he trusted Samson.

"I can't believe Mr. Banner and Charlie are on the wrong side of this thing," Sam said, depressed.

She sat cross legged with her elbows on her knees and her chin in her hands.

"At least, I thought Charlie wouldn't do anything to hurt me," Sam continued.

Christian felt a pit form in his stomach, as he wondered if Sam still had feelings for Charlie. Sam peeked up and looked at Christian, who immediately glanced away. He didn't want Sam to see the hurt he felt by what he thought she was feeling.

Sam sat up and reached for Christian's hand.

"I feel sorry for Charlie," she whispered. "But I love you. I know you wouldn't do anything to hurt me."

Christian turned back to look into her eyes. He had seen terror in those eyes when they hid in the forest and listened to Alexis give play-by-play, but the terror had been replaced by the sparkle of hope Christian longed to look at. A dimple formed next to a smile, and she leaned close to him and pecked Christian on the cheek.

"I have never seen you jealous, Christian Pearson," she said, biting her lip.

"Well, I wanted to crack that punk's head open," Ray said, his eyes closed and his head against the wall, "and I'm not even your boyfriend. I bet Christian wanted to tear him apart."

"Oh, Christian's too sweet for that," Sam cooed.

But Christian would hurt Charlie, or anyone else, if it meant Sam would be safe. He hoped it wouldn't come to that, but at this point, Christian was willing to do whatever was necessary for her survival.

"Sweet?" Ray huffed. "Christian's got a mean streak hiding behind that good-guy image. I bet he would do more than you think to protect us."

"Do you have a mean streak?" Sam asked as she looked into his eyes.

Christian smiled, "Nah, I don't have a mean streak, but I guess if someone pushed me far enough, I would put up a pretty good fight."

Sam scooted closer to Christian and leaned her head on his shoulder as she stroked her nails along his back.

Samson opened the door and climbed into the cab. Christian could feel the truck sway to the driver side again as Samson pulled himself in. The door shut, and Samson shifted the truck into gear.

"Little ones, you stay back behind the curtain," Samson said, seriously. "We gots to go back south, and them bad men are everywhere."

"Do we need to hide in the box again?" Ray asked.

"Nah," Samson said, waving his hand to dismiss the question, and Christian was glad to hear that news.

The radio popped on, and Christian recognized the song. It was from the eighties by a group called A-Ha. Christian peeked through the curtain, noticing the sun setting on the horizon.

"It's getting dark," Christian whispered.

Ray nodded and Sam peeked through the curtain.

"It is getting late," she said, "according to the clock on the dash."

Then the four teens sat quietly and listened to the sounds of the eighties as Samson guided them to their next destination.

CHAPTER
25

They had only listened to five songs from the Retro Monday radio program when the truck began to slow down. The natural light from the other side of the curtain had continued to fade. Only the thin light of twilight remained.

"We exiting," Samson said as he turned off the music. "Can you hear me?"

"Yes," they answered.

"I'm gonna park, and you gonna have to move quickly," Samson said seriously. "They bad men around."

"We aren't staying with you?" Christian asked, concerned.

"No, little man," Samson said disappointedly. "You can't. When I says 'Go,' you go out my other door. Don't stop, little man. You run under two trailers and they be a white van. You get in back door of that white van and close and lock it, and you be quick as rabbits, you hear? When you in the van, you gots to hide under them blankets. Little man, you got it?"

"You say 'Go,' and we go under two trailers into the back of a white van and lock it," Christian said intensely.

"And you hides under them blankets," Samson said, an edge to his voice.

"Go, two trailers, white van, back door, lock it, hide. Got it!" Christian said excitedly.

"Good, little man," Samson said. "I gonna miss you little ones."

"We won't see you again?" Christian said disappointedly.

"End of the road with me, little man," Samson said somberly.

Samson sounded sincere to Christian and Christian reached through the curtain in the darkness and put his hand on Samson's shoulder.

"Thanks, Samson," Christian said.

"They following me right now," Samson said. "So, you definitely gonna have to run like rabbits, quicks like rabbits."

Samson opened the curtain and the darkness in the sleeping quarters equaled the darkness outside. Christian thought that was a good sign. They wouldn't be making the switch in broad daylight.

"It's dark now," Samson said. "And we into the trucks. Y'all move up here."

Samson patted the seat next to him.

Christian moved forward against the door, and Sam and Alexis joined him in the cramped seat. Ray perched on the edge of the sleeping area. Christian watched as Samson slowly drove in between two rows of semi-trucks. Some had running lights on while others sat dark and seemingly empty. When Samson turned right, Christian caught a glimpse of headlights in the rear mirror. It appeared to be a large Suburban.

As they cleared the cab of the truck parked on the end, Samson bellowed, "GO!" surprising Christian, who had his fingers on the latch for the door.

The truck was still moving slowly, but Christian opened the door and jumped to the ground. The truck stopped as Sam and Alexis exited at almost the same time.

"Close the door," Samson ordered as Ray moved to the opening and the truck gears ground.

In one motion, Ray slammed the door and dropped as the truck began backing up. The change of direction caused Ray to land off-balance. He rolled onto the ground but quickly jumped to his feet. Christian grabbed Sam's hand and they crouched to go under the first trailer.

A beeping sound emitted from Samson's truck, announcing his reversal of direction, and the trailer backed in a direction that would cover their escape. Christian realized what Samson was doing; he was backing up his trailer toward the government agents in the vehicle following them, in order to block the road to help them move undetected to the van Samson instructed them to get into. Christian stayed low and cleared the overhang of the second trailer. An old white work van with tinted side windows sat in front of them. Christian pulled Sam to the left, toward the back side, and popped open the rear door of the beat up vehicle. Alexis was right on Sam's heels, with Ray in tow as Christian held the door.

The rear tires of Samson's eighteen-wheeler were just coming into view, and Christian saw the reflection of headlights off the rear door of Samson's trailer. It honked its displeasure at Samson's truck as it continued to back up.

"Quickly," Christian whispered as he pushed on Ray and followed him into the back of the van.

Christian yanked the door shut and pushed down the lock. He turned to see the front end of a black SUV through the van's windshield. He dropped down and held his breath. A light shone into the van and then it was gone.

"They have moved past us," Alexis said.

"Cover up," Ray whispered.

They grabbed blankets from near the front seats. Quickly, Ray and Christian spread them out over the girls and then themselves. Christian noticed a roll of plastic laying the length of the cargo compartment along his side. It looked long enough, so he started to unroll it. It appeared to be painter's plastic, the stuff painters lay down to avoid spills on a home owner's carpeting. He pulled, and the plastic unspooled easily across them.

"At least it's another layer," Christian whispered as he lay flat, trying to calm his nerves.

He closed his eyes and Alexis whispered, "They are pulling around behind us now, and the vehicle is parked. The engine is idling. Stay totally still; the doors just opened."

Christian looked up at the blackness of the underside of one of the numerous blankets they had scattered over themselves to conceal their bodies. The dimness of light appeared behind the fabric. Then Christian saw a beam of light above Sam's face in his peripheral vision. The light moved away and then back again, sweeping above Christian. He heard a tug at the back door, and then a deep voice.

"Leave it," a man said. "Check the front seats. I'll wait here."

"Nothing," another voice answered a few seconds later from up front. "Another wild goose chase, I guess."

"Let's see if Donny can get anything from the truck driver," the deep voice called from the rear.

Christian heard car doors slam shut and everyone seemed to exhale simultaneously.

"Definitely not the good guys," Alexis said. "I could hear someone on the headset barking at them to get back to their patrol of the lot."

"They bad men around," Ray said, trying to mimic Samson. "He sure saved our butts, didn't he?"

The plastic made a funny sound when Christian nodded his head in agreement. They waited silently as the minutes passed. Christian wondered what would happen next, thinking that they were at the mercy of whoever jumped into that driver's seat. Samson had taken direction from someone, and Christian wondered who it was. He hoped it was Mr. Tibbs.

"Someone's coming," Alexis whispered.

They waited like silent statues. Christian heard a key in the door, and then the lock clicked. The van rocked as someone climbed into the driver's seat. Christian didn't move, and neither did The Three.

The ignition coughed once, and then the van rumbled to life. The other door opened, and the van rocked a second time but less than the first. Christian heard the flick of the headlights, and the van started to move forward, slowly at first.

A man with a rough, deep voice spoke from the driver's side, "Don't move, don't get up, and don't make a sound if you want to survive."

Christian's heart pounded in his chest as the van picked up speed. Then the brakes squeaked as the van quickly stopped. Christian heard the whine of a window being powered down.

"Come on, Jackson," the man's voice said. "I've been here for ten hours, and I'm tired of truck stop food. We're going to get something with a little taste to it. You want me to bring something back for you?"

The second person in the passenger seat cleared his throat.

"Sorry, sir," Jackson said, nervously. "I didn't realize you were in here, too."

The window whined again.

"Let 'em through," Christian heard Jackson say before the window fully closed and the van lurched forward.

"Stay down," the driver ordered when he heard plastic move. "We aren't safe yet."

After fifteen minutes, the van slowed to a stop and both men got out. The passenger door opened and closed right away, but the driver door stayed open.

"What was that sound?" Alexis whispered.

"I didn't hear anything," Ray responded.

"It sounded like a gun with a silencer," Alexis said. "Like in the movies. You didn't hear it?"

"Nope," Ray whispered. "You sure?"

"Not completely," Alexis answered.

Christian heard footsteps on gravel outside his side of the van, and then someone got into the driver's side and slammed the door.

Christian assumed the passenger was no longer with them, or the passenger moved to the driver's spot. Only one person got back into the van.

There was a sound of metal sliding near Christian's head, and Christian pulled the plastic away from his face, only to see the opening to the front had been sealed off. The van moved once more, and the driver cleared his throat as if he was going to speak, but he didn't say a word.

"What's going on?" Christian asked, but there was no reply.

Christian banged on the door with his fist, pounding the steel, and still no response. Christian's agitation had gotten the others' attention, and soon they were all uncovered.

"They slid this metal door closed," Christian complained, banging on it again with his open hand.

"Who are you?" Christian called.

The driver remained quiet and Christian became nervous.

Christian moved to the back and pulled up on the rear door's lock, but it refused to budge.

"I can't unlock it," Christian said, his concern growing. "It won't unlock!"

Ray tried to pry at the metal door between the driver and the cargo area, but it was no use. Ray couldn't get a grip on it; they were trapped. Christian moved the plastic and blankets, hoping to find some kind of tool he could use, but his hands found nothing but a couple cans of paint and some brushes.

The van slowed to make a right turn, and Christian grabbed a gallon paint can and slammed it against the window. Nothing!

"This is not normal glass," Christian said as he put his hand against it.

Ray moved toward the rear door and ran his hand along one of the windows.

"It feels more like plastic than glass," Ray said in surprise.

"What is going on?" Alexis said, her voice rising with her fears.

Christian looked out the rear window. Nothing but an occasional streetlight dotted the distant road behind them.

"Who the hell is driving this thing?" Ray said in frustration. "And where are they taking us?"

There was a sound of sliding metal, and Christian turned and saw a narrow slit had been opened near the front. Christian climbed on all fours past Ray and then Sam before putting his face against the door. He had to cock his head sideways to look into the front. The van passed a streetlight, and for a brief second, the driver was illuminated by the outside light.

"Well, hello, Christian," a familiar voice called softly from the driver's seat, and Christian immediately recognized the face looking at him in the rearview mirror. "I knew I would catch up with all of you sooner or later."

Christian turned and slumped with his back against the metal door. He looked at Alexis's rigid posture and could dimly see her wide eyes before the streetlight faded into the distance behind them.

"NO!" she said in disgusted disbelief. "This isn't possible."

Christian nodded and said dejectedly, "Oh, it is."

"Who is it?" Sam asked.

"Banner," Christian said weakly, bringing his hands to his face. "It's Mr. Banner."

END GAME EXCERPT

1

Darkness covered the landscape and Christian could only feel the contours of the land by the occasional dip or rise of the road. The four teens sat motionless and silent in the van as it cruised quietly on the pavement of an unknown highway. A thin light from the front dashboard gave a hint of the outlines of the four phenomenon children trapped in the back.

"Where are you taking us?" Samantha said, breaking the silence of the darkness.

There was no response from Mr. Banner.

"Why are you doing this?" Sam added with a whimper.

Only silence.

"He's not going to tell us anything," Alexis stated, placing a hand on Sam's shoulder.

Sam's body shuddered, and Christian realized she was sobbing.

"We were so close," Christian said. "I can't believe Samson did this to us. Why would he give us up?"

"Obviously," Ray huffed, "he was working for him."

Ray motioned toward the driver's seat.

"I guess it was too good to be true," Alexis added.

"But I don't get it," Christian continued. "Samson could have given us up at any point during that escape from the safe house. Why would he take us all the way to the truck stop before handing us to Banner?"

Christian heard a chuckle from the front seat.

"What is so funny?" Christian asked, the anger growing inside him.

Mr. Banner chuckled again, and Christian responded by pounding his fists against the metal barrier.

"Stop laughing!" he screamed. "Shut up! Shut up! Shut up!"

Christian's hands began to throb, but he continued to pound with all his strength against the wall that separated him from the man who had him imprisoned. The boom of flesh on steel echoed throughout the van and Christian felt totally out of control. As each fist slammed against the metal, the pain intensified and soon Christian was exhausted. His strength lessened as his body fatigued and soon his forehead pressed against the cold steel with his arms dangling limply at his sides. Tears streamed down his cheeks.

A hand gently grabbed his shoulder and pulled him from his position against the barrier, and Christian turned to see the large silhouette of Ray. He led Christian to a spot away from the front, and soon Christian sat against the rear door. The plastic tarp rustled as Samantha crawled across to Christian's position.

"You okay?" Sam whispered.

Christian didn't answer. He stared out the window into the darkness.

"Christian, you okay?" she repeated.

"Just let me rest," he responded. "I've lost my hope."

The radio exploded to life, jarring Christian. The lights of a vehicle passing in the opposite direction slowly illuminated portions of the back, and Christian spied Alexis moving closer to the crack of the opening near the front seat of the van. The opening suddenly closed as the lights of a semi brightened and then disappeared. The 18-wheeler rumbled past them, throwing them into darkness once more.

Christian turned to watch the red lights of the trailer speed away from them. The sounds of the radio were overpowering, almost deafening. Christian covered his ears, mimicking what Sam was already doing.

"Why is it so loud?" Christian shouted, wondering if anyone could hear him over the din.

The roar of the radio continued to blare through the speakers. Christian kept his hands clamped over his ears and brought his elbows together, burying his head into his forearms.

As abruptly as the radio started, it stopped in the same manner. Christian heard the metal of the small opening slide once more and looked up to see the soft light of the dash creep into the back once more. Christian noticed the outline of Alexis move stealthily toward his position in the very back of the van.

She motioned with her hand for Ray to come with her, and they moved slowly toward Christian and Sam. Alexis leaned as close to Sam and Christian as she could, puzzling Christian with her actions.

"He got a call," Alexis whispered in a tone that bordered on inaudible, since Christian's ears were still ringing from the bombardment that had just ceased.

Ray, Christian, and Sam had their heads turned so their ears were as close as possible to Alexis's words.

"I don't want him to know I heard the call," she whispered. "A rendezvous has been arranged somewhere in Arizona."

Mr. Banner cleared his throat. "Alexis, I don't know why I thought that loud noise would keep you from hearing my conversation. I should know better."

"Where are you taking us?" Ray demanded.

"I'll save Alexis the time," Mr. Banner relented. "I have set up a transfer into a more reliable vehicle."

"We trusted you," Sam cried. "How could you do this to us?"

"You forced my hand," Banner responded. "How could I let my phenomenon pupils just disappear into thin air? I have worked too long and hard to allow you to just slip away. And just in case you decide to try something stupid, I should let you all in on a little secret. Once I get you to where I need you, I will release Christian's grandfather and Sam's parents. That should make you think twice before trying something stupid, again."

Sam turned to Christian and he put his arms around her.

"So, you are behind all of this!" Ray roared.

"Yes, Ray," Mr. Banner responded calmly. "I still work for the government and that allows me to make sure things go according to plan, as far as the Phenomenon Child Program is concerned. There are bigger things at play here, bigger than you will ever understand. I'm sorry, but you four are merely pawns in a much larger game."

ACKNOWLEDGMENTS

First, I would like to thank Lisa Pelto and the entire staff at Concierge Marketing. You showed me what real publishing is and put up with me through the process. Thanks to Julie Schram, a wonderful artist who is easy to work with.

I would not be the author I am without the honest input from my readers. A heartfelt thank you goes to Alecia Zauha and Brooke Scott for their young adult feedback on the second book of The Phenomenon Trilogy. I would also like to thank Megan Scott for a parent's perspective, Tiffany and Brent Bradley for the encouraging reviews, and Lynette Dergan, a top notch middle school librarian who would tell me if this book stunk.

In addition, let me express my gratitude to Danielle and Courtney Kirgan and Dan and Vicki Koons for being who they are. These two wonderful couples were merged together to create Sam Banner's parents. These two couples have never met, and I find the irony of that to be quite funny.

And no thank you would be complete without acknowledging my wife and my daughters for putting up with me throughout the entire process of getting this book put together. They were extremely patient with me while I burnt the midnight oil to get this portion of the trilogy done.

Most importantly, I would like to thank my Lord and Savior, Jesus Christ. It is through Him that all things are possible.

CHECK OUT THESE
OTHER TITLES

THE NEW PHENOMENON

END GAME

THE PHENOMENON TRILOGY